A Rogue's Rules for Seduction

"Swear to me you weren't part of this," Willa said tautly.

Dom shook his head. "I didn't know a bloody thing. You think I'd be here if I was onto what they planned?"

"I've no idea what you think," she fired back. "I used to believe I did, but I was proven quite spectacularly wrong."

His jaw tightened. He stared at her for a moment, his tempest-hued eyes locked with hers. A sizzle of something danced down her spine and low in her belly. There'd never been a shortage of attraction between them. Even now, when she hated him to the depths of her being, he exuded a primal energy that drew her in, luring her with potential of what could be if they ever permitted themselves to let go of all restraint.

By Eva Leigh

The Wicked Quills of London
FOREVER YOUR EARL
SCANDAL TAKES THE STAGE
TEMPTATIONS OF A WALLFLOWER

The London Underground
FROM DUKE TILL DAWN
COUNTING ON A COUNTESS
DARE TO LOVE A DUKE

The Union of the Rakes
MY FAKE RAKE
WOULD I LIE TO THE DUKE
WAITING FOR A SCOT LIKE YOU

Last Chance Scoundrels
THE GOOD GIRL'S GUIDE TO RAKES
HOW THE WALLFLOWER WAS WON
A ROGUE'S RULES FOR SEDUCTION

A ROGUE'S RULES FOR SEDUCTION

Last Chance Scoundrels

EVA LEIGH

AVONBOOKS

An Imprint of HarperCollinsPublishers

A ROGUE'S RULES FOR SEDUCTION. Copyright © 2023 by Ami Silber. All rights reserved. Printed in the United States of America. No part of this book may be used or reproduced in any manner whatsoever without written permission except in the case of brief quotations embodied in critical articles and reviews. For information, address HarperCollins Publishers, 195 Broadway, New York, NY 10007.

First Avon Books mass market printing: April 2023

Print Edition ISBN: 978-0-06-308629-6
Digital Edition ISBN: 978-0-06-308269-4

Cover design by Amy Halperin
Cover illustration by Paul Stinson

Avon, Avon & logo, and Avon Books & logo are registered trademarks of HarperCollins Publishers in the United States of America and other countries.

HarperCollins is a registered trademark of HarperCollins Publishers in the United States of America and other countries.

FIRST EDITION

23 24 25 26 27 BVGM 10 9 8 7 6 5 4 3 2 1

There's a reason why every romance I write is dedicated to Zack—because he has been and will always be my IRL hero

Acknowledgments

❧ ❋ ❧

*W*ell, dear reader, we've been going *through it* for a very long time. And it becomes increasingly challenging to keep our belief in happily ever afters. Yet we do. We hold on to hope, not just for ourselves, but for the people around us, our friends, our families, our communities.

First and foremost, I want to thank you, reader, for returning to the world of fiction. If my books give you a moment's respite in the midst of prolonged chaos and uncertainty, then I have done what I set out to do. Hopefully, we can all rise up together, stronger, and make a better world.

Thank you to Nicole Fischer for her insightful notes that put me through the five stages of grief, but always result in a better book. Thank you to Madelyn Blaney for handling the details, the promo heroes Naureen Nashid, Amanda Lara, and DJ DeSmyter, as well as the whole Avon team, who work so very hard. Also special thanks to the Avon art department for giving me the world's most beautiful covers.

Much gratitude to the friends who provided counsel and support, including (but certainly not limited to) Joanna Shupe, Jen DeLuca, Jackie Barbosa, Lenora Bell, KB Alan, Robin Bradford, Martti Nelson, Lauren Dane, Victoria Dahl, Rose Lerner, Suleikha Snyder, Lorelie Brown, Tessa Dare, Anaïs Chartschenko, Caroline Linden (cookie exchange forever), Echo Molina, Erin Pollaro, Adriana Herrera, Sarah MacLean, Christine Rose Elle, Diana Quincy, Nicola Davidson, Sierra Simone, Cat Sebastian, Olivia Waite, and Megan Frampton.

Special thank-you to all the reviewers and bloggers for your continued support and incredible efforts in getting the word out about my books. Your tireless and enthusiastic work is sincerely appreciated.

I was four years old when my mom, Janice, taught me to read. The book was Arnold Lobel's *Grasshopper on the Road*, and it unlocked a whole world of books for me, encouraged by my book-loving mother. Soon after I learned to read, I began writing my own stories. Many, many years later, after I had finished two graduate programs and was struggling to become a published author, my mom and I were in a used bookstore— one of my favorite places—and I was eyeing some history books to use as research. She bought me those books, saying, "I believe in you," and she always did (even when she said she read my romance novels "with [her] eyes closed"). Mommy, thank you for supporting me. I will never stop missing you.

A Rogue's
Rules for
Seduction

Chapter 1

❧ ✳ ❧

Scotland, Inner Hebrides, 1819

𝒥ucking aristos," Dominic Kilburn muttered as the boat pitched beneath his feet.

Through sheer force of will—and using the strength of his admittedly thickly muscled thighs—he managed to keep from tumbling headlong into the churning waters, but it was close. If he wasn't such a stubborn bastard, refusing to let this sea get the better of him, he would have fallen in. Which was a slight problem. He couldn't swim. Men of low birth like his seldom could.

"What has my class done to you *now*?" Finn Ransome asked, standing at the railing.

"This damned sea is rough as a bottle of gin from a Ratcliff tavern," Dom snarled at his friend.

"Being on the water has got your nerves just as

choppy as the waves," Finn noted. "I'm hearing your old neighborhood creeping into your accent."

"Damn gambler's insight." But there was no hiding it. "No matter how many elocution lessons Da made me take, whenever I'm feelin' rattled, I can't stop droppin' consonants like rotten flesh. Guess I'll always be Ratcliff born and bred."

"It's charming," his friend noted.

Dom snorted. "Ain't too many of your class that think so. And you bein' an earl's second son, you got a voice as smooth and cultured as cream from the top of the milk bottle."

Finn also seldom revealed much emotion, not even when a twenty-foot boat heaved and rolled across Scottish waters. The vessel was just large enough to accommodate Dom, Finn, Finn's wife, Tabitha, their luggage, and the skipper—who moved around the craft with the practiced ease of someone who had likely been born on the deck of this very boat.

"You may as well be dealin' another round of faro," Dom accused, "you're so damned composed."

"There's nothing *I* can do about the state of the sea," his friend said mildly. "It stands to reason that I should permit myself to enjoy it. Why are you standing in the middle of the boat? Come to the rail and savor the view."

"I'm stayin' right here." Dom remained rooted to his place in the middle of the boat's pitching deck. "As far away as possible from the rail and the chance of a watery death. I *ain't* sinkin' to the bottom of the frigid Scottish sea."

Not without seeing her *first.* If he was going to end his miserable time in this godforsaken world, he wanted his last view to be of Willa's face. Even if she was scowling at him and calling him every known curse word, it would be enough merely to look upon her one final time. He might not die happy, but he'd die content in the knowledge that she was alive and might have a chance at actual happiness.

Yet he hadn't seen Willa's face or heard her voice in nearly a year, not since the night before that terrible spring day. Dom had run out on her in the moments before their wedding ceremony, assisted by Finn and his brother Kieran, which was bad, but even worse was the fact that Willa was their sister.

"And I fail to see why you'd be angry with my class," Finn said evenly. "Though the British aristocracy *does* have an unequal and unfair amount of power, you cannot claim the gentry can actually affect the elements, and make a sea choppy."

"But it's members of *your* class that decided to have this ruddy house party on some tiny Scottish island," Dom fired back, bracing as another swell lifted the boat high before slamming it back down, "rather than at any one of their countless country houses paid for with others' blood and sweat."

"Oliver Longbridge said his manor on the island would be the perfect place for a house party," Finn pointed out. He barely blinked when sea spray dashed across his face before calmly using a handkerchief to dry himself. "One unfettered by the traditional rules and conduct of polite society, thanks to its removed location. Besides," he added, when Dom would have complained again, "*you* decided to come to the party of your own volition. No one threatened the life of your favorite racehorse."

"Except you and that cursed brother of yours kept wheedlin' me to go," Dom countered. With an exaggeratedly affected patrician accent, he drawled, "'Do come to the party, Dom. It will be ever so droll to escape the tedium of London, and promises to be such a jolly time, there's a chap.'"

Finn laughed. "My God, if Kieran and I truly sound like that, you've my permission to tip me overboard."

"That would mean moving from the safety of where I stand," Dom answered, "riskin' *my* life to end yours."

There was no rancor in his words. Ever since Dom's father had made his fortune nearly twelve years ago through the leasing of dockside warehouses, the companionship of the Ransome brothers had been Dom's sole consolation as he'd navigated the treacherous, insular world of England's elite. Dom would sooner throw himself into the water than hurt his two closest friends.

"I think I see the island," Tabitha Ransome said excitedly.

She came to stand at her new husband's side, and Finn's arm immediately curved around her waist, holding her close. It was a gesture that was at once protective and adoring, just as the expression on Finn's face was protective and adoring. Though he was a man who seldom let anyone know what he was thinking or feeling, those barriers fell away whenever Tabitha was near. For her part, the scholarly Tabitha appeared equally smitten when in the presence of her husband.

Dom's heart clenched. He didn't begrudge Finn his happiness—but it only reinforced just what Dom had lost, and would never have for himself.

And now that both Finn and Kieran had found themselves brides, Dom was left almost entirely on his own to prowl London after dark. Given the grim humor that had gripped him ever since jilting Willa, that meant that most mornings found Dom crawling home after either wearing himself out at the all-hours pugilism academy or trying to find consolation at the bottom of a tankard.

Whether his sore head those mornings came from the punches he took from his sparring opponents or the vast amounts of alcohol he'd swallowed was anyone's guess. But boxing and drinking did the job of distracting him from the fact that he'd lost Willa, would never have her, and had to go through the rest of his cursed days corroded with guilt.

Well—they *used to* distract him. More and more lately, there weren't enough sparring opponents or casks of ale to keep him from sinking into a mire of shame and rage.

And that was the only reason why he'd accepted the Ransome brothers' invitation to join them at Oliver Longbridge's house party on this private island in the Hebrides. Because anything had to be better than his existence now. There might not be a boxing ring, but he could always drain someone else's cellar. He might also sleep better in a different bed, because God knew he wasn't sleeping now.

"It certainly appears the part of a wild, wind-swept retreat," Finn noted as the boat neared the island. He added warmly to Tabitha, "Looks as though it's stepped from one of our favorite gothic novels, love."

"Will you prowl after me as I roam the corridors, holding my candle aloft as I wear nothing but my night rail?" his wife asked with a teasing, affectionate smile.

Finn's eyes darkened. "I look forward to catching you."

Dom kept his gaze trained on the island, growing larger with each moment, rather than watch the intimacy between Finn and Tabitha. From this distance, he could just start to make out details of Longbridge's private retreat. Rocky cliffs formed a border around a beach, and on one of those cliffs perched a three-story stone building with pointed roofs and even a crenelated tower. Behind the manor house stretched rugged terrain, velvet green in the early spring, and though the trees dotting the landscape were minimal, they formed little adornments here and there.

"The island is beautiful," Tabitha said, gazing across the water. "Don't you think so, Dom?"

"I suppose. Kieran's the poet and likely's got any number of pretty and ornate metaphors and similes to rattle off." But for someone who had spent the first eighteen years of his life in the riverside Ratcliff slum, wide open spaces like this island only created a seething uneasiness in his gut, as if there was nowhere to hide, and no means of fighting.

That's all it had to be, just a city bloke's apprehension at being in an unfamiliar environment. Not a premonition.

Dom's mother had been a modern woman of profound sense and reason. She also held a touch of her old Welsh foremothers' superstition. She was always careful with wrens' nests found in the eaves of their tenement, and she wouldn't allow anyone to bring hawthorn flowers into their rooms. Perhaps some of Ma's old beliefs had seeped into Dom, making him susceptible to suggestion. He couldn't shake the feeling that something loomed on the horizon. Something other than the sprawling stone manor house perched atop a lonely and remote island.

It was the sort of place nobs believed romantic but working people like Dom thought were out of the way, hard to care for, a bit frightening, and overall, a substantial pain in the arse.

The best part about this place was that it was far, far away from anywhere that could make Dom remember Willa. Every corner of London was saturated with her—parks where they'd strolled together, tea shops, museums. Everywhere genteel courting couples could be found, and since she was an earl's daughter, that's exactly where they'd gone.

The city was haunted by Willa. Even when she'd fled to the Continent in the wake of their disastrous almost-wedding.

But now she was back in England, back in London. He'd done his utmost to avoid seeing her, which meant hiding at home during the day and only going to the city's seediest corners at night. A prisoner of his own guilt. Longbridge's far-flung Scottish retreat seemed exactly where Dom needed to be, at least for the next fortnight.

"The party's already underway?" Dom asked while the heaving boat drew nearer to the island.

"A week's passed since Longbridge opened his doors to what I've been promised is the most amusing and uninhibited company," Finn said with a smile.

"By *uninhibited*," Dom said dryly, "you mean a collection of sluts of all genders."

"The same," Finn replied.

Dom waited for a kick of expectancy at the prospect. He'd be far away from the wagging tongues, disapproving eyes, and suffocating morals of the ton, and no doubt there'd be plenty of bed hopping. But while the pitching of the boat didn't disturb his stomach, he grew nauseated at the thought of welcoming anyone into his bed. Anyone who wasn't *her*. And since that wasn't ever going to happen, he'd have to settle in for a long two weeks of listening to other people fuck in adjoining rooms.

Worse yet, he might be next to Kieran and Celeste's chamber. Kieran had married Dom's little sister last year, and it was evident through their heated looks and lingering touches that the two were ardently in love. The very last thing Dom wanted to hear was his own baby sister in the throes of passion. If that was the case, Dom would go sleep out on the moor or the heath or whatever these country folk called a big plot of dirt.

Kieran and Celeste had left for the island three days ago, so if, by some horrendous stroke of misfortune, Dom's room *was* next to theirs, hopefully they'd gotten all the passion out of their systems.

Casting a wary eye toward Finn and Tabitha in their own heated embrace on the deck of the boat, he thought it seemed unlikely. In their bachelor days, the Ransome brothers had been infamous, and now that they had both found love matches, they seemed randier than ever, always fondling their brides and whispering things that made their wives blush. It was enough to make a man want to swallow rocks.

Dom turned to the skipper, a bloke with the requisite full gingery beard and knit cap.

"Do you live on the island, too?" he asked the man.

"Where you boarded the boat, in Oban," the skipper answered in an accent so thick it would require ten lanterns to see through. "That's my home. I come back to Mr. Longbridge's as he needs me, but as soon as I drop you folk off, I'm headed back."

"So, you'll return daily to reprovision," Dom surmised.

The bloke only gave him a craggy, weathered smile. "Nearly there."

That wasn't an answer, and apprehension prickled along Dom's nape. He ought to tell the skipper to turn around, but that was ridiculous. It had already taken days on bumpy roads to reach the port, and then there'd been this boat trip of several hours just to reach Longbridge's front door. Turning around now would make him look a ruddy ass, and he'd no real proof that anything *did* await him, so he'd continue on this journey and make himself enjoy this bloody house party. If not *enjoy*, then *tolerate*. As much as he'd been able to tolerate anything since last spring.

At last, the boat reached a small jetty that arrowed

out from the beach. Several uniformed footmen stood at attention, clearly having seen the craft's approach, to await the visitors' arrival. The skipper brought his vessel in and tied off before helping Finn to disembark. In turn, Finn assisted Tabitha in climbing onto the little pier. When it was Dom's turn, he waved off offers of assistance.

"Eighteen years climbing on and off ships," he said gruffly, "I should be able to do this on my own." From the time he'd been able to walk, Dom had worked the London docks as a stevedore, his size and strength invaluable assets. On the wharf, at least. In the ballrooms of the ton, the fact that he was built like a hulking stone tower made him the object of ridicule and disdain.

To hell with those snobs, he told himself, which had been his motto for over a decade.

Thank God he didn't embarrass himself as he stepped from the boat to the jetty. Da might not have been proud of him these last few years, but he didn't disgrace his father now.

It likely *would* have shamed social-climbing Ned Kilburn when the skipper began to hand over the luggage to the waiting footmen, and Dom stepped in to take his bags. Both the footmen and the ship's captain looked perplexed that a man in the expensive clothing of a gentleman not only insisted on carrying his own belongings, but didn't stagger as he bore the weight.

As he watched everything, a corner of Finn's

mouth quirked up. Yet he kept silent. As well he should. Finn and Dom had known each other a long time, and it was precisely their lack of interest in adhering to stifling rules that had made them friends in the first place.

The footmen pressed on, taking Finn and Tabitha's luggage.

"Felicitations on your crossing," a cultured voice said, "and welcome to Creag Uaine. While you're here and beneath my roof, you'll want for nothing, and your every whim will be indulged."

Dom, Finn, and Tabitha turned to see Oliver Longbridge striding up the pier toward them. As usual, Longbridge was dressed in the height of fashion, his exceptionally stylish long coat billowing out behind him as he approached with his hand outstretched in greeting. Longbridge was the son of a Black West Indian father and a white English mother, and he'd made a fortune between his inheritance and shrewd investments. In London, he was a popular and well-respected figure—yet only a select few knew that the decorous Mr. Longbridge held clandestine parties notorious for their unbridled hedonism. The fact that Longbridge was hosting this particular house party ensured that it would be infamous for years to come.

After Longbridge shook Finn's hand and pressed a suave kiss to Tabitha's knuckles, he faced Dom with a wide smile.

"At last, we've pried you away from your beloved London," Longbridge said cheerfully.

"They said you've got matchless cellars." Fortunately, Dom had collected himself enough since
disembarking so that he was able to use his elocution lessons, and could now sound more like a
gentleman.

"And you plan to empty them," Longbridge answered, chuckling. "There are other delights to en-
tice you." He waggled his brows.

"So I've been told, but I've more of a taste for
whisky than anything else."

They began walking from the pier to a set of
wooden steps that climbed up the cliff. Finn was
all solicitousness as he kept a hand at the small of
Tabitha's back, and Dom winced.

"Is there anything else you might desire?" Longbridge asked as they ascended the steep, worn
wooden steps.

Dom frowned at this pointed question. But then,
Longbridge was only playing the attentive host.

"Getting away from London is all I want," he
answered.

"The city is far behind us," Longbridge said
magnanimously. "Here on Creag Uaine, we're free
to do what we like, when we like. Become better
acquainted with *who* we like."

Having been to a few of Longbridge's parties,
Dom had seen his host and the guests eagerly
becoming *acquainted* with many people. Dom

himself had lost the taste for such wild and fickle activity the moment he'd met Willa, and had never recovered that appetite.

Still, he made himself say, "Brilliant," as if the idea didn't completely turn his blood to icy slush.

Finally, they reached the end of the stairs, which terminated at the top of the cliff. Hard not to feel slightly pleased with himself when he was the only one of their party who wasn't out of breath, including the trailing string of footmen.

A gravel path stretched from the top of the stairs to the front of the manor house. This close to it, Dom whistled in appreciation. Sizable as the house was, the manor wasn't flashy, more like a product of the rugged land surrounding it. It sprawled in several directions as if it had grown and evolved with the progress of centuries, and had a charming ramshackle quality in its organic structure. The house wasn't an obvious display of wealth and power that often marked the residences of the elite. This had served as a home, with quirks and minute flaws.

Hearing Dom's whistle, Longbridge beamed. "I like the heap, myself. Came down to me through my mother's side. Legend has it that in its earliest days, it helped repel seaward invasions from the English and there are supposedly hulks of English ships rotting beneath the waves just off the beach. You can see some timbers when the tide is out."

"I'd wager there are more than a few ghosts," Finn noted.

"The dead outnumber the living," Longbridge answered cheerfully. "It would take hours to enumerate them all. There's no shortage of stories."

"Quite fascinating," Tabitha said with a studious look. She patted her reticule before pulling out a notebook and pencil. "I would be extremely interested in interviewing you and your staff to hear about the development of these stories, and the philosophical implications of affixing a kind of consciousness to a place."

Longbridge blinked. "Ah—"

"Later, love," Finn said fondly, guiding his wife toward the house. "For now, let us get out of the wind, fortify ourselves with some wine, and seek the comforts of the house. Then we can discuss all the philosophical implications you desire."

Tabitha nodded in agreement, and Dom and Longbridge shared a look. There had been a few moments last year when Finn had attempted to play matchmaker between Dom and Tabitha, his rationale being that Dom had won a few academic prizes at Oxford, and Tabitha was . . . well . . . Tabitha. Fortunately for everyone, Dom had bowed out, Finn and Tabitha had become smitten with each other, and Dom had managed to avoid having to discuss scholarly subjects before noon.

True to Finn's warning words, the wind was indeed starting to pick up, causing Finn and Dom to hold their hats as Tabitha's skirts and Longbridge's coat flapped.

"Storms happen quickly and with little warning out here," Longbridge said above the gusts. "Inside, I've plenty to warm you up."

He gestured toward the house, and they moved as a group through the arched stone above the heavy wooden front door that did in fact look as though it could hold off a group of English soldiers. Stepping into the large entryway, Dom looked around at the dark wood paneling on the walls, and the many pieces of weaponry mounted on those same walls.

"This is Mr. Brown, and this is Mrs. Murray," Longbridge said, gesturing to a thin man in dark, sober clothing, and a stout, red-cheeked woman with an apron and a ring of keys at her waist. "The butler and housekeeper, respectively. Anything you want, you have only to come to them and it will be provided. No questions asked. Isn't that right, Mrs. Murray?"

"So long as everyone's willing," the housekeeper answered with a charming burr.

As if in response to Mrs. Murray's words, a loud crash sounded in another room, followed by uproarious laughter. Of course—the party had already begun a week ago.

"I'll see to that," Mr. Brown said with a bow.

"And I'm sure that a broom will be required," Mrs. Murray added. "After which, I'll show everyone to their bedchambers."

The servants bowed and curtsied before departing.

In the meantime, the parade of footmen climbed a wide set of carved stairs with their bags. Two servants approached Dom, expectantly looking at his luggage. No hope for it but to give the footmen what they wanted—so he handed them his belongings. Each servant took one bag before heading up the stairs.

"Come," Longbridge said with cheer, "I've got hot toddies and a variety of things to nibble on, all to refresh you from your long journey. This way."

Their host shot a meaningful look toward Finn and Tabitha. Finn's expression didn't change, but Tabitha gave Longbridge a small nod.

Tension constricted along Dom's spine. What the hell was going on?

Still, as Longbridge ushered them toward a chamber just off the entryway, Dom shook his head. He was imagining things. Celeste always said he saw threats where there were none. This was likely the same circumstance. Fists swinging at shadows.

Dom entered the room adjoining the entryway. It seemed a perfectly fine chamber, also paneled in wood, with sofas and chairs scattered throughout, and a fire blazing cheerfully in the hearth. On a table in the middle of the room perched a tray with the promised hot toddies and cakes and sandwiches.

Striding toward the table, Dom picked up one of the steaming drinks and brought it to his lips.

At the same time, a door at one end of the chamber

opened. A woman came through it, speaking over her shoulder to someone.

"Why do I need to come in here?" she was saying. "I was right in the middle of showing Mrs. McDaniel how to cheat at billiards."

The woman drew up short and Dom dropped his hot toddy. Scalding liquid poured over his hands and clothes. He didn't notice anything but the woman.

She had thick brows, a round, elfin face, and dark and piercing eyes, with energy radiating out of her like an invisible storm as she gaped at him.

"Oh, fuck," said Willa.

Chapter 2

❧ ✱ ❧

*W*illa stared at Dom in disbelief. He couldn't be here. He couldn't simply *show up* as if he was some ordinary person who came and went like anybody else. Because he wasn't *anybody else*. He was the man who had taken her heart in his giant hand and crushed it into a pulp, and then left her to be a laughingstock, as she tried as best she could to scrape together what was left into some semblance of a functioning organ.

But here he was, standing in Oliver Longbridge's parlor and gawking at *her* as if *she* was a specter from his past.

His mouth opened and closed, as if he attempted to speak, but no words came out except a strange animal sound. His normally olive-hued complexion had turned ashen, whitening the scar that ran across his chin, and his massive chest rose and fell as he struggled to breathe. His face was leaner than she'd remembered, but his lips were just as improbably full as they'd always been, his eyes the grayish blue of a storm, and he was still handsome in the way that weather-beaten mountains were handsome. He was nevertheless Dom, down to the bump on the bridge of his nose that revealed it had been broken. More than once.

She'd hoped that, in all the times she'd imagined seeing him again, her first response would be anger. Anger was clean. It was pure and it had purpose.

Instead, longing swelled within her. A palpable yearning that swept through her like a tide, urging her to run to him, throw her arms around him, and let the heat of his body soak into hers, warming her from the long frost that had gripped her ever since that day in May.

The day he'd abandoned her at the altar in the moments before their wedding.

Ah, *there* was the rage she wanted. Surging into her with the power of a firestorm.

Spinning, she reached for whatever was closest at hand—a porcelain shepherdess figurine—and hurled it at the wall so that it exploded into thousands of fragments. Dom lifted his arm to shield himself from the flying pieces.

"What," she said through clenched teeth, "are you *doing here*?"

"Finn and Kieran talked me into comin'."

He was upset—he'd regressed into his Ratcliff accent. Good to know that she unbalanced him as much as he unbalanced her.

But . . . Kieran and Finn, her *brothers*, the very two rogues who'd helped Dom flee their wedding, the same two scoundrels who'd been nothing but apologetic since she'd returned from the Continent . . . *they* had convinced Dom to be here?

"I heard something shatter," Finn said, coming into the room with Tabitha on his arm. "I take it the reunion has happened."

She glared at her brother, and then spun to face Kieran, who had the temerity to walk hand in hand with his own wife as if he couldn't be happier or more in love.

"Hopefully, Longbridge didn't have a sentimental attachment to whatever broke," Kieran added blithely.

Clearly, he didn't care that he'd deliberately brought the one man Willa had no desire to ever see again to this house party, to this island.

Oh, God. Her heart slammed in her throat. She was stuck on an *island* with Dom.

She ran from the room, racing past everyone, even Dom. Heedless of the voices crying out for her to come back, she ran. Heavy footfalls sounded behind her, but she didn't pay them any attention as she sped down the gravel path, toward the stairs that led to the pier. The pier where the boat that had brought Dom still waited.

All she had to do was reach that boat, and then she'd be safe. She'd sail away from this infernal place and Dom and all the heartbreak he'd given her, and she would never, never again trust her brothers.

She skidded to a halt at the top of the stairs, and her heart plummeted from her throat to the bottom of her stomach.

The boat was already sailing away.

"Wait!" she cried, waving her hands over her head.

"Come back!" Dom shouted from beside her.

She glared at him. "You've no *right* to want to flee the island. *I'm* the jilted one."

He said nothing, his brow lowering heavily.

"Then again," she added tightly, "this is entirely like you—running away." Turning back to the retreating ship, she tried again. "Ahoy! Don't leave!"

Dom also shouted for the boat to return. They both possessed voices that could get quite loud— she specifically remembered a fight shortly before the wedding where they'd yelled so vociferously at each other, everyone in the vicinity had to cover their ears—and yet, despite their strident pleas for the boat to come about, it sailed on. Until it was no more than a speck approaching the horizon. And then it was gone.

She was trapped on this island with Dom.

Her stomach knotted. "There has to be some way off this blasted chunk of rock," she muttered.

"Longbridge," Dom growled. "He'll know."

Willa ran back into the house. Solid, forceful steps on the stone floor sounded behind her.

Mr. Longbridge was in the parlor, amiably chatting with her traitorous brothers and their wives, as if this wasn't the most catastrophic day in recent memory.

"There *will* be a boat tomorrow, yes?" she demanded without preamble.

The host only smiled easily. "Afraid not. Gordon isn't due back for some while."

"*When?*" she pressed. There must be a finite amount of time that she was stranded on this island, in this house, with Dom.

Mr. Longbridge only shrugged. "Hard to say. We're well provisioned, so there's no specific day that he's scheduled to return. At the least, he'll be back in a fortnight."

Behind her, Dom swore lowly. There was something almost poignant in hearing him use foul language. When they'd been courting, he had tried to keep coarse words out of their conversations, but every now and again a Cockney-accented curse slipped in, as if there was a part of himself he could never fully change. It had thrilled her, to be wooed by a man who was so unlike all the others of her social circle. She'd loved how different he was from everyone else she knew.

Her hands clenched at her sides. This was all Kieran and Finn's doing.

She stormed up to them as they congregated around the fire, Celeste and Tabitha standing with their husbands. At least their brides looked wary, but not her damned brothers.

"You have a hell of a lot of nerve," Willa fumed, "looking at me without an ounce of remorse."

"I'll just see to my other guests," Mr. Longbridge said, slipping out of the room.

"This was a coordinated effort," she said hotly, looking back and forth between her brothers.

"Wheedlin' us both into coming here," Dom added, his voice tight.

"What in God's name did you think to accomplish?" She glowered at Kieran and Finn, jabbing her finger at them. "Deceiving me to . . . what . . . bring me closer to the man who jilted me—with *your* help, I might add—the man who made me the laughingstock of London? How in the hell was this ever considered a good idea?"

Kieran looked unusually grave, and Finn's expression was somber.

"You didn't . . ." She pinched the bridge of her nose. "You didn't seriously expect that marooning us on this island would somehow bring us back together?"

Behind her came the sound of someone unstoppering a decanter and pouring a beverage. A glance back revealed Dom filling a glass to the rim with what appeared to be whisky. He downed the entire drink in one swallow before grimly pouring himself another. This he drank almost as quickly as the first.

She marched over to where he stood and snatched up the decanter, which she put directly to her lips.

Her eyes on Dom, she took several swigs of whisky before setting the vessel down on its table with a heavy thud.

Dom didn't blink. But then, he never did. It had been their mutual flouting of convention that had brought them together in the first place.

"Swear to me you weren't part of this," she said tautly.

He shook his head. "I didn't know a bloody thing. You think I'd be here if I was onto what they planned?"

"I've no idea what you think," she fired back. "I used to believe I did, but I was proven quite spectacularly wrong."

His jaw tightened. He stared at her for a moment, his tempest-hued eyes locked with hers. A sizzle of something danced down her spine and low in her belly. There'd never been a shortage of attraction between them. Even now, when she hated him to the depths of her being, he exuded a primal energy that drew her in, luring her with potential of what could be if they ever permitted themselves to let go of all restraint.

In their courtship and after their engagement had been announced, they'd shared a few kisses, some caresses, hinting that the passion between them could be explosive. Yet Dom had always been too protective of her reputation to go any further. Much to her annoyance.

What she did *not* want now, or ever again, was

to feel anything for him beyond rage. She would ignore the heat that flared into being whenever they were within touching distance. It was merely an unsatisfied urge. Naturally, she'd crave something that she couldn't and shouldn't have.

"What *exactly* was your plan?" she said, turning back to her brothers. "If not to act as my pimps?"

Celeste sucked in a breath, and Tabitha's hand flew to her throat. Red stained Kieran's cheeks, and while Finn still appeared unruffled, his hands flexed. He never did that tell with anyone but her, as if he was still the older brother ready to leap in and keep her from toppling off the railing she insisted on climbing.

"Brutal words, Will," Kieran said lowly.

"Deservedly so," she snapped.

After a moment, Kieran said, "Neither you nor Dom have spoken to each other since the night before the wedding."

"Didn't seem much point in it," Dom said.

"Except," Finn noted, "from that time, both of you have been in spiraling descents. We, that is, Key and I, know that if there's to be any hope of progressing forward, you two *must* talk."

"It's not about me forgiving the man who embarrassed me in front of London?" Willa shot back. "Or forgiving you—not only for your part in it, but your own manipulations in bringing me *here*?"

"Both of you are damn stubborn," Kieran answered, "and if we didn't *make* you communicate, there was no hope of either of you moving on."

"My God." Willa threw her hands into the air, utterly disgusted with the entire situation. "I'd only just begun to accept speaking to you both again, but now that you've pulled another horrendous stunt, it would be miraculous if we ever exchange a single syllable."

She narrowed her eyes. "Is this about that ultimatum our parents issued when you helped Dom in abandoning me at the altar? Oh, yes, I know all about it," she added. "You two and Dom must find respectable brides within a year, or else you don't receive another penny. Two of you have married—to women who deserve far better than you, I might add—and that leaves Dom's bachelorhood standing between you and your allowances. And the year is almost complete."

"Hell, Will," Finn said, having the audacity to sound hurt, "we wouldn't compromise your happiness for money."

"If you'd concerned yourself with my *happiness*," she threw back, "you *wouldn't have helped my groom flee our wedding. Or lured me here under false pretenses.*"

Kieran opened his mouth, presumably to try to defend his and Finn's actions, but Dom spoke first.

"Enough." His voice rang out, deep and decisive. "There's nothin' more to be said. We're all stuck here for the likely future. Best we can do is agree to stay away from one another 'til the next boat comes."

"It's a small island, Dom," she answered coldly. "Staying away from each other is going to prove a challenge."

"Since when have you backed down from a challenge, princess?" He said this in a low, soft voice, intended for her ears only, just the same way he used to whisper his support of her whenever she'd declared that she would do something bold. There'd been that one time when they'd been at the Royal Academy Summer Exhibition. She'd been so incensed at the number of female nudes versus the number of paintings depicting unclothed men that she had privately sworn to Dom that she would tell the whole Academy what she thought of their blatant double standard.

Go and tell them, princess, he'd murmured to her. *They need to know, and who better to hold them accountable than her royal highness?*

To the horror of her parents, also in attendance, she'd stood in the middle of the Academy exhibition hall and clapped loudly. *Bravo, gentlemen,* she'd said resoundingly. *Naked women and men at war. You've shown us that you're as limited in your imagination as you are in talent.*

Stunned, silent shock had followed. All but for Dom, who'd stuck his fingers in his mouth and whistled. Loudly.

She'd adored that about him, how brash he was,

always ready to show the nobs that he might walk amongst them, but he never desired to be *one of them*. In that way, he was perfect for her.

And yet, hearing him encourage her now brought a rush of hot stickiness to her eyes. As if . . . she craved support. Not just anyone's support, but *his*.

She blinked the dampness in her eyes away. There was nothing he could give her that she wanted.

"Fine," she said as icily as she could manage. "If there's one thing we agree upon, it is that we're to avoid being near one another for as long as we possibly can. No matter what my brothers want, we don't have to speak to each other."

He gave a clipped nod. At that little gesture, her heart sank. Only then did she realize that part of her still hoped that he would fight for them to remain together. Yet, just like before, all he did was run away from her.

Chapter 3

❧ ✳ ❧

Dom had never been a soldier, but he'd heard stories in taverns and on the docks. Tales of battlefield horrors. Of men losing vital parts of their bodies to explosions and other sword strikes, but taking far too long to actually die.

Now he knew that he could watch his heart be ripped right out of his chest. Yet he continued to walk and breathe, and, worst of all, feel.

Tabitha and Celeste huddled around a stiff-shouldered Willa, offering sympathy and listening ears.

Dom had clung to some hazy wish. A wish that his former fiancée wasn't completely disgusted by him, or perhaps—and this was an even slimmer hope—that she'd have forgiven him for what he'd done.

But he didn't merit her forgiveness. He never did and never would, and living through this agonizing pain that should have, by rights, killed him, was precisely what he deserved.

Kieran and Finn approached.

"Wise you're being chary about coming near me," Dom muttered. "I'm at least two stone heavier than you, Kieran, and four inches taller than you, beanpole Finn."

"And we've fought you in the boxing ring." Kieran fingered his jaw. "Your right uppercut nearly knocked me into the twentieth century."

Dom stalked away from them, into the hallway. He passed three guests tossing a globe back and forth as they cavorted along the corridor.

"You were damned stupid," Dom growled at Finn and Kieran, who followed him.

The brothers exchanged a glance, which they often did in the silent communication of close siblings.

"We know this can work," Finn said. "We've no intention of hurting you."

Dom said, curt, "You've hurt *her*."

The flying globe hurtled toward Dom. He snatched it out of the air before it could hit him, and threw it back to one of the gentlemen. The man caught it, but winced from the force of Dom's throw. Laughing and cheering, the group scampered down the hallway.

One of the women nearly collided with Willa, just as Willa was coming out of the parlor. The lady skidded to a stop, and then carefully edged her way past Willa, who looked annoyed.

Yet when Willa looked at him farther down the

corridor, her dark eyes gleamed with fury, and her arms crossed protectively over her chest. Her chin came up.

That was good. Better for her to be angry with him than heartbroken. She was always so full of force and determination, and it would have deepened his own self-hatred to see that he'd made her wretched.

"Perhaps," Kieran suggested slowly, "this *could* be an opportunity. To gain the resolution you both seem to need."

Finn began, "Tabitha and I learned that if we talk with each other—"

A harsh bark of laughter escaped Dom, causing Willa to throw him a hard look before striding briskly away. Even when she wasn't full of fury, she wasn't the sort of woman to softly glide from one place to the next, preferring to move with directness and purpose rather than appear a delicate blossom drifting on a breeze.

In motion, her spine was upright, and her hips moved from side to side, drawing his gaze to her ripe shape. When they'd been courting, he hadn't permitted himself more than a quick graze of his fingers along those curves. God, how he'd wanted to, though. He'd wanted to grip her round bottom and press her into him because whenever he'd been near her, he'd been hard and aching and so full of desire for this hurricane of a woman, so unlike anyone he'd ever met.

But he hadn't allowed himself that liberty. For all his family's new blunt, he was a longshoreman and she was an earl's daughter, always far above him.

That hadn't stopped him from wanting. And the hell of it was, he *still* wanted, even when he had no right.

"Talking to her ain't happening," he said to the Ransome brothers.

"But—" Finn began.

"Let it lie," Dom snarled. "I'm already a hairsbreadth away from chucking you both into the sea."

"Our intentions are good," Kieran said with his patented winning smile.

"A good intention is like foxglove—it's meant to be healing, but too much of it is poison."

At that, the Ransome brothers went mute. "Hopefully," Dom went on, "your silence means you're thinking of how the hell you intend to apologize and make good with your sister."

"The same goes for you," Finn noted dryly.

Dom merely stared at him, because there was no way to make good with Willa. Not in this lifetime, or the next.

"Excuse me, Mr. Kilburn." The housekeeper appeared beside him. "I'm free now to show you to your bedchamber, if you'll come with me."

Without sparing a glance for the brothers, he followed Mrs. Murray up the wide stairs, noting that the banister was polished by both the labor of the staff as well as the generations of hands that had held the railing. Back in Ratcliff, things fell apart long before they could get such a patina.

"This way, if you please," Mrs. Murray said once they reached the landing. She gestured down one of the long, wood-paneled hallways.

They walked down the corridor, passing other bedchambers that were already occupied, judging by the personal items arranged on dressing tables.

"That's Miss Steele's room," the housekeeper explained, nodding toward one of the chambers. "And over here is Mr. Cransley's chamber. Mrs. McDaniel has this room," she added.

"Unmarried guests share the same wing?" Dom asked.

Mrs. Murray chuckled. "Oh, Mr. Longbridge likes to keep things informal here."

"No surprise there," Dom said under his breath. He ought to have expected as much, given their host's secret reputation as a libertine.

Mrs. Murray stopped outside a room whose door stood open. She waved her hand toward it. "This is where you'll be, Mr. Kilburn."

Dom peered into a chamber full of heavy, masculine furniture that appeared to be at least a century old, though well-preserved. His bags were already in the room, and a footman was in the process of unpacking them.

"I have a gown that needs pressing, Mrs. Murray," Willa said, stepping out of the chamber next to Dom's. She carried a green frock Dom had liked, since it made her look like an elfin queen.

Yet as she came into the hallway, she abruptly stopped. Her gaze shot to Dom.

"What are you doing lurking outside my bed-chamber?"

"Mrs. Murray's showing me my room," he answered, pointing to the place in question.

Willa frowned. "It's next to mine."

"What?" His body stilled.

"Oh, yes," Mrs. Murray said cheerfully. "It's a fine bedchamber, Mr. Kilburn. The bed is capacious and will easily accommodate a man of your, er, considerable proportions."

Dom's *bedchamber* was to be right next to where Willa *slept*. Where she *disrobed* and *bathed*. And he'd hear it all.

The very definition of torture.

"I'm moving to another room," he said abruptly.

Willa's frown deepened as the housekeeper looked at him with concern.

"Sir," Mrs. Murray said, "I can assure you that this chamber is one of the finest in the house. It stays quite warm even after the fire has gone out, and there's a delightful view of the garden—"

"Another. Room," he said.

The housekeeper spread her hands. "There *are* no other rooms available. Every bedchamber is occupied by Mr. Longbridge's guests."

"This house is huge," Dom said through his

teeth. "Surely there's got to be some corner of the place that's got a cot, a pallet, a pile of hay, *anything.*"

Willa sucked in a breath, but he kept his attention on the housekeeper.

"Well . . ." Mrs. Murray said uneasily. "There *is* one room in the attic that used to be for the tutor. But, sir," she added, hasty, "it's in an awful state. No one has slept there in over a decade, and I'm afraid it's fallen into a bit of disrepair. Quite a chilly spot, and out of the way. You'll have to climb two flights of very steep and narrow stairs, and—"

"I'll take it," he said at once.

"I don't think Mr. Longbridge would like that," the housekeeper fretted. "He prides himself on his hospitality, and to have one of his guests stay in such an uncomfortable room, it would strike at his dignity."

"I won't tell anyone about the state of my room," Dom said firmly. "Say to him I insisted, and it reflects better on him as a host that I was lodged to my liking."

When Mrs. Murray still looked uncertain, Dom went on, "It's what I want, and as a guest of this house, I should be supplied with what I desire."

There was a long pause as the housekeeper seemed to agonize over this decision. He didn't enjoy upsetting the staff, but in this, he wouldn't budge. The idea of being so close to Willa was a torment. Bad enough that they had to share a roof, yet sharing a *wall* was a surefire recipe for even more anguish.

"Very well," the housekeeper said, her shoulders sagging. "I'll tell the footmen to bring your luggage up to the . . . the room."

"My thanks, Mrs. Murray. And if Longbridge gives you any trouble, I'll personally vow that you did everything in your power to deter me, but I was a beast, and insisted on the attic room."

The housekeeper curtsied. "I suppose I should take you up there now, sir. And," she added, looking at Willa, "given the, ah, state of the attic chamber, I will come back for your gown, miss. No need to give it a washing as well as a pressing."

Dom searched Willa's face for some sign that she was pleased he'd changed rooms, yet she continued to frown, her thick brows drawn down like an oncoming storm. He knew that look—because that storm had struck many times. Yet he was a cyclone, too.

"My room, Mrs. Murray?" he pressed.

"Yes, sir."

The housekeeper moved back down the corridor. Dom sent Willa one last nod before heading to follow Mrs. Murray. He could keep the peace a little longer—but a tempest was brewing. And with each moment he and Willa shared a roof, it grew stormier.

Chapter 4

❧ ✽ ❧

How fetching you are in this gown, my lady," the maid said, surveying Willa after she had finished dressing for dinner.

Isla had been assigned to Willa, since Willa had left her own maid behind in London. A few of the footmen had similarly been recruited to tend to the gentlemen guests.

Standing in front of the mirror, Willa smoothed her hand over the emerald-green velvet of her gown. It was adorned with darker green embroidery along the neckline, sleeves, and hem, and caught the light beautifully. Since the climate of this Scottish island was quite cool, even in the spring, velvet wasn't too heavy a choice, and it carried with it a gravitas that she savored—as though she was no one to be trifled with.

"It was always one of his favorites," she murmured. The plush fabric was soft and dense as shadows and bore not a single crease, thanks to Mrs. Murray's attentions.

"One of *whose* favorites, my lady?" Isla asked.

"No one important," Willa answered. She hadn't packed the green dress with Dom in mind. Every time she'd worn it, he'd stared at her like he wanted to feast on her, but that didn't influence her decision to put it on this evening. It had nothing to do with punishing him.

She patted her hair, which Isla had dressed in appealing curls.

"You'll draw all the gentlemen's attention tonight," the housemaid said.

"Precisely my aim." In the few days Willa had been at the house, she'd met a number of handsome and charming gentlemen, and it had been a long time since she'd flirted with anyone.

Anyone who wasn't Dom.

She'd once loved to flirt with him. To make teasing, slightly intimate remarks and touch her ungloved fingers to his and watch his blue-gray eyes darken, observe his jaw tighten. They'd touched often, as if pulled together by an unseen force, and even though their touches seldom went beyond the strictly proper, she'd liked seeing how much he'd wanted her because she'd wanted him, too, just as much. There was something thrilling about having a man so physically and mentally strong be in thrall to her. It had been powerful, heady, knowing that *she* was what he desired.

But not enough. Not nearly enough to make him stay.

She turned away from the mirror. "None of this."

"None of what, my lady?"

"None of waiting on dinner," Willa answered. "I'm famished."

After thanking Isla, she strode from her room. She cast one quick glance toward the room Dom was *supposed* to occupy—he couldn't have fled from her fast enough—before sweeping down the corridor. As she walked, she passed Mr. Gilbert Cransley as he emerged from his chamber.

She knew him from London, of course, because he was a viscount's second son and moved in the same circles as she did. He was a handsome bachelor with a fairly substantial allowance, and she frequently observed him surrounded by ladies.

She'd also heard from Kieran and Finn that Mr. Cransley was a frequenter of wild parties—precisely the sort that Mr. Longbridge threw but she could never go to—so it was no surprise to find him at this manor.

Willa herself was only permitted by her parents to attend the house party because Celeste was to theoretically serve as chaperone, saving Willa the trouble of dragging along a companion.

"Lady Willa," Mr. Cransley said, bowing at her approach. He'd brushed his light brown hair back from his high forehead, which had the effect of bringing attention to his vividly blue eyes. Those selfsame blue eyes sparkled as he looked at her—with far more boldness than would be acceptable at a more sedate gathering. "How delightful you appear this evening in that stunning gown."

"Implying that I do not appear delightful at other times?" She exhaled. "Forgive me, Mr. Cransley. Though my dress is of decent quality, at present, my humor is somewhat threadbare."

"Nothing to forgive," he said smoothly. "Do call me Gilbert."

He offered her his arm and she took it. In the unfettered spirit of the house party, she wore no gloves, and so she felt the excellent material of his coat, as well as the well-developed muscles of his forearm. He was known as a sportsman, and his physical condition attested to this.

And yet her heart did not pound faster to learn how robust he was, and she had no desire to speculate on the rest of his physique. Whereas whenever she'd taken Dom's arm, the feel of his brawn had always made her giddy, and she had hoarded memories of the few times she'd seen him in his shirtsleeves, the fine fabric pulled taut over his shoulders.

As if sensing the direction of her thoughts, Mr. Cransley—Gilbert—said gently as they walked down the hallway, "The advent of your poor disposition seems timed to Mr. Kilburn's arrival."

"A pennant flying at the top of a mountain takes no notice of a slug slithering at the bottom." She lifted her chin.

Her escort chuckled as they reached the top of the stairs.

"And yet," he continued while they descended the steps, "no one would blame you were you to be aggrieved by his appearance here. After all, you *did* call off your wedding on account of his uncouth and intoxicated behavior. Though some tongues wagged at the timing, it was still the wisest decision you could've made, rather than tether yourself to a lifetime of boorish conduct."

She gave a noncommittal noise. Difficult to say that Dom had been *gracious* when he'd permitted her family to tell Society that *she* had been the one to stop the wedding owing to the groom's drunken loutishness. But it had saved her reputation, to an extent, since it would have been entirely unsalvageable if it was known that Dom had jilted *her*. She would have been seen as damaged, used goods, ensuring that she'd never be able to find a husband.

As it was, in the wake of the aborted wedding, she'd retreated to the Continent, for a change of scenery as well as to let the aforementioned wagging tongues find some other scandal to flap about.

"You've nothing to fear," her escort said. "I will serve as your champion here, and protect you from Kilburn."

She was about to snap that she didn't need anyone to protect her from anything. But Gilbert was merely being courteous and fulfilling the role that gentlemen were to theoretically take, which was to shelter women from anything remotely troubling or—God forbid—requiring thought.

And she was more than a little tired of trying to school men. Let them figure life out for themselves and take the blows that hopefully would come.

They followed the sounds of many voices to the spacious drawing room, which, Mr. Longbridge had explained earlier, had been recently remodeled to fit the current fashion for lighter walls and furniture. The other guests were standing in groups, and, after parting company with Gilbert, Willa took a turn around the room.

In addition to their host, herself, and her family, there was also Baron Hunsdon, whose appearance, grooming, and manner seemed patterned after a poet of the Romantic school.

"'*Spirit of Beauty,*'" the baron recited, "'*that dost consecrate / With thine own hues all thou dost shine upon / Of human thought or form,— where art thou gone?*'"

Kieran looked on the verge of throwing a vase at the baron.

Speaking effervescently with Mr. Longbridge was Charlotte, the Marchioness of Shipton, a very handsome woman of middle years. She lived apart from her husband, the marquess, who openly kept house with his mistress in London. From all accounts, it was an amiable separation, and Lady Shipton took full advantage of her unusual circumstances by taking as many lovers as she pleased. It seemed an ideal sort of marriage, come to think of it.

Although, Viscount and Viscountess Marwood were also in attendance at the party, forming a very different picture of what constituted marital joy.

"To be the ideal houseguest is a continual dance between being constantly amusing and remaining excruciatingly polite," the viscountess said to Mr. Longbridge. She had a pleasing East London accent, which she didn't bother to hide. "Both are exceptionally wearying to the host."

Mr. Longbridge threw back his head and laughed, while the viscount regarded his wife with a look that could only be called worshipful.

There was no definitive proof that the wedded state did or did not create happiness—Willa's own parents had been a love match that had, after marriage, decayed into loathing.

Willa had always been determined to live her life the exact opposite of Lord and Lady Wingraves'. Perhaps because they had been led by their hearts when choosing a spouse, they'd pushed her toward making a strategic alliance with a wealthy peer's son.

Instead, Willa had pointedly chosen Dom, who possessed money in abundance but none of the breeding that her parents had insisted on. She'd hoped that, at the least, her own union would never slide into chilly silence and pointed indifference.

But she would never know what being Dom's wife would have been like.

She pressed a hand to her heart to stop its instinctive, habitual ache. God—she was so weary of being angry and sad over the whole failed wedding, and yet the pain refused to fade.

Now, in this drawing room, the man who'd devastated her was conspicuously absent.

"You seem eager to catch a glimpse of someone in particular," Mrs. Eliza McDaniel said. She was a widow with fair skin and hair, and avaricious eyes, and stood with Miss Lakshmi Steele near a window at the far side of the chamber.

"I like to take the measure of the people in any room," Willa answered. She didn't give a fig if Dom was here or wading out into the sea, either to sink or be carried away on one of the strong tides that were no doubt even higher now. A storm was definitely brewing, shaking the window with strong gusts of wind. Heavy rain would surely follow if the gales were any portent.

"You were much the same at school," Miss Steele said. The youngest daughter of a viscount and an East Indian woman of considerable fortune, she and Willa had never been close, and even now regarded each other with wary politeness. "When you weren't bedeviling the teachers with your refusal to conform."

"Little has changed," Willa replied.

"Where is your companion tonight, Miss Steele?" Mrs. McDaniel asked.

"Poor health has confined Mrs. Newton to her room," the other woman answered. "A not infrequent occurrence."

"I suspect that is exactly why Mrs. Newton was hired," Willa said.

Miss Steele's lack of denial was telling. "Before you joined us, we were discussing the positively gothic atmosphere. Who knows what may lurk in the corridors when we are all trembling in our beds?"

"I'm sure I shall scream if I should wake to find a strange figure at the foot of my bed," Mrs. McDaniel answered, shuddering.

"A scream of delight?" Willa asked with a droll smile.

The widow's look turned sly. "There are a few strange figures here that would make for a very intriguing night's activity. Such as that gentleman, who would surely teach me a lesson I'll make sure I deserve."

Willa followed Mrs. McDaniel's look and heat rushed into her face when she realized the widow was gazing at Dom, who had just come into the drawing room.

He always did wear evening clothes well, and tonight was no exception as he filled out his inky double-breasted coat, silver waistcoat, and cream breeches. The stylish, costly clothing contrasted with the rough-hewn build and features, assisted by the carelessness with which he wore his dark hair. It was almost grudging, the way he looked, as if in his appearance, he said, *I'll wear your aristo's togs because I can buy and sell you in a minute, but to hell with you if I'm going to change who I am to make you comfortable.*

Defiant to the end, Dom. It almost made her smile.

She crushed that emerging smile when she realized that she was thinking of him fondly. And that Mrs. McDaniel fancied him for bed sport.

What did it matter to Willa? Dom could take any number of people to his bed, and it made not a whit of difference. He could sleep with scores of lovers and she would go about her merry way, entirely unbothered.

As an unmarried young woman, she didn't have the same freedom with her body. But she could still engage in flirtations, which would gratify her bruised self-esteem. And if she felt any twinge of something hot and acidic in her belly at the thought of Dom whispering lusty praise in some other person's ear—as he had with her when they'd shared stolen kisses—well, she could ignore it. She was very good at pushing through obstacles.

Dom's eyes swept across the room, as if in search of something or someone. Then his gaze locked onto her, hot and direct, and everything in her fluttered with awareness. Almost instinctively, he took a step in her direction.

She did the same, pulled toward him by the force that had drawn them together since their first meeting years ago, when she'd seen only Dom, and every other man had ceased to exist.

Go to him, her body insisted.

What in God's name am I doing? her mind shouted.

Her brothers looked expectantly back and forth between her and Dom.

Abruptly, she turned—lurched, really—and made herself walk to Gilbert. He wore a pleased expression as she neared.

"Lady Willa," he said, smiling. "It has only been minutes but I missed your company already."

"Willa," she answered. "If I am free to call you Gilbert, I insist that the familiarity be reciprocated. If we cannot be at liberty here on Mr. Longbridge's island, where *can* we have freedom?"

Something burning traveled the length of her back, and she glanced over her shoulder to find Dom in the middle of the room, staring intently at her as she flirted with Gilbert. Dom's jaw looked hard as granite and his eyes blazed, but he stayed rooted to the spot.

"Do you think Mr. Kilburn would appreciate my boldness?" Gilbert asked.

"What matters is whether or not *I* appreciate it,"

she answered with a toss of her head. "And I can assure you that I do."

Gilbert's smile widened. "Then I shall be delighted and honored, Willa, if I may escort you to dinner. For I find having you on my arm to be exceedingly charming."

"Any lady can be *charming*," she said, taking his proffered arm. "It's my intention to be unforgettable."

"Whoever considers you forgettable is entirely a fool," he answered gallantly.

"Precisely my sentiments." She looked directly at Dom as she spoke.

Dom only clenched his jaw harder—a muscle actually leapt in his cheek—before moving toward the fire. He turned his broad back toward the room as he moodily stared at the flames, effectively blocking out everyone, including Willa.

She glowered at the wide expanse of dark wool stretching across his shoulders. How dare he look so brooding and enigmatic and untamed, especially in comparison to the sleekly handsome and refined Gilbert. It was like having a spaniel and a wolf in the same room.

Even so, she made sure to rest her hand more firmly on Gilbert's arm, and though Dom couldn't see her, she directed a winning smile up at Gilbert. It was a useless gesture, yet she had to claim some kind of victory, no matter how Pyrrhic.

Mr. Brown, the butler, appeared at the doorway. "Dinner is served."

"We're all far from the constraints of Society," Mr. Longbridge said with a smile, "so there's no need to stand on ceremony. Walk in to dinner on your own, or partner as many people in as you like. No precedence, either. Rules have little place on this island."

Naturally, the married couples paired up and glided from the room, while the two widows and Miss Steele linked arms, chatting animatedly as they walked to dinner. Mr. Longbridge's smile widened when Baron Hunsdon offered him his arm. The two gentlemen strode out together.

"I suppose this means you'll forge your own path, Willa," Gilbert said, glancing down at where her hand continued to rest on his sleeve.

She cast a quick look at Dom. They were the last three people in the drawing room, and he turned away from the fire, his expression grim as he stared at her and Gilbert.

"I would hate to deprive you of my company," she answered Gilbert teasingly.

Her escort laughed. "You are kindness itself."

"This rugged and wild atmosphere has sharpened my appetite." She *would* show Dom that she had moved on. Long ago, she had learned that she could pretend to be invulnerable.

Chapter 5

❧ ✱ ❧

*D*om was the last one to enter the dining room, and his gut clenched when he saw that there was only one available seat left—and it was next to Willa.

A footman held the chair out as Dom approached. Willa looked between the chair and Dom, her chin tipped up, her eyes bright. Unless he wanted to look like the biggest ass in Christendom, he had no choice but to sit beside her.

Huge and clumsy as a barge trying to dock in a tiny berth, he lowered himself down into the ornately carved and plushly cushioned chair. Big as the piece of furniture was, it barely contained him. He was all legs and elbows as he sat, jostling Finn on one side and Willa on the other.

She shot him a look before pointedly turning to Cransley next to her and laughing at something the overbred nob said.

The table shook from the force of Dom's thighs hitting the underside of the wood.

"Easy, old man," Finn murmured for Dom's ears alone.

"Can't help it," Dom muttered back. "This damned aristo furniture's scaled for dollhouses."

"I'm sure there's a boulder on this island to serve as your table," Willa said with an acidic smile. "It will be appropriately impervious to your ungainly movement."

He'd forgotten that she had excellent hearing.

"Everything nobs use is too small." He picked up his fork and glared at the tiny piece of silver. "Too many blue bloods mating with other blue bloods, and what are they left with? Feeble hands and puny cutlery." He cast the fork down onto the napkin beside his plate.

"We'll have a servant fetch a pitchfork from the stables," she answered. "Your giant paws can suitably manage *that*."

"*This* suits me better." He used his hands to grab the small roast bird on his plate and brought it to his mouth.

Eyes wide, Willa watched as he sank his teeth into the meat, chewing with gusto. But . . . she didn't turn away. Her cheeks grew flushed and she licked her lips.

"Quite right," Longbridge said with a nod. "Forks and knives are entirely too fussy for capons." Following Dom's lead, their host picked up his poultry with his hands and took a bite—though his was far more polite than Dom's big mouthful.

Soon, everyone at the table was ignoring their cutlery in favor of their hands, picking pieces of meat from their plates and scooping up peas with their fingers. Even Willa abandoned her fork and plucked a tiny drumstick from her capon, biting into it as she shot him a defiant look.

He stared, fascinated, at her teeth and lips as she ate. She stuck a finger into her mouth and licked it clean.

Thank God he had a napkin to drape over his lap because his cock was very interested in the sight of Willa eating with her hands and licking her fingers.

Shaking his head, he tried to turn his attention back to the dishes arrayed across the table.

"What's that?" he demanded, pointing toward one mystifying platter of food.

"Mousserons à la crème," Finn explained. "Creamed mushrooms. It looks distressing but tastes delectable. Bit hard to eat with one's fingers, though."

A glance toward Willa showed she was busy talking with Cransley, which meant that, with any luck, she wasn't paying Dom any attention.

"We used to dream of food like this," Dom answered to Finn, voice low so hopefully Willa couldn't hear. "Da and me, when vittles were scarce."

"Must've been difficult," his friend mused thoughtfully.

"Back then, I was always hungry, and shoveled down whatever food we could afford. Me and Da needed our strength to haul cargo on the docks." Dom shook his head. "No matter how much my stomach growled for more, though, I tucked away choice pieces in a kerchief to give to Celeste. She'd been such a wee thing back then, all eyes and dreams."

"I'm certain she appreciated it," Finn said. "And if Kieran knew, you'd have his undying gratitude."

Dom regarded his baby sister as she sat beside her husband. Aristo rules meant that, typically, a married couple wouldn't sit together at a dinner party, but as soon as the rules were flouted, they chose to be near each other rather than anyone else.

"She's grown now, of course," he murmured. "A gentleman's wife in elegant clothing and more than enough to eat. But I can't fully shake the picture of her, tiny and barefoot, sitting on the floor of our run-down rooms, helping Ma with the piecework they did to bring in more coin."

Celeste laughed at something Kieran said, and it warmed Dom to see her happiness, and the way that her husband looked at her as if she was an actual, living miracle that Kieran had been lucky enough to witness.

At least one of the two Kilburn siblings was happy. And if it could only be one of them, then it was best that it was her.

"I think the heavens have been torn asunder,"

Lady Shipton said across from him. She nodded toward the windows, where rain hammered against the glass in a sharp, angry rhythm. "Have you done anything to offend the gods, Mr. Kilburn?"

"I offend a lot of people," he answered before taking a drink of wine.

"Surely only those without a suitably robust constitution," she replied, her smile alluring. "It would require quite a lot to scandalize me."

"A dare?"

"If you wish it to be."

Lady Shipton was an attractive woman who wore her carnality like a fur stole, lush and lavish. Yet all Dom wanted to do was smash through the walls and run into the storm.

Willa's distinctive, husky laugh stroked down his back. He'd always loved how she laughed, full and open and deep, as opposed to the harp-like practiced trills that Society ladies were instructed to make, smothering their true selves for the sake of appearing dainty and ornamental.

I'm enjoying myself, Willa's laugh declared, *and I don't give a damn whether you like it or not.*

"Isn't that right, Mr. Kilburn?"

His attention snapped back to the present, and Lady Shipton's sparking eyes and low-cut bodice. She looked at him expectantly, as if she'd just said something and expected a reply. "What's that?"

"I said I wager that you'd be up to any dare

presented to you," the marchioness murmured, "and you'd enjoy flouting expectations as you did it."

He'd experienced his share of propositions, both before he'd entered Society, and after. Usually, they were made by women who thought him a coarse brute and fancied the idea of his big, rough hands on their silken bodies. He'd been glad to prove them right. Of course, once he'd met Willa, he'd stopped responding to those propositions. Nothing was stopping him now from taking up Lady Shipton's obvious offer.

Except his cock shriveled to a husk at the thought.

"My taste for dares has shrunk now that I'm not a boy," he said.

"Who wants a boy, anyway," Lady Shipton said, "when a man will do much better?"

Willa laughed again, and Dom's gaze whipped toward her. She was running her finger around the rim of her wineglass and Cransley was entranced as she did so.

God, she looked so lovely in that green gown. It had been his favorite of hers—was she wearing it tonight on purpose? Was it a message? Defiance, without a doubt. She *wanted* to torment him.

Did ever a man bless the rack that tortured him, praising the machine that pulled his limbs from their sockets, applauding the device that made his existence hell?

"Jealousy can be a powerful weapon, too," the

marchioness said. When Dom turned his attention back to her, she gave him a knowing, sultry smile.

"Jealousy assumes *one* of the parties gives a damn about the other," Dom replied.

"And we know that *isn't* the case," Willa threw in.

"Just so, princess." Dom took another long drink from his glass.

Her lips pressed into a line, and she used the tip of her knife to poke angrily at a piece of fish.

Dom started to rise from the table, but Finn placed a hand on his arm.

"Not yet," his friend advised.

"I know the rules," Dom said lowly. "But I can't sit at this table any longer."

"Try. Politeness might not mean much, but Willa's been watching you all night. She'd be thrown badly if you stalked from dinner like a wounded bear."

"It wouldn't matter to her. She's not even looking at me."

Finn gave a slight smile. "Kieran said you'd won academic prizes at Oxford, but those prizes don't seem to cover astuteness." At Dom's dubious silence, Finn added, "Trust me, Dom. She's quite aware of your presence at the table."

Dom rubbed his chin. Come to think of it, every time he glanced in her direction, her earbobs danced, as if she'd just turned her head away from him.

He stayed seated through the rest of the meal.

There was still a part of himself that could hardly believe that he, a man who'd once slept with rats scurrying across his face, was actually having a sumptuous dinner in an ancient but elegant dining room in an even more ancient but elegant manor house. The clothes on his back could have paid for a year's rent, just as the onyx ring on his finger could have bought months' worth of food.

And yet . . . was this life any better than the tough but honest living he'd eked out in Ratcliff?

At the end of the meal, Longbridge got to his feet. "We aren't going to separate the sexes—in fact, we're all going to repair to the parlor."

The guests murmured, interested and intrigued, and even Dom wondered what the hell Longbridge meant by that.

Everyone filed out into the hallway, though Willa lingered in the dining room, taking one final drink of wine.

Dom lingered, too.

"Princess." He took a step toward her.

She slammed her glass down onto the table, and the servants who had been in the chamber to clear the plates scurried out of the room, leaving her and Dom alone.

"You don't have my permission to call me that," she snapped, color high on her cheeks. "You lost that privilege when you abandoned me at the altar."

His jaw tightened. "I hurt you, and you'll never know how much I grieve over that."

"How can I," she fired back, "when you've said nothing about it? I've no idea whether you're pleased by what you did, or you regret it—and you certainly haven't apologized."

She was yelling now. He looked toward the hallway in case any of the guests lingered there.

"They can't know I was the one to leave," he said grimly. "It'll hurt your reputation."

"What does it matter?" she went on hotly. "There's been too much obfuscation, too many lies strung out to cover the shameful truth, and I'm sick of it. If the world learns what truly happened between us, and my reputation is in tatters, then I welcome it. Anything, other than *this*." She gestured to the space between them, filled with tension and pain.

He swallowed hard, but the words that wanted to tear from him refused to come out.

She shook her head, and disgust filled her voice. "For all your protestations, you *aren't* sorry."

"That I hurt you," he finally ground out, reverting to his old accent. "Yes. Knowin' I caused you a moment's pain, let alone nearly a year of it—I'd sooner gut myself with a cargo hook. Not a second goes by that I don't wish to God I hadn't caused you anguish. And I'm sorry," he continued in a rasp, "so damned sorry I did that. I'll go to the coldness of the grave repentin' that I've done that to you. You have to know that."

"I don't *have* to know *anything*." Her eyes

gleamed. "I don't have to listen to a word you say to me."

"Princess—"

"Mortification. That's what I felt when you left me. You humiliated me in front of my family. You embarrassed me in front of the whole city."

He burned, acid filling his veins. "The last thing I wanted."

"If you think you touched *this*." She placed a hand over her chest and laughed, but the sound was uneven and choked. "You could *never*."

Her eyes were bright, gleaming. Something glossed on her cheeks.

Tears. They couldn't be. Not once in the whole time that he'd known her did she ever weep. She was the strongest person he knew, and yet here she was, insisting that he hadn't hurt her, while tears ran down her face.

Pain slashed through him, jagged and red.

He reached for her. She lurched away from his touch. Wiping at her face, she dashed from the room.

And then he was alone, save for the apology he'd offered but she'd refused.

A few moments later, the servants reappeared, edging into the chamber to clean up after the meal. He waved away offers to get him anything, instead snaring a decanter of some spirit from the sideboard. He took it with him as he climbed the stairs to his room.

As he ascended, he undid his neckcloth and drank straight from the crystal container. The whisky barely burned as it slid down his throat, but it would take a hell of a lot more than what the pretty decanter held to make him feel anything. As he walked, he grabbed a candlestick, since the way ahead would be a dark one.

The location of his attic room was far from where the other guests slept, which was just what he wanted. Yet it meant he could only reach his bedchamber by going up a very narrow set of back stairs that creaked threateningly beneath his weight.

The sound reminded him of the rickety staircase he used to climb. Late at night, he'd go up to his family's cramped rooms after a long day's work, his muscles aching from hefting cargo as big as himself. He'd known he was growing up because the wood beneath his feet had complained more and more, the same way it did under Da's weight, and he'd been proud to know that he was becoming a man. A man of heft and substance. A man who made a difference in the world—or at the least, who could help provide for his family.

The quiet of stairs that were well-built and thickly carpeted was unnerving. It was as though he'd been erased, his significance blotted out.

Fortunately, the stairs he climbed groaned like ghosts under his feet. He smiled grimly before he took another drink from the decanter.

Twelve years had passed since Da had made his fortune, and yet those years felt more like a dream than anything that had come before. Any day now, he expected to wake up and find himself lying on his too-short bed, looking at the water stain on the ceiling, and hearing Ma cough as she prepared their morning porridge.

Every now and then, Willa had wanted to know more about his background, who he'd been and where he'd come from. He'd given her few details, only saying that it was very different from anything she'd known. Earls' daughters didn't need to know such things. And how could he admit to her that there were parts of his old life—one part in particular—that filled him with shame?

She, so strong and so forceful, would have no doubt scoffed and scorned such weakness. So, he'd said little.

But tonight . . . Tonight, she'd wept. She'd rejected his apology and he'd made her cry.

Dom finally reached the attic landing. He bent down beneath the low, sloping ceiling, the top of his head grazing the beams. Rain hammered against the roof as if a band of demon horses galloped over the slate. There were two other rooms off the short corridor—both of them crammed full of the house's cast-off detritus. His bedchamber was at the end, and shadows danced as he strode toward it.

"Fuck," he muttered when he pushed open the door.

As Mrs. Murray had warned, the room was a small one, its furniture rusted and barely holding together. Still, it was better than anything he'd known in Ratcliff.

That had been in the daylight. Before the storm. Now rain streamed in through holes scattered across the roof, revealing just how run-down this chamber really was. There were puddles everywhere, and water steadily dripped down onto his bed. The bedlinen and mattress were fully soaked.

He set the decanter down on the floor and put the candle on the table, then debated his choices. Go back downstairs, where everyone—including Willa—was gathered, find Mrs. Murray, and then be moved into another room, which would be the chamber next to Willa's. Or stay here and endure the night.

With an oath, he shucked his fine evening coat and waistcoat and tucked them into the barely standing clothes press. He pushed up his shirt-sleeves before stalking to the bed and shoving it across the floor so that the rain no longer poured onto it. The mattress was a lost cause, but he wrung out the blanket and at least the pillow was only a bit damp.

After tugging off his boots, he blew out the candle. He stretched out on the soggy blanket-covered bed slats. Predictably, his feet stuck out the bottom of the bed, and the pillow squished beneath his head. The storm continued to bellow outside. It was going to be a very long night.

After many hours, he finally fell asleep, and dreamt of diamonds falling from Willa's eyes.

Chapter 6

❧ ✳ ❦

*W*illa managed to collect herself enough to join the other guests after dinner. She made herself smile through several rounds of card games, but all the while, Dom's words rang through her head, far louder than the storm lashing the house.

Knowin' I caused you a moment's pain, let alone nearly a year of it—I'd sooner gut myself with a cargo hook. Not a second goes by that I don't wish to God I hadn't caused you anguish. And I'm sorry, so damned sorry I did that. I'll go to the coldness of the grave repentin' that I've done that to you.

"The next move is yours, Lady Willa," Mrs. McDaniel said, breaking into her thoughts.

"What's that?" Willa blinked at the hand of cards she held in shaking hands.

"Mr. Cransley has taken his turn, so now it falls to you."

The faces of the other players were smooth and

shiny, their expressions ranging from curious to mildly impatient. She glanced back down at the cards, but they made no sense, just a collection of meaningless symbols, and so she laid them down upon the baize-covered table.

"I forfeit." Without looking back, she rose and walked toward the window, where rain hammered furiously as if it was attempting to pierce the glass.

Laughter from the table was as sharp as the rain, and to remain in this parlor, with these people, pretending that Dom's words hadn't cut down to the core of her being—it was impossible. Restless, she stalked from the chamber.

She drew up short when she nearly collided with Celeste.

"No taste for cards tonight?" Willa asked, glancing back toward the parlor.

"Other games interest me more," her brother's wife answered. She started to move past Willa, her eyes focused somewhere deeper in the house, but Willa clasped Celeste's wrist, stopping her.

"How often have you heard Dom apologize?" she asked, though it was more of a plea than a question.

A corner of Celeste's mouth curved up. "You'd have a better chance of extracting an apology from the storm outside than getting my brother to admit he was wrong. Although," she added thoughtfully, "when he learned that I had been miserable pretending to be a perfectly genteel woman, and didn't want to be engaged to Lord Montford, he was very upset, and remorseful."

"Then he's sincere," Willa pressed, "when he says he's sorry?"

"I take it that Dom has apologized," Celeste said approvingly. "Good. He ought to. What he did was horrendous and worthy of an epic groveling. But you don't know whether or not to accept his apology?"

"A few words aren't going to suture the wound," Willa said grimly.

"They won't," her sister-in-law agreed. "Nor should they."

"That is," Willa added quickly, "if he wounded me. Which he didn't. Only my pride."

Celeste regarded her carefully. "So, it was only injured pride that made you flee to the Continent for nearly a year. Only hurt dignity that drained the blood from your face when you saw him here. Or caused you to destroy some porcelain. Or stare at him throughout dinner as though the very sight of him was a torment and a blessing."

"It might've been more than a blow to my pride," Willa said, grudgingly. "I thought . . ." She swallowed hard. "It doesn't matter what I thought."

"It's all right." Celeste's words were gentle. "There's no shame in admitting that you cared for him. Perhaps you still do."

"I don't *want* to," Willa muttered.

Celeste said softly, "I told my heart over and over again that I *wasn't* going to fall in love with Kieran. But it didn't obey me, and did exactly as it desired."

"I've no idea what my heart desires." A sharp pain radiated out from the center of Willa's chest, and she used her free hand to press against it.

"Perhaps that's what this time on Mr. Longbridge's island is for," her brother's wife suggested. "Listening, truly *listening*, to your heart."

"Am I supposed to forgive him?" Something ached within Willa, something that felt suspiciously like longing. But longing only led to more vulnerability, and with it, pain. *That*, she couldn't allow.

Celeste stroked her fingers down Willa's face. "Forgive yourself for being hurt. There's no shame in it. As for you and Dom . . ." She shook her head. "Both of you must find a way forward. In whatever form that takes. Together or apart. So long as you both can find your way toward peace."

A hard, hot knot lodged in Willa's throat. "Peace seems the furthest thing from me right now. I ran to the Continent to seek it, but the change in landscape only served to show me that I can't outpace something inside of me. If anything, it only showed that I . . ."

She choked back her words. How could she admit, even to someone as understanding as Celeste, what Dom's desertion had meant to her? What it meant *about* her?

"Salome," a man's voice sang from down the hallway. "Where's my lusty Salome?"

"There's no one here named Salome," Willa muttered, frowning.

Celeste's face turned a deep, rosy pink. "I . . . um . . ."

"Salome, I await you in the study for private tutoring. You know what happens to naughty students who are tardy." Kieran appeared at the end of the hallway, and he, too, turned scarlet. "Oh, God."

With dawning horror, Willa looked back and forth between her brother and the furiously blushing Celeste.

"I'm going to bed now and will spend the rest of my life insisting that I saw and heard *nothing*."

Before Kieran or his wife could say another word, Willa ran for the safety of her room.

SOMETIME DURING THE night, the storm had stopped. Mr. Longbridge had said that the weather was mercurial, and came and went with astonishing speed.

When Willa made her way down to the breakfast room in the morning, sunlight streamed in through the tall windows, and birds sang unfamiliar tunes to herald the new day.

She greeted the few guests who were up at this

early hour, and told herself that the tight feeling in her chest was gratitude because Dom wasn't amongst their number. As she considered the array of food on the sideboard, Miss Steele joined her, and together they piled their dishes with poached eggs and toasted bread—though Miss Steele declined the rashers of bacon.

"Strange that the storm made me sleep even more soundly," Miss Steele remarked as they served themselves.

Willa made a noncommittal noise. She'd spent most of the night careening from one side of her bed to the other, though it wasn't the rain or wind that kept her awake. Her mind had been filled with the abject sorrow in Dom's eyes when he'd offered his apology, and his words echoing with what sounded like true remorse. Yet she'd meant what she had said to Celeste—it would take more than a few sentences to make right the wrong that had been done.

And when she had shut her eyes, Celeste's counsel had rung in her ears.

Forgive yourself for being hurt. There's no shame in it . . . Both of you must find a way forward. In whatever form that takes. Together or apart.

There was so much to try to understand, about herself, and how she could possibly take that forward-leading path that Celeste urged her to take.

One thing she did know: she couldn't let him,

or anyone, know how much he occupied her thoughts, or how her body kept turning to him as if seeking out a dark star.

Everyone would think she was weak, and she couldn't permit that. God, how she prayed for indifference toward him.

"Good morning, Mr. Kilburn," Miss Steele said, glancing toward the door.

"Good morning, Miss Steele. Lady Willa."

Willa's spine stiffened at the sound of his deep voice. She shouldn't acknowledge Dom straightaway, yet still she turned toward the entrance to the breakfast room in time to see him stride into the chamber.

His hair was damp, slightly curling, as though he'd bathed first thing this morning. There wasn't anything else remarkable about his appearance—if you didn't count being a mountain of a man in perfectly tailored dark clothing as having a remarkable appearance.

He nodded at the others in the room, but when his gaze fell on Willa, it snagged. She couldn't look away from him, and he seemed equally as fascinated by her, his storm-hued eyes penetrating as he stared at her.

"Did *you* sleep well in the middle of the storm?" Miss Steele asked.

The spell between her and Dom snapped apart as he addressed the other lady. "Takes a lot to rattle me."

Except becoming my husband, Willa nearly said. But there was no point in prolonging the anguish of the past, not if either of them intended to move beyond that hurt.

Instead of taking a seat at the table, Dom strode right to the fireplace. He turned his back to the flames, his hands clasped behind him, and inhaled deeply as if soaking in the warmth of the fire.

Was that . . . *steam* rising up from Dom's clothing?

A servant approached with a cup and teapot.

"If that's not coffee," Dom said, "I've got nothing to say."

The servant bowed and retreated, before returning again with a silver pitcher and pouring coffee into a porcelain cup. Dom downed the whole scalding beverage in one swallow, held out his cup for more, and drank that with equal speed, before giving the cup back to the servant.

Willa continued to load her plate, trying not to appear too obvious as she stared at Dom. Yes, vapor was actually rising from his garments. As if . . . as if they were soaking wet, and struggled to dry from the heat of the fire.

Wet hair. Wet clothes. A storm that had lasted all night. And Dom had spent the evening in a bedroom that the housekeeper had said was in a terrible state. That could only mean one thing.

She battled the urge to go to him, wrap him in thick blankets, and feed him beef tea so he could find some solace and warmth. At the same time, something cold and biting slithered through her belly.

"Good Christ," Willa muttered.

It was too early to feel such conflicting, bewildering emotions, and yet here she was, holding a plate of poached eggs and toasted bread. Comfort Dom, or brain him with a candlestick?

She slapped her plate down on the sideboard and marched to him.

At her approach, Dom regarded her warily. This close, she could see that he was indeed soaked to the skin.

Another bewildering mix of concern and anger seethed through her, and she wished to all the heavens that she could understand what it was she felt for this infuriating man.

"Hell, Dom," she hissed, keeping her voice low so that their conversation couldn't be heard by the nearby guests. "Am I truly so repellant that you'd choose to spend the night in an absolute *mire* of a room where you're *rained on* and risk *pneumonia* rather than have the chamber next to mine?"

A corner of his mouth lifted wryly, and there was almost defiance in his eyes and in the line of his jaw as he regarded her.

"I can handle it," he said simply. "And it's what I deserve."

She rocked back, stunned. This was not the answer she'd been expecting. "What do you mean, *what you deserve*?"

Before Dom could answer, Mr. Longbridge saun-
tered into the room. "With the weather turning so
delightful, I propose a diversion after breakfast. I
will be leading a trek around the island, and we'll
have a picnic from a scenic vantage. A fascinating
place, this island, with centuries of history. Though
the terrain can be somewhat rugged, so if you're of
fragile disposition, I'd warn you to remain at the
house. Strong hearts only."

There were murmurs from the guests as they debated whether or not to venture forth on the strenuous expedition.

"I'll go," Willa announced.

At the same time, Dom said, "I'm in."

They shared a look, practically challenging
each other to determine who would withdraw
first. Though doubt flickered in his eyes, he didn't
back out.

She should stay behind, keeping the distance between them as they'd agreed. But she recalled what
Celeste said on the nature of moving forward. Did
Willa want to remain the same as she always had
been, stay the same person—or did she want to
take the bigger risk?

Willa had constantly prided herself on not being
afraid, yet . . . that wasn't true. There was always a
fragment of uncertainty within her, a small, glowing coal of fearfulness that she tried so hard to keep
banked. Yet it burned all the same. Perhaps now
was the time to face it. If *Dom* could, so could she.

Before that, though, she had something important to take care of.

"Mr. Longbridge." She approached her host, who was humming to himself as he mounded food onto a plate. "Might I have a word in private?"

Following breakfast, everyone going on the trek repaired to their rooms to change into appropriate clothing and footwear. Fortunately, Willa had packed a pair of sturdy ankle boots that would serve her well on rough terrain, and she switched her silk gown for a lightweight printed muslin and coordinating spencer.

The other guests who opted to go on the rugged walk included her brothers and their wives, as well as Miss Steele, Mr. Cransley, and Baron Hunsdon. Everyone gathered in the entryway of the house, with each person suitably dressed and shod—though Dom looked a trifle uncomfortable in the sporting attire of a man of leisure, likely because he was unused to open-air pursuits. These clothes, too, looked damp. Hopefully, the weather was warm enough that he wouldn't catch a chill on the walk.

She shook her head at herself, fretting over whether or not Dom might get sick. He was the most hale and vigorous man she'd ever known. He could battle off the ague through sheer force of will.

For the picnic, Mr. Cransley was recruited to

hold a hamper, and Baron Hunsdon carried two bottles of wine. The bottles kept slipping in his grip, but he insisted he could manage the task. In short order, they set off on their journey.

As large as the house and its grounds were, they quickly gave way to much more uncultivated terrain. The ground was indeed rocky, rising up in low, craggy mountains that loomed over the beaches like slumbering giants awaiting someone to sail in and wake them. There were a few stands of rather scrubby rowan trees, but overall, the landscape was windswept and austere. She appreciated the land's refusal to adhere to conventional ideas of lush beauty. It seemed to take pride in the fact that it wasn't a soft or coddling kind of place—not unlike Dom's refusal to fully force himself into the role of gentleman.

They clambered over swells of rock, walking in a single file with Mr. Longbridge in the lead. Most of the men kept toward the front, though Kieran walked with Celeste, and Willa and Miss Steele followed soon after them.

Willa glanced at Dom, striding nearby. "You needn't shorten your pace on my account."

"Who says I am?" he asked casually as he clambered over a stony outcropping. The movement made the fabric of his breeches pull across his broad thigh muscles, but of course that didn't interest her in the slightest. If she looked, it was only as someone who was interested in anatomy. Well—she was *currently* intrigued by anatomy, but a person could always shift their interests at any time in their lives.

"You're hovering," she noted. "Keeping close in case I or Miss Steele should need your manly assistance?" She gripped the rocks of the outcropping and pulled herself up.

"Miss Steele seems content on her own," he answered. "And you've no need of anyone's help, manly or otherwise."

Even so, he lingered atop the rock formation, very much as if he was waiting to see if she needed his help. Determined to climb without his aid, she hauled herself to the top of the grass-covered boulder to stand beside him.

Miss Steele paused at the bottom of the outcropping. She blew out a breath and shook her head. "If it's all the same, I'd rather have a hot bath and a cup of tea. Enjoy the rest of your trek."

With that, Miss Steele turned and headed back to the house, which now appeared to be a small fairy-sized dwelling far below.

"All that remain are us hearty souls," Willa noted as she watched Miss Steele's figure retreating. "Unless you also want to return."

It was partly a dare, partly a question, and she wasn't certain which answer she wanted to hear.

"I'm a city bloke, it's true, but it's not often I get the chance to see something like this." He waved toward the landscape unrolling all around them. "Wasting it would be a bloody shame."

It was a little aggravating that she exhaled in relief at his answer.

"And I used to think—" He pressed his lips together.

"What did you used to think?" she asked with a frown.

"That this was the sort of thing I wanted to do with you when we were courting." The words came out of him gruffly, as if he was trying to keep them inside. "Instead of all the pretty promenades and tea shops and tame little scenes we used to visit, we could've gone to faraway places, maybe a little rough and wild, where it could've been just us."

"I would've liked that," she said softly. It *did* sound wonderful, away from judgment and preconceived ideas as to who she was supposed to be. Who *they* were supposed to be.

He tilted his head to one side. "That so, princess? You always brightened whenever we'd run into your friends."

"Not always," she admitted. "Sometimes, yes, it was gratifying to scandalize the ton. To be outrageous."

She'd earned a reputation as a hoyden, a reputation she'd purposefully cultivated. It was either that, or be one of those girls browbeaten into docility, which she would never tolerate.

"The way you liked to show me off to your aristo set, princess?" He studied her, his gaze perceptive. "Your big rough dockworker—not one of those reedy, thin-blooded nobs the other ladies nabbed for husbands."

She opened her mouth to deny this. Then closed it again. Because it shamed her to admit it, yet she *had* reveled in the fact that the man she'd chosen to be her husband was exactly the opposite of what Society—and her parents—had demanded of her.

"The way you liked having a princess—well, an earl's daughter—on your arm?"

His lips curled. "Suppose we both fancied shocking everyone. Making 'em clutch their pearls."

"And clutch their diamonds and coral beads and . . ."

They gazed at each other for a long time, the wind whipping around them, the craggy island spreading out in all directions. Awareness spread through her belly and body as all she saw at that moment was Dom, and he looked only at her.

Before, their conversations had been light, teasing, never with this core of honesty. It shook her. It didn't feel good to know that to him, she had represented an idea rather than him entirely wanting her as a person. But then, she'd done the same thing to him. Her chest throbbed as she confronted hard truths about him, and herself.

And yet . . . something about it felt *right*. That they could be truthful with each other in this way, and admit that they hadn't been exactly who they had pretended to be. As if layers fell away, revealing a precious candor beneath.

"Catch up, you two," Mr. Longbridge called back. "Or else we'll eat your portion of the picnic, and you'll have to forage for your luncheon."

The spell between her and Dom broke apart. Leaving behind revelations and disclosures, she snapped back into the moment, and they were once again on a rocky ledge on a windswept island.

"That's no threat," she said with a shake of her head. Moving away from the rocky outcropping, she headed toward a low bush growing nearby. She bent down and plucked several green berries from the scrub. "These blaeberries aren't yet ripe, but I warrant that on the more protected and warmer side of the island, they'll be perfect."

Dom's brows climbed. "Whatberries?"

"We call them whortleberries in England," she explained. She held the small fruit between her fingers. "It's unusual that they'd grow in the Hebrides, especially since they prefer forest floors and growing under tree canopies, but Mr. Longbridge did say that his island was an unusual place."

There was a long silence, and she glanced up to see Dom staring at her, his expression puzzled. "Have I said something strange?"

"Didn't think princesses like you paid attention to things such as wild berries and tree canopies."

Her spine stiffened. "Perhaps I'm not as much of a princess as you thought. Perhaps there's more to me than you *ever* knew."

She dropped the unripe fruit to the ground and

strode ahead. The only reason why her heart pounded was because she walked quickly, and *not* because she was hurt by what he'd said, or who he had believed her to be.

They'd taken a step forward, only to fall even further behind.

Chapter 7

❖∗❖

$\mathcal{T}$he island is, of course, haunted," Longbridge said proudly as Dom and the other guests gathered in a vale between two rugged mountains. "Ghosts, naturally, and the fair folk. You can't find a niche or stone that doesn't have some spirit presiding over it."

"It's a wonder they tolerate the presence of the living and the mortal," Kieran mused.

"Who says they do?" Willa asked. She didn't even look at Dom when she said, "Heaven knows, I've little stomach for human men."

Dom clenched his jaw. The last hour had been spent climbing over and across the island's uneven terrain—and being chilled by Willa's pointed silence. She'd ignored him for the past sixty minutes.

Life was much simpler in Ratcliff, when all he had to deal with was backbreaking labor and earning enough coin to feed and shelter his family, sometimes avoiding someone with a grudge coming after him with a club. Simple, basic needs that weren't tangled up in the knots and thorns of caring about someone. Well, he'd loved his family, but that was different.

"You see this vale," Longbridge continued, pointing to a band of water winding its way between the hills. "Follow it for a quarter of a mile, and you'll reach a bridge that spans a creek. On the other side of that bridge is a small cabin, regularly maintained by my servants. It's a place I favor going to when the activities I wish to pursue are too scandalous even for the main house."

The devil only knew what sort of things Longbridge thought too scandalous, but Dom would have to take the man at his word.

"Whenever I'm in residence," the host explained, "my staff keeps the place modestly provisioned."

"Is it haunted, too?" Celeste asked.

"To the best of my knowledge," Longbridge said with a laugh, "only by the spirits of my tempestuous assignations."

"Is the changing of bedlinen also part of your staff's maintenance of the place?" Kieran asked dryly.

"Naturally," their host answered. "I'm only scandalous in certain regards. Hygiene isn't one of them. Come, let's proceed onward so I may show you the best views."

Everyone followed Longbridge as he began an ascent up a steep hill, with Dom bringing up the rear. He could move faster and keep pace with the others, but his desire for company had fallen off like a diseased limb. Instead, he let everyone stay several yards ahead of him.

It wasn't possible to look at anything other than Willa as she energetically climbed over rocks and across ruts in the ground. She'd once wryly said that her fey looks didn't quite fit in such a dull and boring place like an aristocratic assembly in a ballroom. Yet here, on this wild and uncanny island, springing lightly up the side of a rugged mountain, it was as if she'd found the place where she truly belonged. Her cheeks were pink and her eyes gleamed like a nighttime sea.

Truly, she was one of the loveliest beings he'd ever been lucky enough to behold. And he couldn't stop himself from speeding up his strides, drawing closer to her. Even if he shouldn't.

He'd been a goddamn ass, saying what he had. It hadn't surprised him, that when they'd been engaged, she'd used him to shock Society. Yet, much as he'd worshipped her, he hadn't behaved any better. They laid themselves bare with their disclosures, and there was a kind of comfort in that.

There might've been a chance that the cold distance between them had gotten smaller, that maybe she wasn't as far away as she had been. Then he'd opened his damned mouth, and here they were, strangers sharing the same side of the mountain.

As everyone continued to ascend, Celeste drifted

closer to Dom. She took his much larger hand in her far smaller one.

"Hard to believe we've the same parents," he said, looking down at how different in size their hands were. "You could always do such fine needlework."

"Not by choice," she said, dryly. Then, glancing toward Willa, she added, "Going to have to do better, big brother."

His brows raised. "You heard us?"

"I wasn't trying to, but the landscape carries voices, and . . ." She looked up into his face. "There may be more to her than you know, Dom. More than she'll let you see."

"Why would she feel like she'd have to hide anything from me?" He stared at the straight line of Willa's back as she moved lightly over rocks and around scrub.

"Perhaps when you call a girl *princess*," Celeste mused, "she feels like she has to be one all the time. She might stride across the battlements, but there can be more to her than a crown. She's a person, too."

He frowned. It was so unlike the Willa that he'd known. Or the Willa that the woman herself had allowed him to see. But maybe there was more than a little truth in what his sister said. An hour ago, he'd begun to understand that, and Celeste's words drove the point home.

He hadn't been fair to Willa. Not by a mile.

"Besides," Celeste added thoughtfully, "there are things about *you* that you won't reveal to *me*, and I'm family."

His gaze whipped to his sister. "What do you know?"

She lifted her shoulders. "Very little—and that's the core of it, isn't it? People get so used to pretending to be who they think someone wants them to be. For many reasons. In my case, I had to be the model daughter, the perfect aspiring lady. Never letting anyone know how much it killed me inside."

"I'm so sorry, Star." He squeezed their joined hands, careful not to crush her fingers. "It's no excuse, but I didn't know what it cost you."

She squeezed his hand back, and the strength in her grip surprised him. "I never let you see it. And everything changed for me with Kieran." Her eyes shone when she looked toward her husband, who had paused in his walk to scribble something in a notebook.

"Writing verses again," Dom said wryly.

"Doubtless," his sister said with a smile. "And I cannot wait to hear them."

Dom turned his attention back to Willa. She had stopped to look at the view, her skirts molded to her body, strands of her dark hair coming loose and dancing on the wind.

"Stay close to her, Star," he said, still looking at the woman who had once been his. "Comfort her, if she'll accept comfort. Do anything in your power to help her move forward, and leave me behind."

"Why not try to take the next steps with her?" his sister asked.

Dom looked at Willa so far ahead of him. Climbing, going higher. Soon, she'd reach the top before anyone else, and tower above them like the princess she was. Yet maybe there was more to her than an endless supply of defiance and strength. But what was it? Who was she, without her armor?

A woman who knew about foraging for wild berries, and who had longed for the same thing he had: time away from the eyes of the world. Maybe to breathe a bit freer. Maybe she was tired of being strong. God knew, he'd borne his own share of carrying weight, and even he wearied of it.

"Don't know, Star." He exhaled. "I've lived in rough places, done brutal things. But she wouldn't want me, not if she knew the truth. I'm not who she thinks I am."

"Who are you, Dom?"

Yet he shook his head. Because *that*, he couldn't reveal to anyone. Especially not Willa.

"WE'RE ALMOST TO the vantage point for the picnic," Mr. Longbridge said, waving toward a bluff that perched high above the hills.

Willa blew out a breath. Thank goodness they were nearly at their destination. Clambering over rocks made her feel alive and energetic—but it was also bloody exhausting.

The scenery was spectacular, deeply romantic in the most poetic sense of the word, and full of majesty. And yet all she could think about was what she'd overheard.

Dom's words to his sister, carried on the wind, haunted her. How he'd urged Celeste to help her move on. Most of all, though, his words kept ringing through her head like a bell tolling death.

She wouldn't want me, not if she knew the truth. I'm not who she thinks I am.

How had she not seen it? This brash, bold man never backed down from a challenge and looked at everyone with defiance, as if to say, *I'm as good as you, if not better.* But lurking in his heart was the fundamental belief that there was something in him *she* would reject.

He'd never shown her any of this vulnerability, or said what it was within him that was so shameful.

If only he had. But then, would that have changed anything? Would it have changed *them*?

"Careful, careful," Kieran cautioned Baron Hunsdon as the other man nearly lost his hold on the wine bottles. "The whole fate of our outing depends on your hands. What's a scenic outlook without wine?"

"I've got it," the baron insisted, even as the bottles slipped in his grip.

"Give over." Dom strode up, untying his neckcloth.

"I can assure you that the wine bottles don't need sartorial assistance," Baron Hunsdon asserted.

Dom rolled his eyes. "I'm not trying to fancy them up."

He whipped off his neckcloth—revealing an expanse of bare, olive skin—and quickly knotted the fabric. For such large hands, they moved swift and deft as he tied the linen into intricate loops. Then he took the wine from Baron Hunsdon and slipped the bottles into what became evident was a makeshift sling that supported their precious cargo.

"Safe as a babe in a cradle," he said, handing the contraption back to the baron.

"How did you learn to do that?" Mr. Longbridge asked admiringly.

Dom's smile was small and wry. "Can't earn your coin on the London docks without knowing your way around a few knots."

"How . . . handy." Willa's voice sounded even more breathless than the strenuous climb would warrant. But she couldn't stop looking at Dom's naked throat, and her mind *insisted* on thinking of all the wonderful, clever things his oversized hands could do to her body.

He caught her staring at him. But he didn't jeer. Instead, his eyes darkened, and he said in a husky voice, "I'm very good with my hands."

"Evidently." Despite the brisk wind that stung her face, her cheeks warmed.

No, no, no. Lusting after Dom ranked high on

the list of terrible ideas, including Pandora deciding to have one little peek inside that box.

"At least the wine is safe." Despite the breeze whipping around them, her words sounded too loud. "This climb has made me dreadfully thirsty. And hungry."

Inwardly, she grimaced. Good Lord, could she sound more brainless?

If Dom noticed that she was behaving like the veriest ninny, he didn't say. Instead, he silently watched her with a predator's eyes as she marched past him, leading the way toward the promised vantage point. Hopefully, the view would help distract her from the fact that she was just as enticed by Dom as ever. If anything, her attraction to him was growing by the moment.

The picnic was as delightful as Mr. Longbridge had pledged, with delicious food and excellent wine and lovely views. There were cold meats and cheeses and bread and pies both sweet and savory, plus crisp pears grown in Mr. Longbridge's own greenhouse. Yet Willa's attention kept being pulled to Dom, reclining on the ground, massive and dark against the steel-gray water behind him. When the other guests laughed and talked, he was silent—all the while radiating potent energy that continually lured her in.

Indifference would be so much better than this bewildering muddle of desire and anger and uncertainty. But then, things were never simple between her and Dom. Perhaps she *had* been merely a princess and a prize to him, just as he'd been a kind of defiant trophy for her. But those roles weren't holding any longer. Not in this place that seemed to strip them of their pretenses.

"We ought to head back," Mr. Longbridge said when the last iced cake had been consumed and the wine bottles were empty. "It will give us enough time to rest and bathe before dinner."

"I could grow acclimated to this indulgent existence," Kieran said as he stood. He helped Celeste to her feet and was especially solicitous in brushing stray blades of grass that stuck to her skirts—paying particular attention to minuscule bits clinging to his wife's bosom and bottom.

"As if your every waking moment wasn't spent indulging yourself," Finn answered.

"A sybarite born and bred," Kieran replied. "Much to our parents' dismay."

Finn shook his head. "Can you say you're a Ransome brother if you *haven't* dissatisfied our parents?"

"Other than our eldest brother and eternal prig, Simon," Willa said sardonically, "*all* of our parents' children proved disappointments."

She started to rise, but Dom's broad hand appeared in her vision. After a moment's hesitation, she slid her ungloved hand into his so he could help her stand. How much rougher his skin was against hers, the temperature of his flesh searing.

Hot sensation collected in her palm and shot up her arm to spread through her body. His nostrils flared and he drew in a quick, uneven breath.

He lifted her to her feet as if she weighed nothing more than thistledown. But he held on to her, and she kept her hand in his, staring down at the sight. Until she regained her senses and pulled away slowly, her fingers dragging against his palm. Old calluses lined his skin, but the abrasion made her shiver.

She fussed with her skirts, pretending to shake off any crumbs from the cakes she'd eaten, though she shot a glance toward Dom. He was talking with Finn and Kieran, yet at his side, he flexed his hand.

"Now we return to my humble lodgings," Mr. Longbridge declared once the picnic supplies had been gathered up. "March, my charming army!"

"I'll see everyone back at the house," Dom said.

"You aren't coming with us?" Willa asked in surprise. "How will you find your way back?"

He lifted his wide shoulders. "Got a fair sense of direction."

"But . . ." She turned in a circle. "What if it grows dark and you get lost?"

"I won't be more than a few minutes behind everybody. Don't worry, prin—" He stopped himself, but she knew exactly which word he was on the verge of saying. "I'm a big, grown bloke, and too mean to get into trouble on this little island."

"If you run into a wild boar, you can always snarl him down."

"There, you see." He offered her a cynical smile. "Surly bastards like me always come out on top."

"Forward, my troops!" Mr. Longbridge commanded.

Willa joined the others as they descended the mountain, but she cast a glance over her shoulder in time to see Dom striding down the other side, as elemental as the rocks themselves. He didn't look back.

Chapter 8

❖ ✳ ❖

After Dom returned to the house a few hours later, he swung through the kitchen before heading back to his room. Up and up he went, until he finally reached the closed door to his bedchamber.

He turned the doorknob, yet it rattled in his hand and the door itself stayed shut. Maybe the wood had swollen from all the moisture and needed a jostle to open.

He pushed more forcefully, yet it wouldn't give. One more unsuccessful turn of the knob proved it: the door was locked.

"The hell?"

Someone might have believed the room empty and shut it up. A quick talk with one of the staff would set everything right.

"There's some mistake," he said to a maid he passed on the first floor. "My room's locked."

There was a moment's panic on the servant's young face.

"I don't want to get anyone into trouble," he said quickly at her distress. "It's got to be a misunderstanding. All I need is someone to unlock the door. No fuss."

"Sir, you'll have to talk to Mr. Longbridge," the maid said, dipping into a curtsey. "You'll find him in his chamber, sir. Just down the hall, on the right."

Dom found his host in his bedchamber—which could only be described as a den of sin, with its massive bed and velvet draperies.

"Ah, Kilburn," Longbridge said as his valet helped him out of a coat. "The island didn't devour you."

"Does it have an appetite for brutes?"

Longbridge shrugged. "One never knows what the island might do. But I suspect it likes you, which accounts for the fact that you've returned."

"Your concern for my welfare is touching."

His host grinned. "I always trust the island to take care of the people I like."

"Thanks for that. The maid said I was supposed to talk to you about getting my room unlocked."

"Afraid not, my friend," Longbridge said, allowing his valet to remove his waistcoat.

"Is the key lost?"

"Safe and secure on Mrs. Murray's chatelaine," Longbridge answered easily.

"Then let me back in." Dom planted his hands on his hips. "Or do you want me sleeping on a rock next?"

"As I said, that's not possible. The crux of the matter," the other man went on smoothly, "is that if I allow you to continue to sleep in that . . . I hesitate to call it a *room*, and then you catch the ague and die, well"—he shrugged—"it reflects rather poorly on me as a host. No one's going to want to stay here if they know that *I* was responsible for creating another ghost. Thus, I had all your belongings transferred to the original room you were assigned to. Well, not *all* of your possessions. The soggiest of the lot is currently spread before the kitchen fire, drying out."

"Isn't there *somewhere* else you can put me?"

"The walls groan with the number of guests I'm accommodating, and every single bedchamber is spoken for. That leaves you but one alternative, old man."

Dom exhaled. He *knew* he was being manipulated, likely by the Ransome brothers, yet there was no way to fight it. He was strong enough to knock the door to the attic room down, but in truth, another night in that garret, and he might catch some putrid and deadly sickness. Wouldn't *that* be fucking ridiculous, the strapping, belligerent son of Ned Kilburn meeting his maker not in the midst of a tavern fight, but carried away by disease because he'd insisted on sleeping in a room with holes in the roof, when a snug and luxurious chamber was just steps away?

But that put him next to Willa.

"Go," Longbridge urged. "There's a fire in your room, and down blankets on the bed, and everything's dry."

There was stubborn, and then there was stupid, and Dom liked to believe he was the former but not the latter.

"Fine." He added through his teeth, "Thank you."

"Thank *you*," Longbridge answered as he sat down so his valet could take off his boots. "You've kept my reputation as a host well protected."

"You're a good man, Oliver."

Longbridge smiled. "That's what the world believes, but I'm delighted that, in private, I can prove everyone wrong."

After a chilly trek across the island, the lure of a fire and down blankets was too enticing to resist, so Dom went down the hall to seek out both comforts. As he approached the open door of his room, he glanced up to see Willa emerging from her bedchamber. Her expression remained carefully neutral as she looked at him.

"There wasn't any other place to put me," he explained gruffly.

"It won't present a difficulty," she answered, her voice just as impartial as her appearance.

"If you tap on the wall before you leave your room, I'll stay in mine until you've gone, that way you've got less chance of seeing me."

"That won't be necessary," she replied. "I'm not going to fly into a frenzied rage just from looking at you. I've *wanted* to, but a person can evolve."

"You always had a good throwing arm," he said, unable to keep himself from smiling. "Be a shame if you didn't keep up your practice."

A tiny smile tucked itself in the corner of her lips. "I ought to be a bowler on the local cricket team."

He shook his head. "Their batsmen won't stand a chance."

They stood like that for a moment, cautiously smiling at each other, until Mrs. McDaniel appeared, heading toward her room. The widow didn't speak to either of them, only gave a polite nod as she entered her chamber, yet her presence was enough to wake them from a momentary daze.

Without another word, Willa swept down the hallway. She didn't spare him a backward glance as she turned the corner and disappeared.

Dom let out a long, jagged breath.

It'd be a challenge to be so close to her, see her every morning, and hear her moving around at night before she took herself to bed. But he'd no choice in the matter. So, he stepped into his room.

A bright fire leapt cheerfully in its grate, and there was a deep, plush bed, grand and welcoming. He couldn't stop a rueful chuckle at what he'd been willing to forgo in order to keep his distance from Willa. Clearly, the Ransome brothers had other plans.

A soft tap sounded on the door, and he turned

to see Sam, the footman who'd been serving as his valet, poke his head in. "Sir?"

Dom waved Sam forward, and the footman eased into the room and shut the door behind him. He carried a pitcher of what appeared to be steaming water, a neatly folded towel slung over his shoulder.

"I took the liberty, sir, of bringing these things in to help you get ready before dinner."

Dom rubbed a hand over his face and found his cheeks prickly with stubble. "I skipped my morning shave, and men in my family can nearly grow a full beard within hours."

Sam's eyes widened. "It's like that on my mother's side, sir. Not mine, unfortunately." The footman poked sadly at his own cheeks.

"Cheer up, Sam," Dom answered. "Better to lack a beard than look like a wild beast after just a few hours."

"If you say so, sir." Sam arranged the shaving supplies and pulled out a chair.

"Usually, I shave myself," Dom said. "After growing up where I did, it's not easy to trust anyone holding a razor to my throat."

"My hands are as steady as I am trustworthy, sir. Which is saying something—my father's a minister."

"Hard to take issue with a son of a man of God." Dom sat down and let the footman apply a hot towel to his face, softening the whiskers.

"We'll get you ready to go downstairs soon, sir," Sam said. "Mr. Longbridge likes to keep his guests busy."

"I'd wager he does," Dom murmured.

Longbridge clearly enjoyed his dual existence, both as one of London's most respected figures, as well as a secret libertine. Dom didn't quite envy him, though, hiding an important part of himself. Even though Da had insisted that both Celeste and Dom do everything they could to get rid of all traces of Ratcliff from themselves, it didn't matter how hard Dom tried to imitate the manners of the ton. They always reminded him that he'd never be one of them, and eventually he gave up his efforts.

Only the Ransome brothers had fully accepted him for who he was. Though—he hadn't shown them everything. And he'd been careful in what he'd revealed to Willa.

It had been a coup to become engaged to her. Him, a longshoreman's boy, marrying an earl's daughter. Calling her *princess* seemed right because that's what she had been to him: regal and powerful. He'd glowed with pride whenever they had walked out together, and had loved seeing the wary and irate looks on the nobs' faces whenever they clapped eyes on her on his arm.

Except . . . she was more than that, and a throb of shame pierced him. He'd worshipped not Willa herself, but the *idea* of her.

"After hauling from one end of the island to the

other, sir, you're surprisingly spry," Sam continued, removing the towel from Dom's face before applying a thick coat of lather on his jaw and cheeks. "The other guests from the walk have all surrendered to their beds. It'll be a struggle to wake them in time for supper. And tomorrow, Mr. Longbridge has something *very* strenuous planned."

"Another night in that attic room and I'd not be so spry for whatever Longbridge has on the docket. Suppose he knew that, so maybe he insisted on me moving to a different room." It was entirely possible that Kieran and Finn hadn't been behind him changing rooms.

Dom held himself very still as Sam scraped the straight razor over his face.

"He's exacting, Mr. Longbridge," Sam said between passes of the blade. "But always gives his guests what they want. Lady Willa was most demanding that you be given this bedchamber—oh, careful, sir, I don't want to carve you up like a roast." The footman dabbed a cloth at the tiny nick Dom had caused by jolting.

"Lady Willa insisted?" Dom said, frowning.

"Vociferously, sir. Said she wanted it done posthaste. Do lean back, sir, so I may finish your shave."

Dom obliged, but his heart pounded, and not because Sam held a blade close to his jugular.

"The way she told the staff that a fire *had* to be

ready for you when you came back. And that there had to be extra pillows." Sam chuckled. "A managing type, you might say."

"You might say," Dom said quietly, holding as still as he possibly could, but it wasn't an easy task, not when his already roused body filled with crackling electricity.

Willa should by rights hate him until the end of eternity. But she worked so hard to make sure he was comfortable and healthy. That she would look out for him as if . . . as if she still cared for him.

And he'd been an ass to her, saying the wrong things on their trek. Making assumptions about her that weren't true.

He had to do better by her. In every way. And as soon as he endured this trial by razor, he would.

"There you go, sir," Sam said, cleaning the last vestiges of lather from Dom's cheeks. "Looking fit to impress the Queen."

"It's the princess I want to impress." But no—she wasn't a princess. She was something else, though he was still learning what that was. Dom rose from the chair and pulled evening clothes from the press. Everything was clean and dry, thank God, so he wouldn't look like a complete beast when he joined the others. He selected a black coat, white waistcoat, and buff breeches.

"I ought to do that for you, sir," Sam objected. "Mr. Brown might think me remiss if word got out that I didn't assist you."

The last thing Dom wanted to do was get a servant into trouble, so he nodded and held still as Sam assisted him in the process of getting dressed.

"Still feels strange to have someone help me put on my togs," he mused. "I used to dress in the dark hours before dawn so I'd be ready to meet the ships that needed off-loading. But then," he added wryly, "nobs make all sorts of rules as to what men should and shouldn't do. Rules that are made to make everyone bend to them, proving their worth."

"That's the truth of it, sir."

Yet he would rather make sure that Sam kept his job than prove how different he was from aristos, so Dom let Sam help him into a fresh shirt, and stepped into the breeches that the footman held out for him, then submitted when Sam did up the silk-covered buttons of his waistcoat, and arranged the complex folds of his neckcloth.

"Sir," Sam said in the silence, "would you be so kind as to refrain from speaking to Lady Willa about how she had your room moved?" The footman's face reddened. "I only now remembered that Mr. Brown said I wasn't to speak of it to anyone, and, well . . ."

"You spoke of it. Easy, Sam. I won't say anything."

The footman looked relieved, and went to retrieve a gold-and-pearl stickpin to complete Dom's toilette.

Interesting that Willa wanted to keep her involvement a secret.

He exhaled. Damn, what a maze the human heart was, with terrifying vulnerability at the center of the labyrinth. Would it devour you before you could kill it? Or maybe there was another choice, where both you and the monster lived side by side, until it was no longer monstrous.

Chapter 9

❖✳❖

$\mathcal{D}$on't care for the cook on the venison?" Finn asked Willa.

"What's that?" She frowned at her brother, seated beside her at dinner.

"You're *stabbing* that piece of meat," Finn answered, "and since I'm certain it's already dead, I can only assume the dish has somehow offended you."

"The food's fine." To prove it, she ate a piece of venison, though she couldn't really taste it.

She glanced down the table, toward where Dom sat. It wouldn't be fair to fault him for looking so alluring and severe in his evening clothes. Even so, the hike around the island had been strenuous, wearing her out like a flimsy shoe, and she'd been groggy from her nap afterward, barely collecting herself enough to bathe and dress before the meal.

Yet Dom looked as handsome and dangerous as a hawk as he conversed with Lady Shipton at the other end of the long dining table, and Willa slightly resented the attractive older woman for being the lucky focus of his attention.

Lady Shipton reached out and placed her hand on Dom's sleeve, laughing at something he said. While Dom didn't laugh, he did give one of his heart-stopping half smiles that hitched up the corner of his mouth, which made Lady Shipton bat her eyelashes at him.

"Are you *sure* you don't have a grudge against your dinner?" Finn asked. "You're assaulting it again."

"He's got every right to," Willa muttered.

"Right to what?" her brother pressed. He followed her gaze down the table, to Dom and the marchioness. "Ah."

"That is to say," Willa went on, jabbing her fork forcefully into a roast potato, "*I* don't want him. So, she's welcome to him."

"If you say so," Finn said slowly. "Though, I might add, you're turning that potato into mash."

She lapsed into a moody silence. It really was no business of hers, whom Dom flirted with. She ought to do the same, but when she looked around the table at the handsome men in attendance, a sullen restlessness clouded through her, and her gaze kept turning to Dom.

When the meal was over, everyone rose from the table, but when the guests moved toward the parlor, she walked in another direction.

"I'm going to the conservatory," she announced

to no one in particular. No one followed her when she left—which was fine. Company would only annoy her.

According to Mr. Longbridge, the conservatory was a relatively recent addition, with massive glass walls that sheltered a collection of plants as well as some fruit-bearing trees. A few torches burned, casting bright reflections around her and gleaming on the leaves of the well-tended greenery. She moved up and down the rows, and drew the humid air into her lungs as she tried to banish how attractive Dom and Lady Shipton looked together.

Of course, the longer Willa hid in the conservatory, the more time he and the marchioness had to get cozy with each other.

Willa strode from the glass-lined expanse. And drew up short when she found Dom seated at one of the two chairs positioned at the entrance to the conservatory.

His long legs were stretched out in front of him, and he held a ceramic bowl. His gaze was fixed on her as he spooned something from the bowl into his mouth.

"Want a bite?" he asked casually, as if he hadn't completely caught her by surprise.

She took a tentative step forward and peered into the bowl. "Blaeberries. Ripe ones," she added, astonished.

"Like you said, they were ripening on the other

side of the island." He had another mouthful of berries, which were topped with softly whipped cream.

"That's where you went when you left the group after the picnic." She couldn't have been more astounded if he'd suddenly grown a pair of raven's wings and taken flight. Dom, city born and bred, had used her advice to forage berries.

"They're delicious." He hooked a foot into the other chair and dragged it closer, then pulled a spoon from his coat pocket and held it out.

A clear invitation.

"Don't you want to share them with Lady Shipton?" Willa asked.

"Only you," he answered, voice low, and a tremor moved through her.

Cautiously, she sat and grabbed the spoon. She dipped it into the cream-covered berries and brought a mouthful to her lips.

Dom watched her the whole time, his gaze shadowed and intent. His eyes went even darker when she took a bite.

"Luscious," she proclaimed. Which they were, juicy and abundant with sweetness. "We can share."

They were quiet for a while, wordlessly eating the berries in a silence that was almost companionable—save for the current of awareness that sparked and crackled between them.

"The cream is a good addition," she murmured.

"And it tastes even better knowing I've got a dry room to go back to."

Heat rushed into her cheeks but she didn't look away when their gazes held.

"You would've gotten pneumonia simply from being stubborn," she said defiantly.

He snorted. "Sounds like me." Then, gruffly, "Thank you. For caring. When you didn't need to. Or should."

She tried to shrug, but her heart pounded. "I wish I could just . . . stop. And yet . . ."

It was too difficult to say more. So, she took another bite of berries. Maybe their sweetness could chase away this horrible uncertainty and unbalance that overtook her whenever she was around him.

"Are the berries my thanks for having your room changed?"

"And an apology for saying what I said on the trek," he said, subdued. "That I was so surprised you cared about things like foraging. It was rude and . . . thoughtless. So—berries."

Her heart contracted sharply. His words of contrition touched her—but that's all they were. Not a romantic gesture, and she needed to remember that. "Apology accepted."

"Could you forage for us if we got lost on this island?" he asked.

This was a topic she could speak about easily. "I'm not as familiar with the landscape of Scotland, especially not the Hebrides, so it would be a little more challenging, but if I had to, I'd make sure we wouldn't starve."

"A hell of a talent," he murmured admiringly.

Another blush touched her cheeks. "I learned through mistakes. The first time I found myself out in the wilderness without anything to eat, I nearly poisoned myself. Thank God a farmer found me and knew what to do after eating the wrong mushroom. After that, I turned into a regular scholar of foraging. It was better the next time. I could've lasted much longer if they hadn't—"

Her lips clamped together. But it was too late. He looked at her with sharp perception.

"When was this?" he demanded. "Who's *they*?"

She forced a laugh even as her throat burned. "A long time ago. And *they* are no one important."

How could she have been so careless as to nearly tell him about some of the darkest times of her life? Or what they meant? To him, she was *princess*. Not some unhappy, abandoned girl. That would never fit his image of her, or what she wanted to believe of herself.

She was *strong*, damn it. Every time she wasn't, she suffered. And yet . . .

He didn't look at her with disgust. Or pity. Only concern, and a filament of anger for those who'd hurt her.

"How did you carry all these berries back?" she asked.

It was a naked attempt to change the subject, and his look was pointed, but thankfully, he said, "In my pockets."

A laugh burst from her. "It's a wonder I didn't hear your valet's cry of despair."

"I gave him a dram of whisky and he calmed down."

Her spoon scraped against the bottom of the bowl, and the sound shot disappointment through her. "We've demolished the spoils of your foraging. I suppose that means it's time to join the others."

"I like it here well enough," he said, his voice gravelly.

She did, too, and that worried her. It felt different now, spending time with him. It was so unlike the way they used to circle each other back when they were courting. She'd never been fully at ease around him, always talking and laughing too loudly, as though she'd been trying to prove something. And he was looser with her now, less on edge.

It felt . . . *nice* was too gentle a word. Because these spinning, sparkling sensations along her skin weren't soft and soothing. She felt more alive, more aware, simply by being near him and sharing these fraught moments.

How could she trust that? How could she trust herself, when she'd been hurt so badly—by him?

"Knowing my meddlesome brothers," she said

with forced breeziness, "they'll start making very wrong assumptions about the fact that you and I are both absent. Best to curtail those suppositions."

Expression opaque, he rose slowly when she got to her feet. As they walked toward the parlor where the others had gathered, she couldn't shake the feeling that something important had slipped from her fingers, but she feared the thing she grasped at as much as her body ached with wanting to hold it close.

As soon as she and Dom entered the room, a servant pressed an embroidery hoop into Dom's hands. Another servant presented Willa with a handsome wooden box that contained a row of cheroots.

"Ah, you've joined us at last," Mr. Longbridge said brightly from the other side of the room. "I was waiting for you to announce tonight's entertainment: we're reversing the sexes. What the ladies do after dinner, the gentlemen will now attempt. Likewise, the ladies get to partake in the men's typical post-meal indulgences such as tobacco and brandy."

Startled laughs rose up from everyone. If they were back in England, and at a more typical house party, there would be absolutely no chance that women could take spirits *or* tobacco, and certainly not in front of men.

More embroidery hoops were handed out to the

male guests, while other servants gave glasses of spirits to the women.

"Are the gentlemen *seriously* expected to embroider?" Cransley asked their host when he, too, was given a tambour.

"*Ladies* are expected to," Celeste answered, and sipped at her brandy with a practiced ease.

"Show me the art of it, love," Kieran coaxed, shaking his embroidery hoop like a tambourine.

"Only if you show me how to suck on a cheroot."

Giggling, Kieran and Celeste sat down on one of the sofas, and after a servant presented Kieran with a needle and floss, she began to demonstrate the proper way to thread a needle.

"Will you guide me?" Finn asked Tabitha.

"I know more about the *theory* of embroidery rather than the praxis," she replied, studying the fabric stretched in the wooden hoop. "It's a bit of a terra nova for me."

"Let us explore the new world together," Finn gallantly answered before they, too, found a cozy corner, and were soon laughing and whispering to each other.

Willa eyed the cheroots uncertainly.

"Ever smoked one before?" Dom asked. When she shook her head, he said, "I can give you some help—if you want. Nobody wants a man giving uninvited opinions."

"Whatever guidance you can provide would be

appreciated. I can never resist the opportunity to do something forbidden."

He raised a brow, and only then did she realize how provocative her words had been. But she pulled back her shoulders and hoped that her cheeks didn't turn *too* pink.

"They all look prime." He gestured to the box. "Picking any one is a good choice."

"Now what?" she asked after taking a cheroot. She rolled it between her fingers and the rich scent of tobacco rose up.

"It's not like a cigar—the ends are already clipped." He nodded at a servant, who approached with a lit taper in a candlestick. "You don't want to put it in your mouth before you burn it, so put just the tip over the fire."

"Just the tip?" She arched her brow.

He started, looking at her with disbelief. "How the hell—?"

A laugh leapt from her. "I have varied reading tastes."

"Remind me to look at your library." He shook his head, collecting himself. "When you're burning the cheroot, roll it between your fingers over the flame so everything stays even."

She did as he instructed, the scent of burning tobacco growing stronger. "Oh! It's glowing."

"It's ready. But don't gulp the smoke down, otherwise you—"

"Too—late," she said around violent coughs as

thick smoke filled her mouth and lungs. She bent over, trying not to heave up her rather nice dinner and even more delightful dessert of berries all over the rug. Her only consolation was that the other women in the parlor were also coughing, as though they were a choking orchestra filling the air with their hacking symphony.

A large, warm weight settled on her back, and it moved in slow, soothing circles. Dom's hand. "Easy. I did the same thing first time I had a puff of tobacco. Wound up spewing my ale all over the docks."

"Not—reassuring." Yet the spasms lessened as he stroked over her back. It truly was astonishing, the size of his hand, covering most of her lower torso. What started as soothing turned into hot awareness, his touch reaching all the way through her limbs.

She didn't want her coughing fit to end if it meant he stopped touching her.

Unfortunately, her lungs calmed down, and he pulled away, leaving an ache within her.

"Ready to try again?" he asked. At her nod, he said, "All you're trying to do right now is get the smoke in your mouth, and then exhale it. Doing that a few times will set you on the path."

"I'm not very good at following instructions," she said wryly.

"Not good at it, or don't want to?" His lips quirked.

"The latter more than the former. But my lesson's been learned, and I'm clamping down on my immature impulse to do the opposite of what you tell me to do." She snorted. "What a banner day. Willa Ransome, actually maturing. And you went foraging. We ought to go look for buried fairy treasure, since the day's full of miracles."

"Suppose there's a chance of change in everyone." He said this with easy humor, but then a shadow passed behind his eyes. "Some more than others."

Where did he go, when that darkness crept into him? And how could she bring him back?

"Observe how I've evolved," she said brightly, then followed his instructions by taking quick but not deep pulls on the cheroot. "Hardly a cough."

He nodded his approval, and she liked seeing that admiration on his face—far too much. Yet of all the people she knew, his approval was something worth seeking. It came from a place of experience and knowledge and strength, things that were sorely lacking in her world.

"See, the smoke's turning white." He pointed to the cloud that rose up from the lit end of the cheroot. "That's what you want. All you're going to need from now on is a puff here and there. No need to look like one of those new steam engines."

"You could have another career teaching debutantes how to smoke," she said after drawing on the cheroot, and then exhaling a cloud. "It would be very shocking to the ton."

"I ought to give it a go."

"They'll run themselves ragged trying to figure out who to complain to." She glanced at the embroidery loop he still held. "But the evening's only half-successful. You haven't started your needlework. Take a seat and show us what you can do."

He made a scoffing noise, but when she looked at him pointedly, he scowled before stalking to a chair in the corner and throwing himself into it. Curious, Willa followed.

The hoop was tiny in Dom's hands, and he held it awkwardly. When a servant handed him a box of supplies, he stared at the contents.

"It all looks so small," he muttered. "Flimsy and delicate. Not like these." He held up his thick, long fingers and glared at them.

Really—could anyone blame her for staring at his hands and imagining whether or not they presaged the scale of *other* parts of his body? She might have been a virgin, but she wasn't blind.

"No words of instruction?" he asked, breaking into her salacious thoughts.

She puffed on her cheroot to hide her pink cheeks. "Much as I relish the idea of telling you what to do, with embroidery, I'm almost as inexperienced as you are. So many tried to teach me, and I couldn't ever get the way of it. Needlework's an art—granted one that doesn't get enough credit

since it's *women's work*—and I haven't the talent.
Or patience."

He eyed the needle in his fingers as if it had personally insulted his mother. "There's no chance I
can do this."

"You might surprise yourself."

His glance up at her was doubtful. But he reached
into his jacket and pulled out a pair of spectacles,
which he put on before frowning at the sewing
implements in his hands.

Staring at him would only make him self-
conscious, and yet . . . the sight of him in spectacles
nearly brought her to her knees. *Good God.* It was
criminal that he should be so handsome, the firelight shining off the glass eyepieces as he tried to
thread the needle.

It was unfair that this compelling, alluring man
should come into her life, and have this massive rift
between them, one that could never be breached.

It took him several tries to thread embroidery
floss through the needle's tiny eye.

"Thank Christ," he muttered when he finally
succeeded in his task. He attempted his first stitch
and grunted when a bead of bright red blood
stained the fabric stretched on the embroidery
frame. "Fu—I mean, damn!"

"Does it hurt?"

"Nah—my skin's too thick, but I've ruined the
sodding silk." He tried once more to get the needle through the fabric properly. Yet he must have

stabbed himself again because another drop of blood stained the silk. "Goddamn it."

He surged to his feet and tossed the embroidery hoop to the ground, then stalked to the fireplace. "To hell with this."

She followed, and when he glowered into the flames, she stared at him.

"Don't quit." When the words left her, she heard how much urgency there was behind them. Almost a plea.

He plucked the cheroot from her grasp and took a long draw from it before exhaling a thick cloud of smoke, then gave the tobacco back to her.

Holding up his hands, he growled, "You don't know what it's like to live with these."

"I can't," she said, almost desperate, "if you don't tell me."

He only shook his head. Keeping his silence.

They both held tightly to their secrets. As they stood together at the fire, it was clear that neither would relinquish their hold on them. But if the poison wasn't released, it had the potential to destroy her and Dom from the inside out.

Chapter 10

✧ ✳ ✧

$\mathcal{D}$on't ingest too much," Longbridge sang, coming into the breakfast room, where Dom and the other guests were eating their morning meal.

Dom sat at one end of the table, Willa at the other. They'd given each other distance today, and he cursed himself. He was never afraid, not of any damned thing, but the cost of that was having all the subtlety and caution of a beast. With her, at least, he could *try* to not be a brute. So, he'd been polite but distant today.

At least he'd slept well in his massive, plush bed in his sumptuous, dry room. He had her to thank for that.

"I have a very vigorous activity planned for after we finish here," Longbridge went on. "And don't look at me like that, Ransome, because while I may be dissolute, I'm not *that* far gone."

"No orgies on the lawn?" Kieran said with obvious disappointment.

"Your skin is very fair, my love," Celeste replied, patting his hand. "We wouldn't want to run the risk of you burning in the sun. But," she continued consolingly, "we can arrange for something suitably well shaded later."

"Good Christ." Dom clapped his hands over his ears. "Have a care for your brother's nerves."

"The same nerves that were utterly unbothered when you and my brothers attempted to steal Lord Caulfield's painting?" Willa asked dryly.

Dom couldn't stop himself from grinning. That had been the night he had finally met the Ransome brothers' sister, having heard much about her from his friends. They had attended an exceptionally boring ball filled with the same nattering dullards and had challenged each other to nick a particularly luscious nude from their host's study.

"You were equally steely when you found us," he pointed out to Willa, "and diverted the staff's attention to the kitchen, just as we were on the verge of getting caught. Cool as winter, you were."

Willa gave a careless shrug, but her lips quirked in a tiny, self-satisfied smile. "And then you returned the favor by backing me later."

"Course I did," he answered at once. "Those nob fools didn't realize who they were dealing with, insisting that you couldn't outshoot any one of the bucks."

"You hadn't even seen me shoot," she pointed out.

"I knew you could do anything."

He and Willa stared at each other, smiling with warmth, and he was brought back to that night, the night when everything had changed. She'd been full of courage and vitality, determined to meet the world head-on, and damn anyone who got in her way.

She still had courage and vitality—but he was glimpsing more beneath that steely surface. And the more he saw, the more he wanted to know. But he didn't have the sodding right to any of it, not after jilting her.

The trouble was, he couldn't stop himself from going back to her again and again. She drew him in with undeniable force. Yesterday had proven that— had, in fact, made it even harder to resist her. He'd loved feeding her the wild berries that he'd foraged for her, and watching her smoke a cheroot might've been the most erotic thing he'd seen in his life.

He'd also seen the way she'd ogled his hands. Or the sound she'd made when he'd put on his spectacles. He used to resent that he sometimes needed them, but if he could have Willa look at him like a savory pie, fresh from the oven, well, he'd wear them as often as she wanted.

"Then Lady Willa has a chance at being today's victor," Longbridge said.

Willa sat back, frowning, and Dom did the same. They were both stunned, and many people gave them curious stares.

He and Willa weren't alone. For a few moments,

it had felt that way. Before, during their courtship, and then when they'd been engaged, they'd both been on a stage, acting before the eyes of the ton.

Now was different. The rest of the world was merely a gray, cold blur, with Willa the only source of color and heat.

Kieran asked cheerfully, "From what, exactly, is my sister going to emerge triumphant?"

"You'll soon discover once you finish your breakfasts," Longbridge commanded, "and come meet me outside on the east lawn." With that, their host strolled out of the breakfast room, whistling a tune that Dom recalled had absolutely filthy lyrics.

Everyone resumed their meal, the other guests excitedly debating over sips of tea and bites of bacon what Longbridge had in store for them.

Dom had no idea what was next for him and Willa, yet he'd be a liar if he said he wasn't looking forward to it.

"THIS ISN'T GOING to be an ordinary game of shuttlecock," Longbridge announced as the guests gathered on a broad expanse of grass.

Servants handed out rackets and the aforementioned shuttlecocks to those who chose to play. The rest of the guests, including Finn, Tabitha, Mrs. McDaniel, and Baron Hunsdon, lounged on chairs that hale footmen had carried out, with a variety of refreshments arranged on platters on wrought iron tables.

"You chose this game because of its name," Dom said, folding his arms across his chest.

"Naturally, I did," their host said with a smile.

"The more often we say the word *cock*, the better," Willa said, which startled a laugh out of Dom.

Even to his own ears, his laughter was a strange sound, like a rusted bridge seldom lowered, and it earned him a few startled glances from the others. But Willa looked satisfied.

"What are the rules?" Kieran asked as he shielded his eyes against the bright sunlight.

"As if you do anything but break them," Finn called, earning him a rude hand gesture from his brother.

"He isn't wrong, my love," Celeste noted. She spun her racket in her hand.

"The rules," Longbridge said doggedly, "are as follows. We'll break into teams of two. The winning team is the first pair to reach one hundred successful volleys of the shuttlecock."

Dom scratched his jaw, unmoved by this feat. "Easy enough."

"Except," Longbridge added, "once each team reaches five and twenty volleys, they'll have to stop and sing 'The Maid's Complaint for Want of a Dil Doul.'"

Tittering and a few lusty chuckles followed this announcement, but Dom only shook his head. "At the top of our lungs, right?"

"The louder the better," their host said with a smirk.

"I'll deafen everyone on the next island," Willa sniffed, tipping up her chin.

Dom looked at her proudly. Naturally, she'd face everything thrown at her.

"And sing 'The Lusty Young Smith' at fifty volleys," Kieran guessed.

Another smirk crossed Longbridge's face. "You'll learn your fate *if* you can make it to fifty volleys. And five and seventy."

"What prize awaits the winners?" asked Lady Shipton, posing prettily with her racket. "Something suitably luxurious, I hope."

"Besting everyone will satisfy me," Willa said loftily.

Dom chuckled.

"The winners will receive a rare bottle of wine from my own cellars," Longbridge declared.

At that, everyone cried out in eager anticipation. God—that wine had to be valuable, and too costly to drink.

"Divide into teams," Longbridge instructed, "and we shall begin."

Those guests who were married formed teams, including Kieran and Celeste. That left the unattached guests to find their own pairings.

Cransley was one of the players, and he started toward Willa. But she walked straight toward Dom.

As soon as she stood in front of him, she said, quick and low, "Both of us play to win. If you and I are opponents, then no one is going to emerge the victor."

"True," he allowed.

"If we form a team," she went on, "we're *unbeatable*."

When he didn't answer right away, she said, "We can best Kieran." She glanced toward her brother, who was busy dodging his wife's attempts to swat him on the arse with her racket. "*And* show the rest of these nobs that we're no one to be trifled with."

"Ruthless." Dom leaned closer, trying not to notice her sweet and spiced fragrance, or how the sunlight was already beginning to dot her skin with golden freckles. "Appealing to my desire to beat the aristos at their own game."

"Team up with me, and we'll *annihilate* everyone." Her gaze met his, and determination glowed in the depths of her eyes. "Are you ready to give the others a demonstration of your superiority?"

He gave her a small but vicious smile. "Let's make 'em cry."

IF WILLA WANTED to win, she'd no better teammate than Dom.

She watched him as he and the other men tugged off their jackets in preparation for the game. The number of times she'd seen Dom in his shirtsleeves was minimal, and as he removed his beautifully tailored coat, her breath caught at the sight of his wide shoulders straining against the fabric of his shirt. He was big all over, with appropriately scaled musculature, including massive thighs that strained the buckskin of his breeches so deliciously. Everything about Dom seemed designed to intimidate, which had thrilled her from the first time she'd seen him.

And yet the more she was coming to know him, the more she understood he was far more complex than anyone—including herself—had ever given him credit for.

As he headed back to her, his movements and gaze purposeful and determined, the racket tiny in his enormous fist, she vowed she would do better.

But first, they had a game to win.

He was given a shuttlecock from a servant, and bounced it on his racket with each long stride in her direction.

"You wield that racket like a weapon," she noted when he came to stand nearby.

"Everything's a weapon in the right hands."

"Are your hands the right hands?" She arched a brow.

"Depends on what they're touching." His eyes were hot, turning her whole body feverish and aware, and robbing her of the ability to form a witty reply.

Perhaps this wasn't as well-thought-out a strategy as she'd initially believed.

"We're relying on the honor system to keep track of the number of volleys," Mr. Longbridge announced. He stood with Lady Shipton, so clearly, they were a team.

"That should be a problem for you, Key," Finn yelled from the sidelines.

"There are ladies present," Kieran shouted back, "so I can't give you my full array of vulgar hand gestures. Use your imagination to pick the rudest one. That's the one I'm sending your way."

"Let me assist you, dearest brother," Willa said. "I think he means *this*." She jabbed two fingers into the air.

Dom choked out a laugh.

"On my count," Mr. Longbridge went on, "we'll begin. Three, two—"

Anticipation built, and Willa readied herself, bouncing from foot to foot in preparation. Her heart pounded in expectation of the game to come.

"One," said Mr. Longbridge. "Begin."

A cheer went up from the spectators, and Lady Shipton gave an excited shriek, but Willa's focus honed in on Dom. He lightly lobbed the shuttlecock toward her. She swung her racket, making contact with the projectile but being careful not to hit it too hard to keep it from soaring over his head. A little rush of pleasure burst in her when his racket connected with the shuttlecock, and then she did the same when it arced toward her.

"Fifty pounds says Willa and Dom reach twenty-five volleys first," Finn announced.

Willa rolled her eyes at the fact that her gambling brother had placed a large wager. But at least that wager was in her favor.

"I'm insulted," Kieran yelled as he and Celeste played.

"And I'm a strategist," Finn answered.

"I'll take that wager," Baron Hunsdon said.

Willa wouldn't let herself be distracted, keeping all her attention on the shuttlecock soaring back and forth between her and Dom. It was damn satisfying to hit the projectile, watch it fly, and then see Dom also make contact with it. As they did, she counted under her breath, her excitement growing with each successful volley.

Fifteen. Sixteen. Seventeen.

She heard a wail of dismay from Miss Steele, who was teamed up with Gilbert. Clearly, that team wasn't able to make it to twenty-five. Willa and Dom would surely be the victors.

"Don't get cocky," Dom warned lowly as he batted the shuttlecock toward her.

"This from the man who drank brandy straight from the decanter in Lord Davenport's private study. In front of Lord Davenport." She swung her racket and hit the projectile—though with a little too much force, so that Dom had to stretch out to connect with the shuttlecock.

Forget being too cocky—she couldn't let herself

get unfocused by the mouthwatering sight of Dom in motion.

"Why put the liquor out if you don't want your guests to drink it?" he asked, hardly winded by his effort.

Twenty-three. Twenty-four.

"That's twenty-five," she cried as she hit the projectile.

"There's my girl." Dom grabbed the shuttlecock out of the air and smiled at her, revealing the minuscule dimple just beside the corner of his mouth, and sending her already thudding heart to pound even harder.

"Damn it," Baron Hunsdon said, and handed Finn several pound notes.

"Sing! Sing! Sing!" the other spectators chanted. "'The Maid's Complaint for Want of a Dil Doul!'"

Dom glanced at her. "Know the words? It's a hell of a bawdy song."

"I went to a school for genteel young ladies," Willa answered with a sniff. "Of course I know the lyrics."

That earned her another smile from him, and she had to concentrate to recall the lyrics she'd just insisted she was familiar with.

"At my signal," she directed him. At his nod, she took a breath, planted her feet, and pointed at him.

Together, at the top of their lungs, they sang:

*"For I am a Maid and a very good Maid
and sixteen years of age am I
And fain would I part with my Maiden-head
if any good fellow would with me lie."*

She'd actually never before heard Dom sing, and while her own voice was decent enough—though half yelling a filthy song didn't truly count as holding a melody—Dom's voice was . . .

Was beautiful. A rich, deep baritone with a hint of huskiness that curled beguilingly in her body's sensitive places. He sang without any hint of self-consciousness, even as the spectators clapped along. Her attention wasn't on their audience, instead riveted by the sight of this massive, strapping man singing with a voice that would ensorcel anyone.

It also didn't help her focus that the words unwinding from him were about a girl in desperate need of a lover. The way her own body ached with the hunger for pleasure. Oh, she'd craved another's touch for many years, but, ever since she'd met him, all of her lustful longings had been directed toward Dom.

Who was looking and sounding bloody good at the moment.

She stumbled over the next few words, but collected her wits enough to join him in the following lines.

*"But none to me ever yet proffer'd such love,
     as to lie by my side and give me a shove
     With his dil doul, dil doul, dil doul . . ."*

Dom's voice went hoarse, and together they fumbled over the last part of the verse.

"Oh, happy were I, if I had a dil doul," they stammered together.

The spectators cheered again at the conclusion of the song, and though Dom hadn't appeared affected by the strenuous physical activity moments before, now his face had gone red as a cherry.

He and Willa stared at each other, and she *wished* she didn't have such a vivid imagination, to make her speculate on all the ways she could bring a blush to Dom's cheeks, or the means by which he might make her breathless and flushed, but damn it if she did.

"Now on to fifty volleys," Mrs. McDaniel cried.

"A hundred pounds Dom and Willa get there first," Finn added, but Baron Hunsdon shook his head.

"Your lack of faith only goads me on," Kieran said stormily. "And we just reached five and twenty volleys, so we can catch up."

"Not until you sing first," Willa reminded him. She gave a provoking wave of her hand. "Go on and dazzle us with your vocal brilliance."

As Kieran and Celeste began their own round

of singing, Willa turned back to Dom. "We'll be halfway to fifty by the time they finish."

"Bloody right, we will." He held up his racket, and at her nod, served.

It was a trifle difficult to pay attention to lobbing the shuttlecock back and forth as the other teams began to reach the twenty-five volley milestone, and the air was filled with the cacophony of many voices belting out lines about giving maids shoves with dil douls.

Yet Willa was determined to be the victor of this game, and so she did her best to shut out everything surrounding her that wasn't Dom. And the shuttlecock.

Damn it—why were all the words today very close to the same word for a man's genitals?

And why did Dom look more and more appetizing as he moved with athletic grace to hit that ruddy shuttlecock? Later, she could let her mind run riot, imagining him lightly sheened with sweat from his exertions doing *other things*. Right now was about reaching fifty volleys before anyone— especially Kieran—did.

Forty-eight, forty-nine.

"Fifty!" Dom declared as she successfully propelled the shuttlecock back to him. "Now what?"

Mr. Longbridge didn't stop swinging his racket as he called, "You see the glasses of wine my servants are filling?"

She noted a footman pouring ruby-hued liquid into tall glasses on a silver tray. When he was finished, there were four full goblets, the sunlight gleaming in the wine.

"The next feat is to drink two glasses of wine as quickly as possible," Mr. Longbridge explained. "Only when your goblets are drained can you proceed on to the next milestone."

The spectators whistled and clapped at this latest development, and Dom shot her a concerned glance.

"Before you ask," she said, striding toward the footman with the wine, "this is well within my capabilities."

"Right. School for genteel young ladies." Dom was quickly beside her, and together they reached the servant with their drinks. "They taught you lots of useful skills."

"All my abilities were part of an independent course of study." She took one of the goblets, and Dom did the same.

"What else? Spitting? Brawling?"

He tipped his head back and as he was swallowing his wine, she said, "A thorough and complete reading of the Lady of Dubious Quality's erotic oeuvre. *The Highwayman's Seduction* is my favorite, especially when he kisses her beneath her skirts."

Dom promptly spat out his wine. Fortunately, he managed to turn his head in time to spew the

liquid on the grass, rather than on her or the footman. But it had been a close call.

"That doesn't count as drinking a glass," Gilbert
protested in the middle of singing.

"Another for Mr. Kilburn," Mr. Longbridge instructed his servant.

The footman poured more wine for Dom, and
he shot her a wary glance before bringing the glass
to his lips.

"I promise not to talk about shuttlecocks, dil
douls, or filthy books," Willa vowed, crossing her
heart.

"Comforting," he said before drinking.

Kieran and Celeste were just reaching their fifti-
eth volley, so there was no time to spare. This was
also not the moment to daintily sip at her wine—as
if she ever did such a thing—and so Willa followed
Dom's lead, doing her best to down her first glass
in a single swallow.

He made it look much easier than it was, and she
was forced to take several gulps before draining
the last of the wine. It might have been an excellent vintage, it might have been ditch water. She
barely noticed the flavor as she hastily moved on
to her second full goblet.

As she speedily drank down the beverage, she
kept an eye on her brother and his wife. Kieran
and Celeste were starting on their first glasses
of wine.

Surely Miss Beckford would have been horrified

to see one of her former pupils gulping wine so quickly that it trickled from the corners of Willa's mouth. She had to angle her body to keep anything from dripping on her gown, and if there was a moment when she'd ever looked less elegant, she couldn't recall it now. But it didn't matter. Victory was all that signified.

Even so, Dom watched her with what appeared to be admiration. He had already downed his second glass, but if the alcohol affected him at all, he didn't show it.

A pleasant warmth had settled over her somewhere between the first and second goblets of wine. Yet as she set her now empty glass on the tray, the ground beneath her feet tilted slightly.

"Easy." Dom took hold of her elbow, his fingers on her bare flesh, and the warmth of the wine turned into a raging heat that poured through her. It had to be the alcohol, surely, that made her skin so sensitive. It had nothing to do with the fact that Dom's flesh was searingly hot, or that the pads of his fingers were slightly rough and callused.

"I'm fine," Willa insisted. She would simply ignore the faint slurring of her words. "Less' keep going to seventy-five." She eyed Kieran, who was beginning his second glass. "Got to beat 'im."

"You said you could handle your wine," Dom noted sternly, "but you're already foxed."

"Not a bit," she insisted. "Surely the wine can't have affected me so quickly. Although," she added with a frown, "I didn't eat much breakfast, and maybe I had juss a few bites of dinner."

She patted her stomach. "Not a lot in here to sponge up m' wine. And what are you doing, walking around with sush hot hands? Big hands, too," she mused, looking down at where his broad palm covered her elbow and his fingers wrapped around the crook of her arm. "Makes me wonder how much of me you could cover with 'em."

Someone tittered, but Willa ignored them, instead looking up at Dom through a pleasant haze.

"We should stop," he said, his brow creased with worry. "Get you out of the sun, too."

"And let *them* win?" She smirked at the other players. "Not a fucking chance."

Chapter 11

❧ ✳ ❦

Dom held Willa, torn between wanting to tend to her in her fuddled state, and letting her loose so they could win this damn game.

"Have a care, Kieran and Celeste are pulling ahead of you," Finn announced from the spectators.

Willa tugged herself from Dom's grip. "Not for long."

He could give her what she wanted, but he'd keep a close watch on her. If she seemed in danger of getting hurt, to hell with the game, he'd take care of her. After making certain that she was able to stand on her own, he took his position opposite her, and served.

Despite the fact that she was in her cups, she was determined to persevere, returning all of his volleys. She'd shown focus before quickly guzzling two glasses of wine, and somehow, *after* guzzling two glasses of wine, her focus had narrowed further. Nothing existed but hitting the shuttlecock arcing back and forth between them.

He'd never played games like this in Ratcliff. No one had the budget for useless things like rackets and fussy little projectiles made of feathers and cork. Instead, they used to take bundles of rags and kick them like footballs. The boys and girls in the lanes were rough in their play so it wasn't unusual to come home spattered with blood—either his or his opponents'.

The chance that he'd *ever* learn genteel games would have been nil, had it not been for Kieran's kindness to him at Oxford, teaching him in the ways of sport when his class and ignorance of such activities kept him from joining any leagues.

As if aware of his thoughts, Kieran shouted over to him, "Is *this* how you repay your teacher?"

"Always a risk that the pupil bests the master," Dom answered, keeping his attention on the volleys between him and Willa.

"We'll ruddy see about that," Kieran called back. "Seventy-three, seventy-four. Seventy-five!"

Dom swore under his breath. He *had* to make certain that Willa won. But their team was only two volleys behind, and moments before Longbridge explained the next task, Dom and Willa reached the needed seventy-five.

He and Willa and Kieran and Celeste all faced their host, waiting for their instructions. A stab of brotherly concern lanced him to see his little sister swaying on her feet, her cheeks flushed from exertion and two hastily downed glasses of wine. But Kieran had a steadying arm around his wife's waist, and Dom was busy looking after Willa.

"For your third and final task," Longbridge said in the middle of batting the shuttlecock to Lady Shipton, "you must run a circuit through the Untamed Garden before returning here and finishing the last of the game. And *both* teammates must make the journey. If you don't know where the Untamed Garden is, the servants will show the way."

He nodded toward where a footman stood, pointing toward the western side of the house.

"I saw that garden yesterday," Dom confided to Willa, "on my way back to the house. I know where it is."

"Then less' go," she insisted.

When he took a step in the direction of the garden, she followed, but her legs wobbled beneath her.

"Not a good idea to run," he noted with concern.

"Won't win if we *stroll*," she insisted, then glanced at Kieran and Celeste, who started to run. Kieran held Celeste's hand, since she didn't seem quite steady on her feet, yet they were making good time. "But we have to go *now*."

He spun around and presented her with his back, lowering down slightly as he did so. "Climb on."

A moment went by, then she clambered onto him, looping her arms around his neck. He gripped her legs, and then and only then did he realize that this might not have been a sterling idea. Her body pressed firmly to his, and her skirts rode up so that he held tightly to her thighs.

He even—God help him—touched the silken skin above her garters.

"What are you waiting for?" she demanded. "Go! Go!"

Swallowing hard, Dom took off.

It wasn't the easiest thing to do, running with a full-grown woman clinging to you like a barnacle. Luckily, he was strong, and could carry her easily. Less luckily, all he could think about was that her crotch kept bouncing against his back, and that she had also read dirty books by the Lady of Dubious Quality, and had formed clear ideas about what she would like done to her crotch. *Kisses beneath her skirts.*

Run, you bastard, he reminded himself.

Just ahead, Kieran and Celeste were rounding the corner of the house, where a nearby footman pointed them to the garden. Celeste wasn't fully balanced, but she put up a valiant effort to sprint.

"We'll never pass them," Willa lamented.

"Hold tight," Dom answered through clenched teeth.

Summoning all his strength, he ran at full speed. His thighs burned as he sped past Kieran and Celeste, and he shut out the curses Kieran threw at him. Holding tightly to Willa, he bolted down a gravel path, and then into the aptly named Untamed Garden.

"Duck down to cover your face," he gritted to Willa.

Thankfully, she didn't question his reasoning, which became apparent when branches whipped at him and surely would have cut her had she not protected herself. He felt her cheek press against his shoulder.

Ignoring the stings and scrapes, he instead concentrated on not tripping on the uneven ground.

Up ahead was the stone pavilion, marking the middle of the garden, but behind him he could hear Kieran's and Celeste's footfalls.

A servant was positioned inside the pavilion, and called out, "You're to go back the way you came, sir, after making one lap around this structure."

His lungs burned as he sped around the pavilion, yet he wouldn't give up and he *definitely* wouldn't drop Willa.

He passed Kieran and Celeste on their way to the pavilion, and the temptation was too much for Willa, because she called out to her brother, "This is our race to lose."

"And lose it, you will," Kieran wheezed as he ran. "You—"

"*Later*, Willa," Dom insisted.

"We *are* going to win," she said in a quieter, less certain voice, once Kieran was behind them. "Aren't we, Dom?"

"Sure as hell going to try."

That seemed to satisfy her, because she was silent once more. They broke free from the garden's wildness and he dashed back the way they had come. Ahead, the spectators cheered at their approach.

Reaching the portion of the lawn where the game was taking place, he fought to stay standing, and to carefully lower Willa down until her feet touched the grass. He bent over double, bracing his hands on his thighs as he fought for breath.

Willa's face appeared as she crouched down in front of him. "Water? Wine? *Anything?*"

"Just . . . the . . . victory," he growled.

She handed him his racket, and, when he felt slightly certain he wasn't going to die from a cardiac seizure, he straightened. Just in time, too, because Kieran and Celeste approached—though they looked bedraggled as they staggered across the lawn.

"I'll serve," Willa said, sounding steadier than she had earlier.

He could only nod.

The next five and twenty volleys were the most important of his life. Tension climbed moment by moment as the shuttlecock arced back and forth between him and Willa, climbing, each stroke of their rackets making excitement and the need for release climb higher.

Back and forth, back and forth. The rhythm

building and building. They were in perfect har-
mony, every swing and hit raising the tension.
Ninety-eight. Ninety-nine.

And then . . .

"One hundred," Willa cried with the final successful volley.

For the first time in over a decade, Dom feared he
might spend in his breeches. And it wasn't helped
when a triumphant Willa tossed her racket aside
and launched herself into his arms.

"The victors," she exclaimed jubilantly.

Groans rose up from those teams that were still
competing, including Kieran and Celeste, while
the spectators cheered and lifted their glasses in
salute.

"The winners are Mr. Kilburn and Lady Willa,"
Longbridge announced.

Dom didn't care. He was aware of one thing,
and one thing only.

It had been over a year since he'd had Willa in
his embrace. And now that she was holding him,
and he her, every moment was to be savored. She
was abundant with curves, simmering with energy
beneath his hands, and as she bounced excitedly
on her feet, her breasts did a damned nice thing
that felt incredible against his chest. He pressed
his face into the crook of her neck, inhaling her
spiced fragrance deliciously underscored by the
tang of fresh perspiration. And a hint of wine.

He stiffened. Whatever affection she felt for him

now was because of the two glasses of claret she'd downed like a sailor not twenty minutes ago. He'd be a fucking bastard if he took advantage of her in her drink-befuddled state, or believed that she truly wanted to be in his arms. No matter how much he wanted her there.

Carefully, he removed himself from her hold, and urged her backward so that there was plenty of distance between them. His hands dropped to his sides but the feel of her burned into his skin.

She blinked in confusion, and a moment later, she looked hurt. Then that was gone, too, as she turned to face Kieran.

"You will *never* again best me, brother," she announced haughtily. "From this moment forward."

"Misjudge her at your risk," Dom added.

She cast him a quick glance, one he couldn't read, before aiming her attention at a winded Kieran.

"I yield to the champions." Her brother held up his hands in surrender.

Longbridge approached, a bottle of wine in each hand. "As promised, your prizes."

"I forfeit my reward," Willa said, turning faintly green. She glanced at Dom and she appeared far more wounded than suffering from a sore head or sick stomach. "And I've played enough games to last me the rest of my years."

At that, she spun on her heel and marched with surprising speed back toward the house.

"These are yours," Longbridge said.

Dom tore his attention from Willa's retreating back to see their host holding both bottles out to him.

"If you want them," Longbridge added.

"I want them." Dom took the wine from the other man. It didn't matter if it was the best vintage or tasted of actual sunshine and diamonds. All that he cared about was if the wine could get him good and drunk, drunk enough to stop feeling the pain that cleaved him apart whenever he hurt Willa.

Chapter 12

❧ ✳ ❧

*W*illa spent the next few hours in her bedchamber, nursing a sore head and an even more tender heart.

Damn it, what did Dom *want* from her? One moment, he was her greatest champion and ardent admirer, making certain she triumphed over her brother, and the next, he literally pushed her away.

"Are you in terrible pain, my lady?" Isla hovered anxiously by her bed. "That was an awful groan you just gave. Shall I fetch some laudanum?"

"A club to the skull will suffice," Willa answered. "Anything to hasten me to unconsciousness."

"I don't have a club," Isla mused, "but Cook's clootie dumplings are quite stodgy, so they might serve."

"No mention of food, if you please." The queasiness in Willa's stomach was partly due to the aftereffects of hastily consumed wine, but mostly from the spinning top that was her response to Dom, and his wildly oscillating behavior toward her.

The best she could do, given the circumstances, was brazen it out. But then, she'd always been good at being brazen. Being vulnerable, on the other hand, was much more difficult. And terrifying.

"There *is* an old family remedy," Isla said as she dabbed a cool cloth on Willa's forehead. "It tastes much worse than a peat bog, but cures a bout of crapulence within minutes."

"*Worse* than a peat bog?"

"Aye, my lady."

"Yet effective." Willa exhaled, which sent a bolt of white pain through her head. "You'd earn my gratitude if you mixed some up for me."

"Back in a trice, my lady."

Isla was true to her word, and returned a few minutes later with a mug of something that was as thick and sludgy as the promised peat bog, with an oily sheen glossing its surface.

"What's in this?" Willa asked, wincing as she sat up to drink the concoction.

"If I told you, my lady, you wouldn't drink it. Best not to smell it, either."

"Better to dwell in ignorance." Pinching her nose, Willa tipped the mug back, drinking down its contents. She blessed her lack of gag reflex as she swallowed the viscous mixture that had a flavor reminiscent of rotting cabbage, but not quite as pleasant.

The effects could be felt almost immediately. Willa's pounding head subsided to a soft throbbing, and her stomach went from a roiling sea to a calm lake.

"My God," she said in wonderment as she stared at the mire of remains coating the bottom of the mug, "you could make a fortune selling this to aristocratic men."

During her brothers' bachelor days, she imagined, they would have paid substantial amounts for a cure like Isla's.

"Aye, but I'd rather see them suffer for their overindulgence." Smiling wryly, Isla took the mug back from Willa. "If you're feeling well enough, Mr. Longbridge has invited all the guests to the beach. Most everyone is down there already, but should you like, I can change your clothes in no time and you can join them."

"Is Mr. Kilburn down there, too?"

"The great big fellow? Sam says he dresses like a gentleman but talks like a working lad, and is far nicer than most of the other nobs—I mean the other genteel guests."

"That's the one." Willa slung her legs around to sit at the edge of the bed, and to her relief, the room didn't spin. Her heart, however, swung in her chest like a pendulum at this accurate description of Dom.

"Aye, I believe he's gone to the shore." Isla peered at her. "Or you could stay here, my lady.

Just because you've recovered from too much drink doesn't mean you have to tromp around and spend time with anyone you don't want to."

It wasn't a surprise that Isla and the other servants were aware that there was something going on between Willa and Dom. Underestimating the staff's perspicacity and knowledge was always a mistake.

Willa *could* stay in her room. Hide. Avoid whatever it was that brewed between her and Dom.

She got to her feet, and her legs were far stronger beneath her than she would've expected.

"I'm going out," she said to Isla.

"WHAT IN GOD'S name are they doing?" Willa asked from the shore. A group of four men, including Kieran, Gilbert, Viscount Marwood, and Baron Hunsdon, had piled themselves into a rowboat and were beating their oars against the waves as their small vessel lifted up and down on the surf. They were yelling indiscernible things to each other and to anyone on dry land who bothered to listen.

The others, including Mr. Longbridge, Finn, Tabitha, Celeste, and Lady Marwood, promenaded along the water's edge, occasionally shouting encouragement to the would-be seafarers. Dom stood on his own, watching the scene from the beach, his arms folded across his chest, and shook his head. No doubt wondering at the foolish pursuits of the gentility.

"Enacting the siege of Troy," Miss Steele said beside her.

"Good Lord." Willa shook her head. There really was no defensible position for aristocrats' pastimes.

"I'm coming for you, fair Helen!" Kieran bellowed to Celeste, who waved a scarf overhead.

"Are they trying to land or are they taking to the open waters?" Willa asked.

Miss Steele shrugged. "I don't think *they've* determined that, yet." She cautiously eyed Willa. "You seem to have recovered from this morning's indulgences. But then, I'd expect no less."

Willa tilted her head. "What do you mean?"

"At school," the other woman explained after a pause, keeping her gaze fixed on the men in their pitching boat. "The rest of us were always struggling to stay on the right side of Miss Beckford's rules. You didn't even attempt to appease the old dragon. Flew right in the face of her statutes and regulations—but every time she'd punish you, you came roaring back. Nothing bothered you. So, it stands to reason that a few too many glasses of wine wouldn't hinder you."

"I see," Willa murmured. She did her best not to remember those years at school, full of terror and shame and attempts to mold her into the kind of young lady her parents and Society demanded her to be.

"Do you know," Miss Steele said with a self-deprecating laugh, "how in awe of you I was? I daresay you . . . well . . ."

"Go on," Willa urged.

The other woman grimaced. "You *terrified* me. Perhaps because you truly didn't seem to care what punishment Miss Beckford threw at you. And it seems you were *always* being punished."

"Obedience and I were never on speaking terms." Yet she turned to Miss Steele with a troubled frown. "I didn't know I was so frightening."

"The fault's mine," Miss Steele replied, sheepish. "I was so dreadfully homesick for India, and my amma. Once you found me in the closet, crying. You told me to dry my face and stand up—but I just couldn't. I felt so ashamed of myself for not being as strong as you."

"My God." Willa's eyes suddenly burned. "What an utter shrew I was to you."

"That's not the word I would've used," the young woman answered softly.

"I can think of others," Willa muttered, "that are far more crude and just as appropriate. The truth is . . ." She swallowed. "I wasn't nearly as strong as I pretended to be, and to insist that *you*, a mere *girl*, far from home . . . to demand that you somehow swallow down your pain and pretend that it didn't affect you . . ."

Turning to Miss Steele, she said urgently, "That was wrong of me. Very wrong. And I'm so terribly sorry that I wasn't there to give you the comfort you needed. I can't excuse my behavior. Only . . . I didn't . . . I *don't* have much experience being consoled, or anyone to tell me it was all right to cry."

Miss Steele's eyes went wide. "Then, if you don't mind me saying, *I'm* terribly sorry."

Though Willa tried to laugh, it wasn't a successful effort. "If I was as bloody tough as I'd claimed to be, I wouldn't have run away from school so much."

"You *did* seem to do that quite a lot."

Learning how to forage had become a necessity, since Willa's appearance at a villager's home or at a farmhouse, asking for food, would've caused the residents to notify the school. Yet invariably she was found and dragged back, and punished all over again for her transgressions. She'd been beaten, denied food, locked in her room on freezing cold days with no fire and no blankets, permitted to wear only her shift.

When she'd been fourteen, she'd actually made it all the way back to London, back to her parents' house. They'd been horrified, naturally, by her appearance on their doorstep. She'd been bedraggled, exhausted, undernourished. Despite her desperate plea to remain at home, they'd returned her to the school. Well, they themselves hadn't done it. They'd hired someone, and *that man* had hauled her to Miss Beckford's.

From then on, whenever Willa had run away, she'd picked other destinations. Bath. Brighton. Cheltenham. Anywhere she thought she might be able to disappear. Her brothers had been at university, so they hadn't known until much later that she'd made several escape attempts from boarding school.

It hadn't mattered, though. Perhaps driven by fear of the earl and countess's anger if she truly did vanish, the school's administration always made sure she was found and brought back.

Come to think of it—it made sense that after Dom had jilted her, she'd run away again. In that case, she'd fled to the Continent. But then, just as in her girlhood, her escape attempts hadn't helped. She'd been trapped in one way or another.

"I wasn't . . . a very *happy* person back then," she said slowly. The sudden realization was a painful one, the way in which a child's body ached as it grew. "And I'm afraid I turned most of my unhappiness on the other girls at school. Including you."

It made sense, now, that Dom's abandoning had hurt so much. Part of her had believed it was because of the unhappiness that lurked beneath the surface of her brashness. As if, because she wasn't a wholly joyful person, she deserved to be cast aside.

Her throat tightened at the thought.

"All of us were in the midst of personal battles," Miss Steele answered.

"You're very kind to excuse my behavior." She took in a deep inhalation of briny sea air. "Do I *still* terrify you?"

"A little," the other woman confessed.

"I'll do my best to be less terrifying."

"Please don't, Lady Willa," Miss Steele said quickly. "I would like to be a bit more terrifying, in fact, and would hate to think that you'd dimmed your light merely to make someone else feel better about themselves."

"Perhaps a happy medium can be reached," Willa mused.

"Terrifying, yet approachable," Miss Steele suggested.

"I hope this means that we can be genuine friends now." Willa smiled at Miss Steele, a sincere smile, and she exhaled when her smile was returned. "Please, call me Willa."

"It does. And I'm Lakshmi." She looped her arm through Willa's.

Warmth spread through Willa, chasing away the chill of old and bitter memories. She didn't want them to touch her any longer. They only served to hold her back, and keep her in a place of fear.

She shot a glance at Dom. He wasn't standing all that far away—perhaps he'd overheard her conversation with Lakshmi. But his attention was fixed on the men in the boat, who were struggling to bring it to shore. Dom scowled at their efforts to combat the waves, which kept pushing the small vessel back from the beach.

Dom suddenly strode into the sea, water churning around his boots and then his thighs as he approached the boat. With one hand, he grabbed the craft's prow.

"What is Mr. Kilburn *doing*?" Lakshmi asked, astonished.

"I don't know," Willa confessed.

She gaped as Dom hauled the boat and its four passengers toward the beach. He looked like an old sea god, shadowy and determined, dragging a quartet of hapless sailors to safety.

At last, he pulled the prow of the boat to the beach and let it drop. The men inside the vessel tumbled out onto the sand, a heap of limbs and curses. Dom stood over them, hands on his hips, shaking his head.

"You sodding nobs need to respect things you can't control," he growled at the men at his feet.

Dom's gaze went straight to Willa, rooting her to the spot. A thrill clenched low in her belly at his primal display of strength and determination, and even from the distance between them, there was no mistaking the heat that flared in his eyes as he stared at her.

It wasn't the waves pounding the shore that roared inside her.

"Good thing the sea's nearby," Lakshmi said dryly. "In case a fire breaks out."

Yet there wasn't enough water in the whole world to drown the flames that now licked through Willa. They would burn her to ashes, if she wasn't careful.

"I see a boat on the horizon," Finn noted.

Willa's heart leapt as she peered toward the sea. There was indeed a small boat dancing on the waves. Was this to be her escape from the island, and a chance to flee from Dom? She wasn't so certain anymore. She shot a glance toward Dom, and he wore an equally conflicted expression.

While everyone on the shore nattered to themselves, Willa stared at the boat. Dom appeared in her peripheral vision as he, too, watched the boat.

She held her breath for goodness knew how long, and wasn't certain whether her dizziness came from lack of air or the fact that she didn't know if she was quite ready to leave this island, and Dom. They were just beginning to understand each other better—but did she *want* to understand him better?

The boat drew closer to the island.

"You're squeezing my arm rather tightly," Lakshmi noted.

"Apologies." Willa released her hold on the other woman.

Dom glowered at the vessel as it neared. But then—

"It's turning away," Lakshmi said. "I suppose it's a fishing boat."

"I imagine so." To her own ears, Willa's voice was faint, and she hoped it wasn't relief that made her words soft.

Yet Dom's glower had vanished and he appeared . . . satisfied.

Neither of them seemed to want off the island, but she didn't care to examine what that meant. Only a few days ago, she'd been so certain what she had required. Yet minute by minute, with each moment around him, she realized she didn't know *what* she truly desired.

Chapter 13

✦ ✳ ✦

*O*nce the guests had returned from the beach, Kieran and Finn proposed an activity just for themselves and Dom.

Now he found himself with the brothers on one of the estate's sprawling lawns. After loading and cocking his pistol, Dom took careful aim, training his sight on his target. He was more familiar with the feel of a cargo hook or blade in his hand—firearms were too dear for a dockworker to own—but he'd been given instruction to know the best way to hold a fine gun, such as the prime ones provided by his host. The smooth wood of the grip fit nicely in his large hand, and he held it comfortably, neither too tightly so that the recoil would snap his arm, nor too loosely that he might lose his hold when the gunpowder went off.

"Are you going to fire or are we all contemplating the best ways to wipe our arses?" Kieran called from his place on the sideline.

"This coming from the bloke who was sixteen before he learned how to clean his own arse," Dom answered levelly without looking away from his target.

"How dare you impugn my brother," Finn said dryly. "He was *fourteen* when he learned how to clean his arse."

"Fuck off, Finn," Kieran answered affably.

"Both of you," Dom growled. "Shut it. Or I'll get so distracted I'll forget where I'm supposed to aim and shoot off someone's bollocks. That is, *if* either of you overbred aristos *have* bollocks, and not silk bags filled with custard hanging between your legs."

The threat of having their testicles "accidentally" shot was enough to silence the Ransome brothers, leaving Dom free to fire.

He drew in a breath and held it as he squeezed the trigger. There was a flash and a puff of smoke as the flintlock fired. The apple perched atop a low stone wall burst apart in an explosion of pulp.

"Go frig yourself with a chain mail glove," a genial Kieran said as he reluctantly applauded Dom's shot.

"Go write a sonnet about your waistcoat collection." Dom handed Finn the pistol.

As Finn loaded the flintlock, Kieran threw a rude hand gesture at Dom. In response, Dom made an even ruder noise with his mouth. Kieran grinned at him, and Dom felt the beginnings of a smile tug at the corners of his lips.

It was almost like old times. When the three of them tore through London, caring for no one and nothing, determined to wreak as much havoc as possible in both sanctioned and unsanctioned places throughout the city. Back then, Dom had learned that he didn't give a rat's arse about anyone's opinion of him. He'd dwelt in a paradise of selfishness, and the Ransome brothers were exactly the two men to help feed that egotism, since they were also fueled entirely by thoughtlessness.

"All my sonnets are love poems now," Kieran answered with a smirk.

"Odes to your life as a slut?" Dom asked dryly.

"All dedicated to Celeste" was Kieran's answer. "Those indiscriminately lascivious years are behind me, and I thank God that I'll never need to return to them. She's all I want now."

Much as he was glad his friend and sister had found their domestic bliss, heaviness settled in Dom's chest. There'd never been a shortage of women in his bed. They were fascinated by his origins, his size, so lovers had been plentiful. He'd had rules for how to seduce all those highborn ladies, perfected over years of cleaving a path through ballrooms and bedchambers. Never go after a woman who wasn't interested. Always be clear that he wasn't in the market for anything serious. Give his lover pleasure, and then go about his business, on to the next.

All that had come to an end when he'd met Willa.

He'd stopped taking paramours long before they began courting. It hadn't been on purpose. But every other pleasure and pursuit hardly seemed worth it when *she* was in the world.

When she'd accepted his proposal, he had hardly believed he heard her correctly. Surely this brilliant blaze of a fine lady wouldn't want a baseborn churl such as him. Yet she had, and he'd never known such triumph as he'd pressed his lips to hers.

But then had come that day, that godawful day when his past crimes had risen up again. No matter how fine his clothes or how much French brandy he swilled after a sumptuous dinner, he was still a gutter-dweller with blood on his hands. It shamed him. And he hadn't been able to let her see his shame.

He'd pulled away from her without any explanation. Then fled like a coward.

The smile that had just started to curve his mouth withered and died, and he turned away from the Ransome brothers.

A strained silence fell between himself and the brothers. By this point, Kieran and Finn seemed used to his changeable moods, and they murmured quietly to each other as he gazed off toward one of the craggy mountains jutting up from the island. Maybe someone had first come to this place in search of solitude, away from the struggles of the world, but then one of Longbridge's more social ancestors had decided to build a sprawling manor house that hosted scores of guests, including Dom. And Willa.

"Shoot again, Dom," Kieran said cajolingly. "We've a bucket full of apples and I'm certain they're all perfectly happy to be turned into applesauce."

"Thanks just the same," he answered over his shoulder. "I'll let you two buffoons vie for the title of the island's least inept marksman."

Sensation danced along his skin, an awareness that made him turn back in time to see Willa, Celeste, Tabitha, and Miss Steele all tromping out of the house. A long scarf dangled from Willa's hand, snapping in the breeze.

A hundred yards away, the women stopped their march. The wind molded Willa's skirts to her legs, revealing the temptingly ripe curve of her hips and arse as she strode toward him and her brothers.

"Are you three done murdering innocent fruit?" she asked, coming to stand a few feet away. "We're playing blind man's buff and don't want to wind up accidentally getting shot. An ignominious end."

"Take your game elsewhere, Will," Kieran answered. "We were here first."

She made a disgusted noise. "Just throw rocks at your targets. Or each other. That way, you only hurt yourselves."

Kieran rolled his eyes, and Finn shook his head, but the brothers answered in unison, "Whatever pleases you, Will."

She smirked, triumphant.

Dom could only chuckle at her typical display of bravado.

But then . . . there was something else beneath her boldness. Her words to Miss Steele circled him. He'd never known that she'd endured so much. She had never told him. She was a fighter who'd faced soul-crushing adversity. And he'd believed her a pampered princess.

He felt her gaze on him now, a careful regard that seemed to reach all the way inside of him. Her expression was thoughtful, as if she was trying to figure out something written in code on his heart, and he wasn't certain if the notion was disturbing . . . or set his body and soul to blazing.

"That was an excellent shot you took a moment ago," she said after a moment.

"Had a prime teacher," he answered.

A flush crept up her cheeks. *She* had been his teacher. Soon after they'd first met, they had gone to a shooting range and she'd been an unexpectedly patient, thoughtful tutor, showing him the best ways to shoot. Not just pistols, but rifles, as well. She'd carefully gone over all of the steps needed to load, the best ways to aim, and how to fire without falling on his behind.

It'd actually been something of a miracle that he'd been able to absorb her lessons, since she'd had her body pressed close to his as she showed him how to properly hold the gun and sight his target. The sensation of her snug to him had been far more explosive than any gunpowder. He could still feel her, even now, in a hot echo along his flesh as the woman herself currently stared at him with rosy cheeks—as if she, too, recalled that afternoon at the shooting range. As if she, too, had been so overwhelmed with the delicious torture of those hours that she'd also gone home and been forced to make herself come with her own hand.

He hadn't had a climax since he'd arrived at this island. With her room beside his, the past night he'd heard her move across the floor and imagined her preparing for bed or taking a bath. Knowing that she was steps away made it impossible to bring himself off—too inflamed by her nearness to do anything but lie in bed, aching. He wasn't a quiet man when he climaxed, and the thought of her hearing him come was both agonizing and arousing.

"Teaching something is easy," she answered, slightly breathless, "when the pupil's so eager to learn."

Instinctively, he took a step toward her. To his shock, she didn't back away. She swayed closer to him, her own gaze on his lips, and he couldn't fucking remember why he should keep away or why he'd ever fled from her.

"Are we doing this or not?" Miss Steele called across the lawn.

Dom jolted as he and Willa seemed to both come

back to attentiveness at the same instant. Slightly dazed, she blinked and looked around as if she'd forgotten where she was.

He put needed distance between them. He might be a scoundrel, but he wouldn't seduce someone he'd hurt. Especially in front of her brothers.

"Go on with whatever it is you're doing," she said with a vague wave of her hand. "I've my own game to play."

With that, she spun on her heels and strode purposefully toward where the other ladies waited. It would have been wiser not to watch her go, but he'd never been wise where she was concerned.

"Clearly, we brought you both here for a reason," Finn murmured.

Dom didn't listen. Instead, he watched as Tabitha stood behind Willa and tied the scarf around her eyes in preparation for blind man's buff.

Once the scarf was secured, Tabitha, Celeste, and Miss Steele spun Willa around in circles several times, then danced away the moment they let go. Willa staggered a little once she stood on her own. The ladies' cries of "blind man" drifted across the lawn, but despite the covering over her eyes and her disorientation, Willa charged after them.

She was utterly courageous in her pursuit, nothing hesitating or uncertain in her steps while chasing after the other women.

"Damn," Dom said lowly, admiringly. "She's fearless. Despite . . ."

"Despite what?" Kieran asked.

"Did you know?" Dom asked, spinning to face the brothers. "That she used to run away from school?"

Kieran's brows lifted. "She told you? We never could get a word out of her about it—but I eavesdropped on our parents when they fought and blamed each other for having such a defiant daughter."

"She kept her silence with me, only—I heard her talking with Miss Steele. They were at that school together."

"We'd only learned about it years later," Finn said. "The numerous attempts to flee from that place. She never said exactly why she would try to escape, but I was able to figure out that the administration didn't care for her independent spirit, and used punishment and force to break her."

"Our mother and father wanted a pretty little ornamental daughter," Kieran said grimly, "not an actual human being, and she refused to obey."

"And before that, there were those governesses," Finn mused. "Each one more of a dragon than the last, and all fond of caning."

Dom's fists clenched at his sides. "They struck her?"

It wasn't odd that children were physically punished for alleged crimes, but never would he have believed that a genteel lady like Willa would have borne the brunt of such brutal methods.

Kieran scowled, and even Finn frowned angrily.

"Even starved her," Kieran said darkly, "when they found her reading books we'd bring home from Eton. But she endured it until the governesses couldn't suppress her, and they shipped her off to England's harshest academy for girls. Guess they thought that would do the trick. On one of her escape attempts, she even made it to our home in London. But our blessed parents sent her straight back to the school."

Fury scoured Dom, hot and caustic. He'd known, to some extent, that relations between Willa and her parents were strained, but never had he believed she'd been subject to so much awful abuse. Not only from the earl and countess, but everyone in positions of authority, all of them insisting that there was only one way to be a proper female. All this time, he hadn't known what fueled her rebellious spirit. Like a fool, he'd been charmed by who he believed was a lively but spoiled lady.

She wasn't a princess at all, and much more than the aristocratic prize he'd sought for himself. He'd been just another person in a long line of fools who expected something from her. There was a sensitive woman beneath her bravado, and he had been too focused on all her perceived toughness to realize that. To give her the tenderness and acceptance she needed.

There was a triumphant shout and Dom turned in time to see Willa holding tight to Celeste. Willa tore the blindfold from her eyes and gave another cry of victory, while the other women—even Celeste—applauded.

Dom stuck his fingers in his mouth and whistled loudly in appreciation. The way he had when they'd been at the Royal Academy.

Beaming, beautiful, Willa didn't curtsey. She *bowed*. Like a champion, because that's what she was.

THE FOLLOWING DAY was brisk and breezy. Perfect, Longbridge asserted, for flying kites.

Dom joined a collection of guests out on one of the sweeping lawns. He strode beside Kieran and Celeste, his sister carrying one of the kites provided by their host, though his attention was on Willa.

She'd made good on her word, and was talking cheerfully and openly with Miss Steele while they loped along the grass. If Miss Steele had been intimidated by Willa in the past, that was gone now, both women laughing and sometimes whispering into each other's ears.

Willa might have put her awful past behind her, but Dom couldn't. The thought that she'd sought her parents' help, only to be turned away, gutted him. And he'd been the bastard who had jilted her, another rejection in a series of them. Damn him for hurting her all over again.

"This spot is ideal," Longbridge announced when they'd reached the middle of the huge lawn.

The guests broke into smaller groups, including Kieran and Celeste in one pairing, and Finn and Tabitha in another. Dom stuck his hands in his pockets to watch the couples as they tried to get their kites into the air.

Willa and Miss Steele struggled with their kite, each taking turns holding the paper-and-wood object and running to see if a breeze could catch it and lift it skyward. Yet after the fourth go and still no success, Miss Steele shrugged and went to take one of the glasses of sparkling wine a servant had on a tray.

Willa turned to Dom. "Advice on getting this ruddy thing airborne?"

He strode to her and examined the kite. "Back in Ratcliff, we pieced ours together with twigs and bits of found paper. Nothing this nice. And we could never get enough wind between the tenements to make anything fly for more than a few feet. Fun, though," he added, smiling at the memory.

She glanced at him before returning her attention back to the kite in her hands. "It's a simple enough contraption. Between the two of us, we ought to figure it out. *They* have."

Kieran and Celeste had gotten their kite into the air, and she held the line as they laughed up at the sight of the object dancing on the wind. Finn and Tabitha, too, were grinning madly at each other as Finn wrangled their kite into performing acrobatic swoops and dives. Both couples looked happy in a way that Dom could never imagine.

"It wouldn't have worked," Willa said softly. So softly he almost didn't hear her. "You and me."

"If we'd actually gone ahead with it and gotten married when we'd planned on it?" Dom exhaled as the truth of her words struck him. "A disaster."

"We wouldn't have had what my brothers have with their wives." Her lips twisted into a wry smile. "I'd thought I was ready, but I wasn't. Such a foolish girl."

"And I was a clumsy brute. Not quite the stuff of ideal husbands." He would have stalked around the house like an unchained animal, snarling and snapping, quick to take offense and quick to lash out.

"Could you imagine? The terrible fights we would've had?" She chuckled ruefully. "There wouldn't have been a single piece of unbroken porcelain in the whole house."

"We'd need brooms in every room."

They were quiet for a moment as acceptance settled, a kind of truce brought about by mutual understanding. He'd been so certain back when he'd offered for her that they were perfect for each other, but he'd been too blind to see what she had needed.

"Don't think that you're forgiven, though," she added pertly.

"Never," he answered.

They went silent again as they watched her brothers and their wives taking delight in each other, an openness between the married couples that had always been absent with Dom and Willa. At least, it *had* been absent. The space between them now was easier, looser, each moment unlocking doors that he hadn't known were shut. Now that they opened, the hard-knotted tension in his body released.

He wasn't *comfortable* around her, though. Not when he was aware of every part of her, from the curve of her wind-pink cheeks to the long line of her neck and the small swell of her breasts beneath her jacket. Her lips, soft and the color of petals.

In the past, they'd only kissed briefly, but damn him if he didn't want a longer, deeper taste of her now. She might have the flavor of the tannic tea they had drunk minutes earlier. Or maybe she had a sweetness, like berries. She might have a savor all her own, one he'd want to drink down and swallow whole.

God, how he ached to learn *all* of her.

He never would. But that didn't stop him from wanting.

She shook her head as she looked at the kite in her hands. "Maybe this can't happen."

"We don't need to give up yet." To his right, Finn and Tabitha were successfully flying, and even reserved Finn's face was bright with happiness. "They've got the hang of it. We'll try what they're doing."

For a moment, it seemed like Willa would refuse, but then, "No one started by running."

"That made it crash."

They regarded each other for a long moment as
the wind swirled around them.

"Can I?" He reached for the kite. "I'll keep my
back to the breeze. That should get the wind where
it needs to be."

She plucked at the string in her hands. "I'll hold
this and you hold the kite. Move out a bit. No—
farther," she added when he took a few steps away.
"Keep going."

"You sure?"

Her expression was dry. "I assure you that in
this instance, I don't mind you backing away."

"Fair enough." He paced a distance from her, the
string stretching between them, until several yards
separated them. As he walked, the wind tugged
more and more at the kite, and it seemed a living
thing in his hands, eager to be free. "Now what?"

"Let it go," she called across the expanse.

He hesitated. The kite could simply fall to the
ground, all energy exhausted before it even got
started. But what was the harm in trying? Especially because what had been tried before hadn't
worked.

After taking a breath, Dom let go of the kite. A
laugh broke from him as it soared into the air, rising high and even dancing on the breeze.

"We did it!" Willa's laugh carried to him on the

wind. She held the string, her eyes fixed skyward, glittering with pleasure to see the kite wheel and spin, free of earthly rules and limits.

His heart also wheeled and spun in his chest, seeing the happiness in her face. He might not be able to take away the pain of her past, including the hurt he'd caused her, but at least for now, he could give her this. It wasn't everything, yet for this moment, it could be enough.

Chapter 14

❧✳❧

$\mathscr{A}$ drizzle set in after an hour, forcing the guests inside. Restless, unsettled, Willa paced through the house, finding nothing that could hold her interest for long. Her body felt taut, as if in readiness for something that loomed close, yet frustratingly out of reach.

She'd no idea where Dom had disappeared to, but she *wasn't* looking for him. He could do what he pleased with himself—they'd no obligation to each other.

Yet still . . . where *was* he?

When she entered one of the house's innumerable parlors, it was no surprise to find Finn, Kieran, Celeste, and Tabitha playing cards. Well, her brothers and Celeste played cards. Tabitha's attention kept wandering to a book in her lap.

"It's all right, sweet," Finn said affectionately when Tabitha had to be reminded that it was her turn. "You needn't stay and play. Go and read, if that's what you desire."

Tabitha looked momentarily relieved, but then frowned. "If I understand the rules of cassino, you need four players."

"I'll take the fourth seat," Willa volunteered.

Finn's wife smiled her gratitude as she yielded her chair to Willa. Tabitha perched at the edge of a sofa and became immediately absorbed in her book.

With expert hands, Finn dealt.

"It's nearly impossible to beat you at any sort of game such as this one," Willa said, studying her cards, "but I'm determined to at least give it a try."

"You've only to ask and I'll teach you the best strategies," her brother answered.

"You'd give up your advantage?" she asked, surprised.

"I'll instruct you in strategy," Finn said with a smile, "but I'll still win."

Kieran and Willa shared a pleased look. For as long as she could remember, Finn had never held himself in high regard—which was entirely the fault of her parents and Finn's teachers, who mistook his struggles with reading as both laziness and stupidity. But ever since Tabitha had come into Finn's life, with her unshakable belief in her husband's brilliance, he'd been far more confident, and that delighted the younger Ransome siblings.

"You should be grateful," Kieran said with a

snort as he laid down a card. "Finn's been a parsimonious bastard when it comes to showing *me* how to win at cards."

"So, you've never divulged any secrets to Key?" Willa pressed.

"It's the prerogative of older brothers to lord their advantages over their younger brothers," Finn replied, which made Kieran lob a coin at him.

"Dom isn't your brother," Willa pointed out. "Perhaps you've given him some advice with cards."

"Advice and Dom are two concepts that have never enjoyed much interaction," Finn answered, taking the coin and flicking it back at his brother. "Hardheaded, he can be. About nearly everything."

"I'm finding," she said slowly, "that even though I was engaged to Dom, there are parts of him he never told me about. Hidden sides and secrets he keeps alluding to. I own," she went on, capturing a card from the middle of the table, "that I didn't press him for his history. That fault's mine."

"And he keeps himself locked tight as a strongbox," Finn noted.

"Not one for divulging much, is Dom," Kieran said, then scowled when he couldn't capture a card. "Even when he's in his cups, he holds fast to what's in his heart."

Willa looked back and forth between her brothers. "You've known him for over a decade. Surely there are aspects of himself that he's told you about." When Kieran remained silent, she turned to Celeste. "As his sister, surely you can give me *some* insight into him."

Celeste tapped her cards to her mouth. "I can't speak for him—he's master of his own truth. What I *can* say is that whatever you thought of his life in Ratcliff, as difficult and dangerous as you may have believed it to be . . . it was a hundred times worse. He did his best to keep me protected from it, but the brunt of its brutality fell on him."

"How?" Willa whispered.

Celeste shook her head. "Many of the details aren't known to me. As I said, he sheltered me— the same, I suspect, as he's sheltered you."

Desperate for more understanding, Willa placed a hand on Celeste's wrist. "Is there *anything* you can divulge?"

"He used to come home late at night," Celeste said after a pause. "And I could tell by the haunted look in his eyes that he'd seen and done things . . . things of which he was ashamed. They pained him."

Willa's mind spun as she tried to picture what exactly had befallen Dom, yet all she could summon were vague images, blurry depictions of things she had no experience with.

"I'd prayed," Celeste continued, sorrowful, "that once Da made his fortune and we left Ratcliff behind, there'd be some happiness for Dom. If anything, it got worse. *I* had to be perfect, but there was nothing Dom could do to make anyone accept him. He's proud, and puts on a brave and brazen mask, yet when he'd come home on holiday from Oxford . . . there were more shadows in his eyes. I think he'd hoped to find some respite there from the battleground that was his life. But I don't believe that was the case."

Willa rubbed at the center of her aching chest. Turning to Kieran, she noted softly, "That's where you met him. You saw what happened at university."

"It was . . . disgraceful," Kieran said darkly. "The hazing. The bullying. He was five times bigger and ten times more intelligent than any of them, and yet the so-called gentlemen students of Oxford mocked and harassed him. Tearing up his books. Shredding his robes. Letting pigs into his rooms so they could foul up the floors."

"Oh, God." Willa swallowed around the hot coal in her throat.

"He wanted to brawl," Kieran continued, his jaw tight, "but knew he was on precarious grounds as it was, being a commoner against the gentry, and would be expelled if he fought back. So, he bore it all, but spent his nights at a boxing academy."

"It was a place where he could unleash himself," she murmured, her throat continuing to burn from the thought of the impossible, horrendous situation Dom had faced, and how he withstood it.

She'd recognized that his life had been far different from hers. Rougher. Though she'd never realized quite how much more brutal. She'd taken pride in believing her fiancé was unlike the men of the ton, but it had been a shadowy understanding of who he was.

"I'd known . . ." Willa barely saw the cards in front of her. "I'd known there were challenges he'd faced, but never the depths of his struggles. He'd said nothing about it."

"Nor would he," Celeste said quietly. "Prideful, he can be."

Willa exhaled softly, ruefully. She and Dom were a pair. Ostensibly, she belonged in the world of the ton. An earl's daughter, popular despite her insistence on flouting convention, with a substantial dowry. And yet she'd always worn her carefully constructed mask, just as she had when at school. As though nothing could touch her and she laughed in the face of any censure.

At her heart, though, fear lurked. And that fear made her even more afraid that someone might see and guess that she was far less sure of herself than she ever let anyone know.

Then there was Dom, prowling on the periphery. Part of Society but never belonging.

They'd each used the other. He'd been the perfect, shocking choice for bridegroom. And she'd been a prize for him. But even beneath that, they'd gravitated toward each other, instinctively understanding each other even with barriers between them. Something within themselves found a kindred soul in the other.

Yet—"I still cannot understand him. He proposed to me, and then, weeks before the wedding, suddenly became surly and withdrawn. Then everything changed. Why?"

"That," Kieran said grimly, "I can't tell you. Whatever happened, he's said nothing to me or Finn."

"Or me," Celeste added.

Frustration bubbled in Willa like a hot spring. Try as she might, she could not untangle the knot that was Dom. Yet the longer she spent with him on this island, in this house, the more it became clear that simply walking away was less and less possible.

On her own in one of the house's libraries, Willa studied the chessboard in front of her. She'd set out all the pieces in a specific arrangement, one that had been plaguing her for years, and as she sat in a wingback chair next to the fire, she frowned over the layout.

The rest of the guests were in another room, having repaired there after dinner, and music from the pianoforte drifted through the library's open door like a half-remembered memory.

"Oh, damn," Dom's husky voice said behind her. "Didn't expect anyone else to be here."

She turned in her seat to see him in the doorway,

resplendent in his evening clothes. There was something so magnetic about him in the austere combination of black and white—it had attracted her when they'd been courting, but now he carried even more allure.

"You're not dancing with the others?" she asked.

"It never came naturally to me." He moved into the room, and the firelight caught on the pearl that glowed from the folds of his neckcloth.

"You always seemed to enjoy dancing with me," she noted.

"I *did* enjoy dancing with you." He walked to a table that held a crystal decanter and glasses. "Felt so damn proud of myself, whirling you around ballrooms."

"Only proud of yourself?"

His smile flashed as he poured a tumbler of whisky. "Randy, too, getting to touch you like that when we waltzed."

"You weren't the only one," she said under her breath. Between feeling his hewn strength under his clothes, and the rhythm of their bodies, she'd always left the dance floor flushed and excited.

At least he was also aroused whenever they'd danced together.

He held up his glass. "Want one?"

"Please."

After filling another tumbler, he walked it to her. They watched each other over the rims of their glasses as they sipped, and the searing interest in his eyes heated her far more than the whisky.

A pop in the fireplace startled them both. He tore his gaze from hers to frown at the chessboard, and then the empty seat opposite her.

"Where's your opponent?"

"In here." She tapped her temple. "Well, more like the recollection of my opponent is here. My father used to have the board set up like this."

"And you played him," Dom guessed.

She snorted. "Father played against some of his friends, and Simon. But it was *unseemly* for a girl to learn the strategies required to win." She swallowed a mouthful of whisky as she examined the pieces on the board. "I used to watch from the side of the room."

"When you were supposed to be doing your needlework."

A laugh flew from her. "The stitches were beyond my abilities, yet I *knew* I could excel at chess—if given the chance. What was it Lady Catherine de Bourgh said about playing the pianoforte?"

"'*If I had ever learnt, I should have been a great proficient.*'" He smiled, and she smiled in return.

"I read books on chess and played myself, but I couldn't ever figure out how I could beat him when the board was laid out this way." She had the black pieces, while her invisible father had the white pieces.

Dom leaned against the back of her chair. The line

of his jaw flexed intriguingly as he drank his liquor. "The hell if I know. Never learned how to play."

"I'd wager you would be ruthless but effective." She glanced up at him, then waved toward the chair across from her. "You could help me now."

"Did you miss the part where I said I never learned?" He looked appalled. "Blokes like me are only good for lifting heavy things, not daintily maneuvering chess pieces."

"Said the man who went to Oxford," she added wryly.

"If blue blood doesn't get you into university, money buys your way."

"I know for a fact that you're not simply a brute." She remembered what Kieran said about his time at Oxford, and her heart squeezed.

He lifted one brow. "Wasn't that what you liked about me, back then?"

A flush crept into her face. "I was shortsighted and utterly lacking in seeing beyond my own nose. People can change." When he hesitated, she said, "I'll tell you everything you need to know. Just think how you'll be able to beat the aristos at their own game," she added, cajoling.

He gave a knowing smirk, clearly aware of her manipulations, then lowered himself into the other chair, his legs long and heavily muscled as he crossed them. Once settled, he gestured for her to begin her lesson.

Quickly, she ran through the basic rules of

chess. "It's all strategy and thinking several moves ahead, and yet no matter how far in advance I plan, I can't seem to find the weakness here. And everything I've tried costs me too many men." Annoyed, she waved toward the chess pieces, taunting her from their places on the board.

He finished his drink and set his glass on a small table beside his chair before slipping on his spectacles. Leaning forward, he braced his elbows on his knees and propped his chin on his interlaced hands as he scrutinized the game.

A bolt of unmitigated lust tore through her. He was such a fascinating interplay of contrasts—powerfully built, cerebral, strapping, thoughtful—her body was in a riot. Every aspect of him enticed her. But she couldn't, wouldn't, act on this unwanted desire. Not if she wanted to keep herself safe.

Even so, she was half-dizzy with the urge to straddle him as he sat in his chair, have his hands grip her thighs as she took his mouth and rubbed against him. He could even leave his spectacles on as she feasted on him.

"A sacrifice might be the way to win," he said, completely unaware of the shameless direction of her thoughts.

"What's that?" She blinked through a haze of desire.

Dom pointed to the king. "He's partially surrounded by his own men, keeping him defended and hard to reach. But if you could trick your opponent into completely encircling the king, he'd be choked and couldn't move if attacked."

He demonstrated by moving several of the pieces, black and white, until the white king had a protective barrier of other chessmen around it.

"That . . . might work." Thoughts of stripping Dom fled—well, they didn't *entirely* disappear—as she also leaned forward and considered his proposed strategy. "I have to admit, the idea of besting my father because he's too preoccupied with defending himself is awfully delicious."

"Though I don't know which of the pieces could breach the defenses," Dom added, his brow creasing.

"The knight could do it." She held up the horse-headed chess piece. "If I maneuvered him into just the right place, I could take the king."

She demonstrated her idea, until there was only one move between her and checkmate.

"And now it's done." Dom's smile was slow to develop, but when it fully bloomed, it dazzled her.

"I'd been racking my brain for years, trying to solve this." She gave a disbelieving laugh. "Thank you, Dom."

He looked puzzled. "For what?"

"Between the two of us, we finally found a way to beat my father."

"The honor's mine." He reached across the chessboard, clasping her wrist. His gaze shot to where he grasped her—her pulse hammering against his fingers—and then to her face. His breath came quickly, just as quickly as hers. His thumb stroked over her sensitive skin.

She half prayed, half feared that he'd give her the slightest tug to pull her toward him, so that their lips could meet and she'd finally give in to the hunger that had been building inside her with each moment she spent near him.

But she couldn't. She *shouldn't*. Not if she wanted to protect herself.

Slowly, she pulled free from his grasp, and sat back in her chair. She rubbed at the place where he'd held her, aflame with awareness, as she stared at him.

He shifted. With a slight wince, he subtly adjusted himself in his breeches, and it was then that she realized that they had both gone too far to return to any semblance of sanity, any hope of landing on a stable shore, and the thought was both terrifying—and enticing.

Chapter 15

❧ ✽ ❧

*L*uckily, Willa left the library before Dom did. He waited several minutes, mentally reviewing the different sizes of cargo ships, until his cock stopped standing at attention.

What the *fuck* had he been thinking, touching Willa like that while they'd been completely alone? Thinking he wouldn't want to drag her into his lap and show her all the ways he could give her pleasure? He'd seen the way she'd eyed him before that, heat in her gaze as if she'd thought the very same thing, and god*damn* it if he didn't hunger for it, too.

When he could finally get to his feet without showing the whole house his erection, he headed straight to his room. He took a hot bath and downed a healthy glass of whisky—and yet after slipping into bed, sleep stayed away.

Edgy energy surged in him as he lay in bed. He tried to hold still so he might hear the creak of the floorboards in Willa's room next door. But there was silence. All the guests had gone to bed, so likely she was fast asleep.

He should try to rest, too, but no matter how many times he fluffed his pillow or turned onto a different side, all he saw when he closed his eyes was her: beaming at him as she held on to the kite string, her earnest face as she'd insisted that he had the brains to learn chess, the heated way she'd stared at him when he'd been stupid enough to touch her. Even worse, he was tormented by vivid imaginings of things that had never happened, including her hitching up her skirts to reveal the silken flesh of her thighs. Thighs that, thanks to the shuttlecock game, he now knew the feel of.

"Fuck," he groaned, sitting up as he flung back the covers. He swung his legs around to sit at the side of the bed and dragged his fingers through his hair. It wasn't getting easier, being on this island with her. It was, in fact, getting worse.

Tension crackled through him all the time, which he would have relieved with a good old-fashioned frigging, but with her steps away, and her being the main source of his torment, taking himself in hand was out of the question.

He stood and pulled on his discarded clothing. There was no point in bothering with a waistcoat or neckcloth, so he donned only a shirt, breeches, boots, and greatcoat. Somewhat dressed, he decided to forgo taking a candle with him—no point in alerting anyone to the fact that he was suffering from insomnia brought about by pure erotic frustration—then opened his door and went out into the hallway.

A light appeared at one end of the corridor, so he ducked into an alcove and pressed himself against the wall. A banyan-clad Baron Hunsdon tiptoed past before sliding into Longbridge's room.

Before Dom could step out of the alcove, another light appeared. This time, Mrs. McDaniel glided down the hallway before she, too, eased her way into Longbridge's room.

A moment passed. And then another. No one left Longbridge's bedchamber.

When Dom was sure that no one *else* was going to join the party in their host's bedroom, he stepped out of the alcove and hurried as noiselessly as possible to the stairs. He descended the steps quickly, though it wasn't easy given the darkness, before crossing the entryway and sliding out the front door.

Moonlight gleamed down like a sidelong glance, which gave him enough illumination to stride to the wooden stairs leading to the beach. Slight unease crept along his neck to be out of doors at this hour—he was used to being out after dark in London, yet it was still a bit unsettling to be on his own in the middle of nature. He held tightly to the railing as he went down the stairs, keeping his focus on his feet so that he didn't go toppling down and break his neck.

When his boots hit the sand, he breathed out in

relief. The beach stretched out in a pale crescent, and waves tumbled to the shore in endless arcs, running to the sand, and then retreating to leave shining ribbons in their wake.

He strode along the beach. Slogging across the uneven surface would tire him out, and if it didn't, at least he had something to look at besides the wooden panels of his bedchamber.

"Dom?"

He drew up short. She stood a few feet from him, a figure in a long, pale coat, her dark hair like a streaming banner in the breeze coming in off the ocean.

"Willa?" He needn't have asked—even in the hazy light of the moon, he knew her shape, and felt the vitality that was only hers.

"You want to be alone," he said at once. "I'll go."

"There's only so much solitary, moody beach-side haunting I can do," she answered. "But if it's *two* people moodily haunting a beach, that's much more tolerable."

In silent agreement, they began to walk, her strides matching his. A wild, reckless happiness rose up in him. But he'd no right to it. No right to *her*, no matter how much his body and heart insisted that she was his.

IF SOMEONE HAD told Willa a year ago that she and Dom would be walking side by side down this moonlit beach—*without* her attempting to drown him—she would have very sincerely told that someone to piss off.

Taking a nighttime stroll with the same man who had devastated her? Impossible. Ludicrous. She wouldn't have ever permitted him to be that near her, or believed that she'd be able to tolerate his presence for more than the time it took to pull her hand back and slap him across his rugged, almost handsome face.

Yet here they were, strolling next to each other, though it wasn't exactly peaceable, the silence between them. Having him so close by, dark and rumpled and dangerous-looking, she was afire with awareness of him. His size. The smoldering life force that vibrated from him. As well as the fact that they were completely alone on this dark beach, as if everyone in the world had vanished, and she and Dom could do whatever they pleased with no fear of reprisal or judgment.

"On my way out of my room," she mused, "I saw Gilbert Cransley sneak into Lady Shipton's room."

"And I watched Baron Hunsdon *and* Mrs. McDaniel go into Longbridge's bedchamber," Dom said. "No shortage of nocturnal carrying-on with the nobs."

"Not *all* of us nobs," she replied, stepping around a clump of seaweed. "Unmarried ladies aren't encouraged to act out a French farce. Yet," she added, throwing him a glance, "men can do as they please. My brothers are offensively happy in their marriages, so they wouldn't be part of the bedchamber antics, but you are unwed and at perfect liberty to seek out nocturnal entertainment. Instead, you're trudging along a beach. With me."

She tried to speak lightly, as if his reply didn't matter, and yet her breath held as she waited for his response.

"That bed-hopping tomfoolery is for aristos."

Her exhalation came out far more loudly than she would have liked, because he shot her a surprised look. She quickly turned her gaze toward the waves rolling to the shore.

"You used to cavort quite vigorously," she pointed out, still striving for an offhand tone, "with my brothers as company."

"I played the part of rakehell," he said thoughtfully. "But all that came to an end when—"

"When what?" she pressed when he suddenly went silent.

"When I met you," he admitted.

She stumbled slightly, but pretended that it was the sand that fouled her steps. With purposeful carelessness she asked, "Why should that make a difference? Most men continue their sundry trysts and affairs regardless of their more sanctioned entanglements."

His wide shoulders lifted in a shrug. "No point in it. I'd nothing to prove, especially after we got engaged."

"Do you regret it now? Not carrying on in your rakish ways, when the engagement came to nothing?"

He stopped walking, and she did, too. They faced each other at the very edge of the water, the sea surging close to their feet, yet she barely heard the waves.

"It wasn't nothing," he said in a gravelly voice. "It brought us here."

"I wish there'd been another way to get here."

His jaw tightened. "I hate that I hurt you. I'll curse myself for it until my last breath."

She did and did not take comfort from his regret. "I haven't come to peace with it," she confessed. "And yet . . . much as I hate to admit it . . . my brothers were right. The only way is forward."

He gave a short, clipped nod.

"Though right now," she added, "I've had enough of trudging through sand and need a rest."

She lowered herself down to the sand, and he did the same, stretching his legs out in front of him. As they sat quietly, watching the water, she picked up a piece of driftwood and turned it over and over in her hands, feeling how the waves had polished it nearly to a lacquered finish. But people weren't like driftwood, they didn't get smoother as life knocked them about. If anything, they grew rougher and more splintered.

"I was wrong," he said abruptly. "Calling you *princess*. That's what I thought you were, high up in your tower, above all of us struggling peasants. It doesn't fit, though."

"*Witch*, perhaps," she suggested wryly.

"*Lioness.*" His gaze was warm on her, chasing away the chill of the breeze. "Powerful, yes, but not invulnerable. There's tenderness there, a deep and feeling soul, and that makes your power all the more incredible."

Her heart stuttered. "No one's ever described me that way before. No one ever *saw* me that way."

It was frightening, and extraordinary. She wanted to flee and she never wanted to leave this beach.

He brought his hand up, slowly. She went still, her breath coming faster and faster as his broad and fever-hot palm cupped her jaw.

The shadows surrounding his eyes deepened and at that moment, he was as dark and forbidding and seductive as Hades, ready to spirit Persephone away to the depths of his underworld kingdom.

"For all that we're to move forward," he rumbled, "here we are, pulled together like a tide."

"A tide that causes ships to collide and wreck." She couldn't look away from his mouth, so contradictorily lush in his rough-hewn face.

"Maybe we should surrender to our fate and go under." He brought his lips closer to hers, yet they didn't touch. His exhalations were warm, scented with tobacco and whisky, but uneven across her face.

"I'll never permit myself to sink," she said, breathless.

"You can hold on to me." His voice was as dark and fathomless as the sea. "I won't let you drown."

Unable to fight the pull of desire between them, she closed the distance. Her lips found his. Sensation jolted through her at the contact of skin to skin. For a moment, he held himself motionless, and the thought came, brief and humiliating and terrifying, that he didn't want this. Didn't want *her*.

But then he groaned like a man losing a war, his fingers tightening their hold on her as his mouth opened to hers.

This was nothing like the kisses they had shared before as a courting couple stealing moments where they could. Those kisses had been soft and sweet and respectful sips of each other—yet now, *now*, there was nothing gentle or reverent about how they greedily devoured one another.

His lips were firm and commanding, and yet she would not yield easily, meeting his strength and demand with her own. She dug her fingers into the hair on the nape of his neck even as her hand— her whole body—trembled. Their tongues stroked against each other, the feeling echoing in deep and needy places within her.

"For so long," he growled into her mouth, "I've ached to taste you again."

"Am I . . . what you remembered?"

"No memory compares," he answered between hungry kisses, "to the truth and fact of you."

She rose up on her knees to angle herself better and take more of him. While he continued to cup her jaw, his other hand slid around her back to splay just above the curve of her arse. The inferno of his skin burned into her, chasing away the year-long chill that had settled into her bones.

Their bodies moved together, and he lowered back to lie upon the sand as she straddled him.

She gasped against his lips to feel his thick, hard cock press into the juncture of her thighs. He froze, as though holding himself back to spare her from his body's need, but she would have none of it. Pushing her hips into his, she ground against his length, streaks of pleasure arcing through her at the exquisite sensation and brought even higher by his groan of ecstasy. He arched up, rocking into her with his heavy cock.

This was so much better than anything she'd ever experienced with her own hand, and far superior to her fevered imaginings of what it might be like if she and Dom ever surrendered to their desire. It was real and ungainly and crude and delicious.

God—if she had known what it would be like between them, this combustible, this glorious, she would never have let him go. She would have chased him across the globe, demanding the joining of their bodies.

"Jesus, Willa," he snarled as he trailed his lips along her neck. "You're . . . you're so . . ."

"I *know*," she panted. "And you're . . ." She pressed her hips into him, his hand snug against her arse to bring them even closer together.

A moan escaped her at the perfect feel of him, but she was desperately frustrated by the layers of fabric between them.

It wasn't enough. After what seemed a lifetime of waiting and wanting, she craved more of him. More for herself.

She grappled with her skirts, hiking them up. At the same time, she fumbled at the fastenings of his breeches.

"Willa—wait," he rasped. "*Willa*. Stop."

His hand grasped hers, stilling her.

She went motionless, though she gasped and shook and *burned*. Beneath her, his whole body heaved up and down.

"You don't want to do this?" She hated the uncertainty in her voice and yet she couldn't prevent it. At his jagged chuckle, she snapped, "Don't laugh at me."

"Lioness," he said, his voice uneven, his Ratcliff accent strong, "if I laugh, it's at myself, because I'll never stop desirin' you. There ain't *nothin'* in the world I want more than to be inside you."

Heat surged through her, centering between her legs and in her breasts. "But you stopped me."

"'Cos," he said, closing his eyes, "this is exactly the *wrong* thing for us to do."

She sat up as the fire within her cooled to ice. Everything inside of her turned brittle and frozen, but that didn't stop the throb of shame that pulsed in her veins. "I see."

Her throat burned as she shook sand out of her skirts. "*I'm* the one who ought to laugh at myself. Because, as wise as I thought I was, when it comes to you, I was and will always be a simpleton. The blame now belongs to me. I should have known better, but, ridiculous as I am, I honestly believed it might be different between us. That you wouldn't humiliate me again."

She forced out a laugh. "I ought to charge admission. 'Come and see Willa Ransome, England's Greatest Fool. Trying to make love to the man who abandoned her at the altar.'"

The last words came out choked as tears threatened to overwhelm her.

"It ain't like that." He got to his feet, and adjusted himself in his snug breeches.

"How can I believe you?" she demanded wildly. "How can I believe anything between us?"

"Because," he growled, "the fault's mine. It always has been. Years ago . . ." He dragged his hands through his hair. "I did somethin'. Somethin' terrible. And it'll never stop standin' between us."

"What was it?" she pled.

His fists knotted at his sides. "I can't say."

"Damn it, Dom." Her throat burned and she wanted to scream and weep in frustration. "You can tell me. Whatever it is. Only, you can't keep threatening me with this secret of yours, and then keep it to yourself. That's not fair. Just *let me in*."

He shook his head, and moonlight gleamed on his wet eyes. "If only I could. But it ain't possible. I can't put that burden on you."

Her shoulders sagged as hopelessness overwhelmed her. "There's no way to go back, and we aren't moving forward. We're stuck here, in this whirlpool, going round and round until we're sucked under."

"Lioness," he rasped. "I wish it was different. I wish *I* was different."

She turned to the sea and its vastness, stretching out endlessly, and yet it didn't seem nearly as endless as this distance between her and Dom. Every time she thought they were drawing closer, she realized how wrong she was.

GETTING OUT OF bed the following morning was a challenge. How could she face anyone, how could she face *him* after last night?

Yet she wouldn't permit herself to cower. She'd run away to the Continent, and she'd fled the night before. It was exhausting—and fruitless—to keep bolting when that changed nothing.

And, God, how she wanted to change.

She rose from bed and opted to dress herself rather than summon the maid. It wasn't entirely an easy feat, clothing herself without assistance, but fortunately she had packed a few quickly donned gowns. She could arrange her hair so that it didn't look as though she'd spent the remaining nighttime hours restlessly turning from one side of her mattress to the other.

She'd been aware of Isla coming in just after dawn to light the fire, but had feigned sleep to avoid conversation.

Now staring at herself in the mirror, she grimaced at the purple crescents beneath her eyes, yet there wasn't anything she could do about them. She rubbed her palms against her face. Hopefully, the color she summoned in her cheeks would serve as a distraction.

What she'd face with Dom today, she didn't know. But she couldn't avoid it.

She stood from the dressing table, strode to the door, and pulled it open. A small object caught her attention, placed as it was just on the other side of the threshold.

She bent down and picked it up. It was a little figurine, carved from driftwood into the form of a tiny lioness.

The workmanship was a touch crude, as if it had been done with too large a knife, but there was no mistaking what it was, or who it was from.

Her fingers tightened around the figurine, its

shapes pressing into her flesh. She'd never known that he had any skill with carving, but she pictured him staying up, all alone as the house slumbered, to carefully craft the small lioness. For her.

She held the lioness to her chest, holding it snug to her beating heart. Whatever she and Dom were to one another, they were far from done with each other.

Chapter 16

❧ ✳ ❧

$\mathcal{D}$id I see what I saw last night?" Kieran asked as Dom stepped inside from taking a very fast walk around the grounds.

The weather had warmed, and Dom dragged the back of his hand across his sweat-slicked forehead. Even though he'd done his level best to tire himself out by practically running the perimeter of the estate, he didn't have his usual release of the boxing academy. Damn, but he needed it, though. After last night, coming so close to pleasuring Willa in the sand, he was on the verge of exploding.

But at least he'd had enough presence of mind to stop himself before sinking into her, the way he burned to. *Some* part of him was thinking clearly.

"I've no idea what you saw," he answered, striding past Kieran. "So, I can't say whether or not you saw it. Jesus," he added with a shake of his head, "I'm spouting fucking nonsense."

"You and Willa, last night," his friend explained as he trotted after Dom.

Dom stopped in his tracks. "What *exactly* do you mean?"

Ice flooded his muscles. If Willa's brother had seen the way Dom and Willa had been *this close* to making love . . . then it was only a matter of moments before Kieran punched Dom in the face. Even poets could be pushed to violence if their sisters were involved.

"Celeste and I were just heading up to our bedchamber from the conservatory after . . ." Kieran cleared his throat, and Dom was grateful his friend didn't finish that sentence. "Never mind. But we both saw you and Willa coming up the stairs, back from the beach."

Dom exhaled. Thank God Kieran had only seen them returning from the shore.

"We'd gone for a walk," Dom explained gruffly.

Kieran stuck his hands in his pockets as he regarded Dom with interest. "How fascinating."

"Nothing *fascinating* about it," Dom said, dour. "Just two people walking next to the water. It happens all the time."

"Except *these* two people used to be engaged, and things between them appear to be thawing. *Are* they thawing?"

Dom blew out a breath. "Hell if I know. We go forward, and then back, and it's a bloody confusing ⁀e."

"Does she know the steps?"

"We're both lost," Dom admitted. "How to go onward, I've no fucking idea."

Everything was so sodding confusing, except for the fact that he couldn't stay away from Willa. And he wasn't sure she wanted him to stay away.

"I see." Kieran stared at the space over Dom's shoulder, looking into nothingness, but seeing something, because a pleat of thought creased between his eyebrows.

Dom didn't trust that look on his friend's face—not by a mile.

"Well," Kieran said brightly and abruptly, "I'm certain some kind of answer will present itself. All we need is faith in the movement of the celestial spheres."

Dubious, Dom said, "The celestial spheres aren't the only things that are spinning."

"Prepare yourselves for delight," Longbridge announced. He strode into the parlor where most of the guests—Dom included—had gathered to read or write in their diaries or sketch or whatever the hell it was nobs did when they were trying to fill the long, empty hours of their days.

Dom himself was attempting to read *Persuasion*, and, as engrossing as the novel was, his attention kept drifting from the book to across the room, where Willa was bent over a small desk, frowning over something she was writing in a clothbound journal. No doubt recording for posterity what a ruddy confusing mess everything had become.

Sunlight through the open curtains gilded the tender line of her neck, illuminating all the soft, downy hair that curled up from her nape.

He gripped his book tighter, but the feel of its pages was no substitute for touching her, and the scent of the paper and leather couldn't compare to the fragrance that rose up from her flesh.

Dom knew *exactly* what she smelled like because he'd inhaled her deeply as they'd kissed on the beach. And he craved more of her scent and the feel of her and her taste . . . all things he shouldn't desire.

She looked up now at Longbridge's entrance, and her frown deepened when a sturdy footman trailed after their host, carrying a large wooden trunk.

Dom fought the urge to roll his eyes. Longbridge was doing his best to be hospitable and attend to his guests' entertainment, but, my God, could there be *one* moment when there was nothing to do but sit and brood? Dom had a lot of brooding to do. He was actually something of an expert in it.

At his employer's signal, the servant set the trunk down and opened it.

Longbridge plunged his hand into the trunk and lifted out what appeared to be a toga. "For you, my dearest guests."

"An orgy?" Kieran asked excitedly from his place beside Celeste on the sofa.

His wife patted his hand. "Always hoping. That's what I love about you."

"I cannot vouch for what happens afterward," Longbridge said, now pulling out a sword made of paper, "but before that, we'll disport ourselves marvelously with some amateur theatricals."

A round of applause went up from the guests, though Dom noticed that Willa halfheartedly added to the clapping. He himself kept his hands occupied by holding his book.

Amateur theatricals seemed a bloody odd thing to do, but then again, they'd done something similar in *Mansfield Park*. Although that had turned out to be a disaster for everyone involved.

The orange tabby cat that occasionally showed up to lounge beside the fire decided that these activities were simply too much for its peace of mind, and quickly left the room. It surely knew better than any of the humans.

"There's to be a theme?" Willa asked, rising from her desk and approaching the trunk cautiously.

"Saucy scenes from history," Longbridge exclaimed with cheer.

Willa took an immediate step backward.

"And *we* are to act these scenes out," Dom surmised.

"Precisely." Their host beamed.

Standing, Dom snapped his book shut. "My thanks,

but I'll be in the audience." There was no bloody way he would clomp around onstage, awkwardly stammering lines, appearing like the veriest oaf.

"The same for myself," Willa added. She cast him a curious, cautious glance, as she had been doing all day.

If she was afraid he'd tell somebody about the fact that they'd done more than walk on the beach, she was dead wrong. As if he'd blab to *anyone* what an agonizing ecstasy it had been to kiss her again, to feel her passion and fire and all the wondrous things that made her Willa. As if he'd give an outsider details about something that was private and intimate, reserved only for himself and her.

And never to be repeated. He had to remember that. He shouldn't have encouraged her to give in to their attraction when they'd been on the beach last night—regretted it now that he'd had that taste of the passion between them. But damn it, he'd *wanted* her so badly, and been a selfish, greedy son of a bitch.

No matter how much he was engulfed in flames with desire for her, or that half of him felt as though it was missing because he could not touch her or lavish her with the pleasure she deserved, he couldn't have her for his own.

Longbridge's face fell, but Cransley quickly said, "It does sound like an utter delight. I'm in."

Now grinning, their host tossed the paper sword

to Cransley. "You shall be Ares. Who will be your Aphrodite?"

Lady Shipton's hand went up, and Longbridge handed her a diaphanous gown. Then he pulled out what looked like several gauzy pieces of fabric.

"Who will wear—or remove—the seven veils of Salome?" he asked.

Before Longbridge had even finished his sentence, Celeste had leapt to her feet and snatched the veils from his hand. Naturally, Kieran looked as though he'd been given the keys to a king's treasure room.

"You know I lose my head to you, love," he murmured when she returned to the sofa, filmy pieces of fabric in hand.

"Perhaps I *won't* be in the audience," Dom muttered. He'd little desire to see his baby sister dance seductively in front of her drooling husband. What they did in the privacy of their bedchamber was their business, but like hell would Dom watch it play out onstage.

Longbridge returned to the trunk and removed a wig and coat from the previous century.

"Aha! Who shall take the role of Casanova?" their host exclaimed.

Baron Hunsdon stepped forward. "I volunteer."

Longbridge's eyes gleamed as he pulled a long cape from out of the trunk. "I have a brilliant idea. I shall play Don Juan, and the scene shall be between the two most infamous libertines, Casanova and the Spaniard, each attempting to seduce the other."

The guests broke into another round of applause and Baron Hunsdon appeared extremely pleased by this development.

"Are you certain we cannot inveigle you to participate, Lady Willa?" Longbridge asked. "I've many more costumes to choose from—you can be whoever you desire."

"My thanks," Willa answered. "I'm happy enough being myself."

She retreated to the writing desk, as if putting distance between herself and the prospect of acting in a dramatic performance. All day, in truth, she'd been in retreat, speaking seldom to anyone. In his few interactions with her today, she hadn't ignored him, though when they had exchanged words, she'd been polite but reserved.

As if she, too, tried to figure out what they meant to each other or what their next moves should be.

"Lady Marwood," Longbridge said, turning to the viscountess. "This is a holiday for you, a playwright of considerable fame, but would you be so kind as to create a few lines for us? Each scene will be extemporaneous, but they'll be introduced by a narrator. You may play the part yourself, if you so wish it."

Lady Marwood had been sitting at a small table, playing cards with her husband and Miss Steele. At Longbridge's request, her mouth curved into a wry smile.

"Come now, my beloved," the viscount said with a laugh. "Affect disgruntlement all you please but you're all but slavering at the prospect of flexing your artistic muscles before the distinguished company."

His wife shot him an even more wry look. "Am I so transparent, Cam?"

"As glass, Maggie." Lord Marwood picked up his wife's hand and pressed a kiss to her knuckles, which brought a blush to her cheeks.

"And a poem from Kieran," added Celeste.

"If you think my words are worthy of sharing the stage with Lady Marwood," Kieran said with what seemed a halfhearted attempt at modesty.

"Without doubt, I do," Celeste insisted, wrapping her arms around her husband's neck adoringly.

Dom swallowed hard as he tore his attention from these scenes of domestic happiness. His gaze collided with Willa's. It seemed they both didn't know what to make of other people's marital bliss when they themselves were lost in a thick fog of confusion, blindly feeling their way.

"Splendid," Longbridge said, clapping his hands together. "All the thespians will spend the afternoon readying themselves for tonight's performance. Rehearse as much as you think it necessary—though the more impromptu their dialogue, the better. Meanwhile, those who are part of the audience will assist in preparing the stage

and scenery. The ballroom will serve as our the-
ater. Curtain goes up at nine."

While their host spoke, servants trooped in
carrying paint, brushes, fabric, wood, and tools.
Willa took a paintbrush, and looked over which of
the paints she meant to use.

Dom gratefully seized a hammer, feeling its comfortable weight in his hand. Though most of the
work he'd done at the docks had been loading and
unloading ships, he'd now and then been pressed
into service repairing crates that split during trans-
port. There was something deeply satisfying in
putting to rights that which had been broken.

The lioness figurine had been a foolish impulse.
He oughtn't to have made it or given it to her. For
all he knew, she'd consigned it to the fire—which
wouldn't have been a surprise. But he'd had to
show her that he saw her differently now. Saw her,
and appreciated her. And while he couldn't undo
the pain he'd caused her in the past, maybe something small like a little wooden lioness could lead
to a better future for her, one where she cherished
herself as he did.

THE DAY PASSED in a flurry of activity. It was a
bit of a blessing, as it kept Dom busy and not able
to brood too much. Yet the trouble with working
with his hands was that it often left the mind, and
heart, free to wander.

He hammered nails and sawed wood to construct the scenery, but the pounding rhythm of his hammer didn't allay his body's continuous hunger for her. Thank God they'd stopped when they had last night. Because if he'd gotten even a hint of what it would be like to make love to her, no force on goddamn earth would have been able to keep him from wanting more.

Carrying one of the flats, he passed her on his way to the ballroom. They both paused as Mrs. McDaniel and Miss Steele transported a length of curtain fabric down the corridor, making it impossible for anyone else to move until they had cleared the hallway.

"You've . . ." He set down the wooden flat and gestured to Willa's face. "There's some paint."

She rubbed at her cheek but the streak of blue remained. "Did I get it?"

"A little to the right." When she unsuccessfully tried to remove the paint, he said lowly, "Hold still."

She did, even when he bent close to her and carefully stroked his fingers across her cheek. The paint had mostly dried, so it came off in flakes, but he went slowly, attentively, as if personally responsible for removing every last trace of the pigment from her skin.

"Can't have you walking around like some woad-streaked Pict," he rumbled.

"Striking terror into the hearts of everyone who beholds me." Her words were breathy and, truth be told, he was having a hard time remembering how to inhale and exhale calmly. Her flesh was so soft beneath his fingertips, and he could just catch little puffs of air from her mouth on his skin.

He was close enough to see her gaze drop to his bared forearms. At some point, he'd removed his coat and rolled up his shirtsleeves, since aristo clothes were rubbish for doing any kind of actual work.

It was a bit embarrassing, the size of his bulging forearms, because they marked him as anything but a gentleman.

Raw hunger flared in Willa's dark eyes. Her tongue darted out to wet her bottom lip.

Jesus fucking God almighty.

"Any . . . paint left?" she asked, almost panting.

"It's gone," he growled.

"Are you . . . sure? There might be a little remaining . . ."

"Maybe here . . ." He stroked his fingers along her jaw, its softness like a flame within him. And then, because he was a mean and selfish bastard, he traced one fingertip down the length of her throat, stopping just above the high neck of her dress.

Her lashes dropped, and she let out a soft, barely audible moan.

His breath came fast and rough, but he'd be damned if he could stop touching her.

If he'd planned that the day's physical labor

would drain his body's demand for her, that had been a bloody stupid thing to hope for. Because it was all he could do to keep from pinning her to the wall with his much larger body, tenderly wrapping one hand around her throat, and taking her mouth in a hard, needy kiss.

Judging by the heat in her gaze, she entertained the very same ideas.

She shook her head, took a step back, and then another, before hurrying past him as if she feared what she might do when presented with dangerous temptation. The same temptation that continued to scorch a path through him.

He wanted her, that much was certain. It was as certain as the fact that she wanted him. But if they gave in to the hunger that blazed between them, there'd be no going back. She'd learn the truth about him, and when she left him, he'd be destroyed.

Chapter 17

❖

*W*illa strode into the ballroom-turned-theater for the evening's performance, heading toward the two rows of seats that had been set up for the audience in front of the lantern-lit stage, when a slightly panicked Tabitha rushed toward her.

"There isn't a moment to spare," her brother's wife said. Tabitha cast a glance toward the other guests in their chairs, fanning themselves and chatting eagerly in anticipation of the entertainment. "You *must* hurry."

With surprising strength given her scholarly inclinations, Tabitha grasped Willa's arm. She pulled Willa toward the stage's makeshift wings, which had been created by hanging velvet curtains from a quickly assembled scaffold.

"Hurry for *what*?" Willa asked.

"Mr. Longbridge has decided that he wants a tableau vivant flanking his scene with the baron," Tabitha explained. She drew Willa behind the curtain on stage left. It was shadowed back here, but there was enough light to see that fabric and a golden belt studded with paste jewels were draped on a chair. "Something to highlight the action onstage. Here—put this on."

Tabitha thrust the fabric and belt at Willa.

At Willa's questioning look, Tabitha clarified, "You're to be Hippolyta. The belt is your girdle."

"There's a Hercules, I'm assuming," Willa said.

"The ninth labor of Hercules, to be exact," the other woman said. "The legendary hero was tasked with obtaining the jeweled, golden belt of Hippolyta, the queen of the Amazons."

"Some tellings of the myth suggested that Hippolyta and Hercules became lovers," Willa noted. "Then it all went to hell and turned into a battle between Hercules and the Amazons."

"In that version, the hero slays Hippolyta."

Willa rolled her eyes. "Typical."

Presumably, the tableau that Mr. Longbridge desired only included the more romantic part.

Willa examined the filmy and revealing costume. It resembled an ancient Greek peplos, fastened at the shoulders with brooches of faux gold, and made of gauzy white silk. Whoever wore it would be quite exposed—but then, formal etiquette and propriety were two guests that hadn't been invited to this house party.

"Hurry," Tabitha urged. "The scene is going to begin shortly."

"Why *me*?" Willa asked, frowning. "There are other women who could play the part—especially as there's no dialogue."

"Mrs. McDaniel hurt her ankle and Miss Steele was too fatigued after the day's labors. Make haste," Tabitha added in an urgent whisper as the audience quieted. "Lady Marwood is about to introduce the scene."

For a moment, Willa considered refusing. But then, what was the harm in it? All she had to do was strike a pose and hold it as Mr. Longbridge and Baron Hunsdon attempted to seduce each other. No one would be paying any attention to her, not if it meant watching two renowned roués work their alluring wiles on one another. And it was unlikely that any of the guests would return to London full of tales of Willa in a revealing costume, not when they'd all cast aside decorum themselves.

And Dom would see her in this scandalous ensemble. She played with fire, and yet welcomed the burn. Anything was better than this suspended state, balanced between the past and the unknown future.

"Help me with this," she said to Tabitha.

With a look of relief, her brother's wife moved to assist Willa in removing her gown and donning the costume. It wasn't exactly easy to manage the task in such a brief amount of time, and in such a confined space, but in short order, Willa stood in the diaphanous peplos. There had been no hope for it but to remove her stockings, since they would have looked patently ridiculous worn with the provided pair of golden sandals. Hippolyta's famed girdle was cinched about her waist, causing the fabric to drape most provocatively around her hips. Though she'd removed her stays, she still wore her shift, which might have spoiled the costume's appearance slightly, but it was impossible for Willa to take the stage in front of her family with nothing beneath her long tunic.

"For Your Majesty." Tabitha placed a paste-encrusted diadem on Willa's head. "Now, the performance awaits you."

Her brother's wife motioned for Willa to take her place onstage.

Willa took one deep breath before striding out in front of the audience. She was alone, no sign of either Mr. Longbridge or the baron, and a tremor of unexpected nerves shook her as she felt the eyes of a dozen people on her. She was used to drawing attention to herself at balls through admittedly unruly behavior, but standing on a stage seemed entirely different. More exposed, somehow.

"Here's Hippolyta!" someone in the crowd cried.

"And here comes Hercules," somebody added.

Clad in a short chiton and draped in a faux lion skin, a bewildered-looking Dom emerged from the other side of the stage.

Oh, hell.

Meanwhile, she caught sight of Mr. Longbridge and the baron standing at the back of the ballroom. They were in costume, but far, far away from the wings. And Tabitha returned to her seat to give Finn and Kieran a nod—as if she'd carried out her assigned task.

Two things struck Willa simultaneously.

The first: she and Dom had been set up. *Again.*

The second: Dom was wearing *very* little clothing, revealing acres and acres of his densely muscled body, including his impossibly wide shoulders, sculpted arms, and taut, hewn thighs that were easily as wide as some people's torsos.

When she'd been on the Continent, she'd attempted to distract herself by taking a few art classes that had included live models of all sexes. And while there had been a tiny scrap of fabric draped across the male model's nethers, the rest of his body had been entirely bare. His form had been extremely agreeable, rivaling an ancient statue for sheer musculature, and the time Willa had spent sketching him had indeed provided her with a few hours of pleasant distraction.

She'd thought herself very sophisticated for an unmarried woman, seeing an unknown and well-formed man almost completely nude.

But that had been nothing, *nothing*, compared to the jaw-dropping sight of Dom in his tiny costume.

Great God in heaven, she knew he was of substantial size and possessed a brawny physique, yet the truth of him went beyond all her knowledge and imaginings.

Not only that, he was barefoot, and his feet were, quite simply, *enormous*. And the papier-mâché club he carried looked like a reed in his massive hand.

That meant that *all* of him was similarly proportioned.

Despite the fact that she stood onstage in front of over a dozen people, tricked by her own kin, exposed and lost, her gaze arrowed straight to Dom's groin. It was as if, fueled by the certainty that he was gigantic in every capacity, she could look nowhere else.

She'd *felt* him last night, but that was a far cry from *seeing* how the chiton's short skirt clung to a large and distinctive bulge at the top of his thighs.

Someone in the audience whistled, and she snapped to attention in time to see Dom's own astonished, ravenous gaze moving over her as she stood in her revealing costume. She felt him everywhere: on the lines of her legs beneath her thin skirt, skimming over her hips, lingering on the shapes of her breasts so provocatively displayed by the draping fabric. His eyes went dark, and his jaw flexed.

A flame of arousal flickered low in her belly, which was ruddy inconvenient as she was *standing onstage* as a direct result of her family's manipulations, and she didn't know what to do with the monstrous, overwhelming desire that kept pulling her toward Dom.

Yet she *was* onstage, and theoretically, she was supposed to be playing the role of the Queen of the Amazons for a tableau vivant. Perhaps if she struck a pose, Mr. Longbridge and Baron Hunsdon would come up and actually act out their seduction scenario.

Awkwardly, she stood with one hand in the air and the other on her hip, hoping she resembled some figure on a painted urn. Dom must've had a similar idea, because he, too, affected a stance, flexing his bicep as if to enact Hercules's display of fabled strength.

Unfortunately for her, it also made the muscles of his upper arm bunch in a far-too-beguiling manner.

She and Dom posed like that for several moments. But nothing happened. Mr. Longbridge and the baron remained at the back of the ballroom. Watching.

"A scene, a scene!" one of the audience members called. "Speak!"

The cry was repeated by others, growing louder and louder, until it thundered around Willa. She glanced uncertainly toward Dom. He appeared just as doubtful as she did, until, at last, something had to be done.

She was Willa Goddamn Ransome and she didn't back down from a challenge.

She moved to the center of the stage. When Dom lingered in his place by the side, she made a quick motion for him to join her.

He took an uncertain step toward her, and then another. Finally, they stood with a few feet between them.

"Now what?" he said, sotto voce.

"Now pretend that you're Hercules and you're trying to seduce me into giving you my girdle," she hissed back.

He stared at her. "Truly?"

"Yes, truly," she said lowly. "*Do it*, Dom, or we're going to look like even bigger asses up here."

He cleared his throat, and then, in a stilted voice, he said, "Uh, fair Hippolyta, Queen of the Amazons, I stand before you—"

"Louder!" somebody yelled.

"With passion," another person added.

Dom's gaze snapped to hers.

Despite the furious blush in her cheeks, Willa tried to maintain a regal posture as befitting a queen of female warriors.

"I stand before you," he continued in a more emphatic tone, "to plead for your indulgence, not as a hero, but as a man. A man humbled by your glory."

Her mind spun as she tried to think of a proper response, something that Hippolyta might say when presented with Greece's legendary pinnacle of strength.

"I am not swayed by your flattery. They are words I've heard before."

"What can I do," he answered, pressing a hand to his heart, "to show a great queen that I am sincere?"

"Kneel." It leapt from her before she could stop herself, but hell, the command felt right. "Demonstrate to me that you are deserving of this favor you seek."

To her shock, he didn't hesitate. Instead, he immediately sank down onto his knees. Doing so put his face level with her breasts, and his own chest heaved up and down as he seemed captivated by the sight.

And, God, if *he* wasn't a delicious spectacle, this massive man fully displaying his impressive physique, kneeling before her.

The role took her over. Tipping up her chin, she walked slowly around him, inspecting him as a ruler might consider her subject. She granted herself the pleasure of trailing her hands across his chest, along his shoulders. His muscles tightened and flexed beneath her palms as if he barely held himself in check. And yet he did. He remained kneeling as she studied him.

"Does Greece's man of strength kneel to show that he is respectful of my power?" She raked her fingers through the coarse silk of his hair. "Is that how he intends to lay claim to that which belongs to me?"

His throat moved and his eyes shone. "Any wild thing—like myself—can be strong. I kneel because there is so much more to you than mere strength. And there is power to be gained by that."

She stood in front of him, her fingers still tangled in his hair, and their gazes held. All notion of performance was forgotten. The audience disappeared. The only thing that signified was Dom, on his knees in front of her, showing her that he believed she had depth and complexity, and that those parts of her should be celebrated.

"Then you renounce your claim on my possession?" she demanded. "There is aught else you want?"

"Let me bide awhile with you like this," he said, his voice gruff. "If I am what you desire, then use me as it pleases you."

Her breath came hard and fast as she warred with the desire to take and take—and give and give.

"I *will* use you," she answered. "And if you please me, I will grant you what it is you seek."

"And if I don't please you?" His words were a low rumble.

"Then I will set you to more labors until you *do*." She stroked her fingers across his mouth.

His tongue slipped from his lips and he licked her.

She gasped. At the sound, he surged to his feet and swept her up, into his arms. It was like being lifted aloft by a storm . . . the ground simply disappeared beneath her and she was dimly aware of being carried off the stage. In a distant corner of her mind, she registered the audience applauding, followed by Mr. Longbridge and Baron Hunsdon enunciating as they took their places for their performance.

Dom kept going, striding out of the ballroom and down the corridor. He went on, through the house, until he shouldered open a door, and then they were outside. Even then, he didn't stop, moving with deliberate purpose . . . into the Untamed Garden.

The foliage was dense around them as he stalked down the path. There was no illumination other than moonlight, and in its paleness the stone pavilion at the center of the garden took shape. A moment later, they were inside the structure.

He lowered her, and she slid down the long, solid shape of his body until she was on her feet, molded to him as her arms looped around his neck. She pressed against him as if she was the moonlight itself.

His eyes were dark fire as he stared down at her, and from deep within his chest as if from the very center of his being came the plea, *"Use me."*

Chapter 18

❧ ✳ ❧

*W*hatever the fuck was happening, Dom didn't want it to stop.

Her ripe body pressed to his, Willa looked at him, lust hot in her eyes.

The scene they'd acted onstage had been no performance. It was as if in her regal but revealing costume, she'd embodied the queen she truly was, a queen who was also sensitive and vulnerable, and he was all too eager to worship both parts of her.

He growled, "It's takin' all of my command over myself not to haul you up onto the railin', plunge my hands up your thin skirts, and stroke your sweet little cunt until you come again and again."

Never before had he spoken so crudely to her, but the words had been ripped from within. They'd been building inside of him, a volcano gone too long without erupting.

It was shadowed within the pavilion, lit only by the moon, but even in the semidarkness he saw the blush suffuse her face, and heard her sharp inhalation.

"All I've dreamt about," he rasped, "since I met you. Givin' you pleasure. Hearin' your sounds, and feelin' the tightenin' of your flesh around me as you came."

She swallowed audibly as his fingers skimmed over the bare flesh of her arms. "You claimed otherwise, but for all I know, ever since you started courting me, you've been amusing yourself with other lovers. Maybe you've been rogering half of London while I played the part of deserted bride."

His fists curled at his sides. "Why would I want to touch anyone who ain't you? How can I take my pleasure with someone else? Since the night we first met, I haven't fucked anyone. Only my hand."

It was a bare, raw admission, one that left him utterly defenseless.

A long moment followed, his heart thundering in his chest. Everything mattered now, every expression on her face and word from her lips weighted with significance. It had all been building up to this reckoning.

"Whatever you demand," he said, guttural, "I'll give it to you. Not to earn your forgiveness, but to give you back everything I stole from you that mornin'. You want me to go, I'll go. You want me to make you come, I'll do that. Everythin' you want is yours."

Her gaze was a hot and palpable thing moving over his face and body, and he swallowed a groan as it lingered on his groin. There was no denying that his cock was impossibly hard, his loincloth doing nothing to keep him from tenting the front of his tunic.

"Show me," she urged. "Prove to me that you've been true to me."

"Anythin'."

"If, in my absence, you've become such an expert in pleasuring yourself, I want to see your skill."

He gaped at her. Surely, she didn't mean . . .

"Do it," she insisted. "You wanted me to use you—here I am. Using you. Take your cock out and make yourself spill while I watch."

"Hell," he growled, so excited he nearly came then and there.

"*Now,*" she ordered him.

Hands shaking, he tugged down the loincloth beneath his tunic. His pulsating cock sprung out, so incredibly hard even his own fingers barely met as he circled it. He groaned at the feel of his hand on his aching flesh.

"Oh, my God," she whispered, her widening gaze fastened on the sight. "That's . . . that's . . . How do you . . . how can you . . . the *size* . . . ?"

"It's big, sweetheart," he admitted without pride because the proportions of his cock were a fact, "but never like this. Just with you."

Though her eyes were hazy with lust, she shook her head as if trying to collect herself. "Stroke it. Slowly."

"*Fuck, yes,*" he rumbled. Before he could do as she commanded, he licked his palm.

"God help me," she whimpered.

"God ain't helpin' either of us now." His attention never moving from her face, he wrapped his fist tightly around his cock and began to thrust into it. The fluid leaking from his slit coated his hand, and each stroke was delicious pain, shooting fire through him with the movements of his fist and instinctive shove of his hips as he watched her watch him.

Her eyes blazed with heat, her hands drifting up to cup her breasts, completely unaware of the movement. She had no choice but to find her own pleasure while seeing him chase his.

It was, by far, the most exposed thing he'd ever done. And he was so aroused that he had to clamp his teeth together to hold back his sounds of pleasure.

"Let me hear you," she whispered, as if knowing his battle.

"I'm very . . . loud."

"Even better."

He let himself go, groaning his ecstasy. The sound echoed within the pavilion, and likely tore through the garden so that it could probably be heard in the house, but he didn't give a fuck. The only thing that mattered was watching her lips part and her eyes turn even more glassy with desire as he let her know exactly what she did to him.

"Faster," she urged.

He needed no other command. Growling, he stroked his cock hard and swift, using exactly the kind of force he craved. This had always been a private thing, something he did to relieve the constant demands of his body. It wasn't *exactly* shameful, but he did it alone and treated it like a necessary task that was to be gotten through quickly so that he wasn't always plagued by desire.

Yet . . . to do this in front of Willa . . . to do this *for* Willa . . . because he wanted her . . . He ached for a fast release, relieving the near agony of this pleasure, and he also wanted to savor every moment, displaying himself for her, teasing out his ecstasy beneath her demanding gaze.

Her thighs shifted beneath her lightweight skirts, the rounded shapes rubbing against each other, chasing her own needs, and her hands massaged the small forms of her breasts. She was just as powerfully affected as he was, inflamed by the sight of him doing this wonderful, raw thing in front of her, at *her* command.

His climax gathered hotly at the base of his spine.

"Do it," she panted. "Bring yourself off while I watch."

Her demand was all it took. With a long, pained

growl, he came. His seed shot from his body in pulse after pulse. It had been a long time since he'd climaxed, and so his release was an eternity of pleasure that spattered upon the ground.

Finally, his body was wrung dry. His knees sagged and he had to grip the railing to keep himself upright in the aftermath. No matter how drained he was, though, more energy surged through him to have done this act in front of her, and to see the fierce hunger written sharply across her face and ablaze in her eyes.

"Your turn," he said as he tucked his depleted cock back into his loincloth.

More color stained her cheeks. "I can't do that in front of you."

"Oh, no, sweetheart." He gathered enough strength to stride to her, and wrap his hands around her hips. She trembled beneath his palms. "I ain't deservin' of that at all. But *you* deserve to come. Over and over until you can't take any more. And *I'm* going to make that happen. Tell me I can make that happen."

She drew in a jagged breath, and fear streaked through him that she might actually refuse.

Then, she said, "Kiss me first."

At once, he claimed her mouth with his in a long, ravenous kiss. Her lips opened to his immediately, her tongue stroking his with velvet licks that reached down all the way within him, making his sated cock twitch with the need for more.

He cupped her face, his thumb brushing against where her pulse throbbed in her throat. She leaned into him and gasped in his mouth as her fingers threaded into the hair at the base of his neck. A growl escaped him, pleasure coursing through his body.

Without breaking the kiss, he moved his hands to her waist and lifted her onto the stone railing. It was wide enough to support her, and brought her high enough so that their faces were level. They devoured each other as though it had been years and not a day since they last kissed.

"I have to touch you, lioness," he rumbled into her mouth. "Let me feel your sweet cunt on my fingers. May I?"

"*Yes*, Dom, yes," she gasped.

He gathered up her skirts, the silky fabric bunching on his bare forearms in prelude for the pleasure that was to come. Her full thighs were deliciously smooth beneath his palms and shaking as he stroked them. Higher he went, her breath coming faster and faster, until she cried out when his fingertips brushed the outer lips of her quim.

At once, he stilled, fearful that he'd accidentally hurt her or done something she didn't want.

"Don't stop," she urged breathlessly. "Jesus, Dom, if you don't touch me between my legs, I'm going to die."

"I won't let that happen, sweetheart," he vowed. His finger slipped between her lips. "*Fuck*, you're so wet."

She soaked him at once, glossing his skin with her arousal. He found the taut bud of her clitoris with his thumb and swallowed down her moan when he circled and stroked it. As he caressed it, he slowly, reverently began to ease one finger inside her. But she was tight, so gorgeously tight, and he had to sink into her by bare degrees.

"Dom," she moaned when at last he was fully within her.

"Want more?" To his own ears, his voice was a feral animal's.

"Everything."

God, how he adored her.

He slid a second finger into her, and she cried out, her head tipping back, when he found the spot inside of her that was swollen and demanding. Holding himself in check, he waited, giving her time to adjust to the feel of him. His fingers were thick—not as thick as his cock—and she was new to this.

Were he a better man, this thought would have made him stop. But they were at last giving in to their need for each other, and it would have taken a literal act of war to tear him away from her.

As he waited for her to grow accustomed to him, his thumb moved in circles over her clitoris, and she began to push her hips into him. She moved as though driven by instinct and need alone.

"That's it, lioness," he urged her as his fingers

stroked in and out of her. "Use me. Fuck my hand and get what you need."

Her fingers clutched at his shoulders as she did just that, rocking into him with her legs wide open, trusting him to hold her as she chased her desires.

That trust nearly brought tears to his eyes. He blinked them away—this moment was for her alone.

He drove into her and caressed her clitoris as she rode his fingers, her moans coming low and fast. Until she stiffened and cried out with her orgasm.

Nothing was more beautiful than Willa as she came. If he could pick only one sight to see for the rest of his days, it would be her, eyes closed, lips parted, as she abandoned herself to her pleasure.

"God above," she said when the tremors subsided. Her voice was thick, as if she was drunk.

"I ain't done with you," he said, gruff. "Not until you're hoarse from screamin' your pleasure."

His fingers still deep within her, he sank to his knees on the rough stone.

"Oh, lovely girl," he murmured as he beheld her flushed, glossy flesh. "So ripe. So ready."

"I used to think about this," she confessed. "About what it would be like to have you look at my . . . my . . ."

"Come now, lioness," he chided lowly. "No shyness from the woman who made me frig myself raw in front of her. Call this beautiful cunt by its name."

More color stained her face and she was practically panting. "My cunt."

He snarled as arousal clawed through him. He didn't think that, after spilling so much seed, he could be hard again so quickly.

"I tried to imagine it," she said breathlessly. "How you'd look at my cunt. If you'd like it . . . or if . . . you might not . . ."

"Oh, I like it," he insisted, his voice grating. "I *love* it. I thought about it, too. Would bring myself off every night, sometimes twice, just picturin' your lovely pussy. This pretty, unashamed part of you. Wet for me. Demandin' my fingers, my cock, my tongue."

She moaned as he punctuated his words with a thrust of his fingers. Her flesh tightened around him.

"That scene you liked in that filthy book," he growled. "Where the man eats the lady's cunt. That's what you want. That's what I can give you."

"God, yes," she gasped.

With his free hand grasping her hip so hard it would surely bruise, Dom bent down and licked her—one long, slow, thick glide of his tongue over her folds. She cried out, but instead of pushing him away, she gripped the back of his head and brought him even closer. Lightning coursed through him to be commanded by her, to serve her. And by God, would he serve her.

She was wet silk against him, spiced and earthy.

He swirled his tongue around the bud of her clitoris, then took it between his lips and sucked.

As she moaned, her fingers dug into his scalp, and the stinging reverberated all the way down to his cock. He continued to suck and tongue her, while he thrust in and out of her passage with his fingers, making certain to graze against that deep, swollen spot within.

Her ankles hooked behind his back, imprisoning him. As though he would want to be anywhere but here, scraping his knees raw while he devoured her cunt.

"Only dreams are this good," he growled against her flesh.

"No dream," she gasped. "All of this is real, and *I'm* real."

"Then I ain't wastin' this opportunity."

He lapped at her, sometimes using the flat of his tongue, sometimes teasing her with the tip. Her flavor filled him, and he happily drowned in her as he paid homage to her cunt. His hips couldn't stop from thrusting as he plunged his fingers into her, wanting so badly to be inside of her in every conceivable way.

Her thighs shook. He held tightly, keeping her secure, as she bowed back and cried out with the shaking strength of her orgasm. Still, he didn't stop, selfishly wanting to bestow as much ecstasy upon her as he could. He went on eating her, fucking her with his hand, until she came again, and then he made her come once more because he was a villain.

He would have gone on, greedy son of a bitch that he was, but she gently pushed him away.

"I can't . . . I can't take any more," she whimpered.

He stopped at once. After carefully sliding his fingers from her, he gave them a thorough lick, then kissed the tender flesh of her thighs. Slowly, reluctantly, he tugged down the fabric of her skirts. But he didn't want to rise, not yet, and laid his head on her knee.

She stroked his hair, smoothing the now damp strands, and it was so fucking *domestic* and *tender* that tears sprang to his eyes.

His own knees burned, and he was certain he'd lost several layers of skin to the stone floor. Hopefully, it would leave a scar, so he could remember this night for the rest of his cursed life.

It was an awkward, silent return trip to the house. They walked side by side, tension stretched between them. He longed to thread his fingers with hers, but she kept her arms crossed over her chest, as if protecting herself, and so he kept his hands hanging at his sides.

His ruddy ridiculous costume itched. As he'd suspected, his knees were torn and slightly bloody, but he didn't mind that.

He kept glancing over at her, searching her face for some sign of pleasure in what had just happened. Instead, her gaze was distracted, a tiny crease notched between her thick brows. His stomach tensed as if preparing for a blow—and yet none came. She remained quiet and far away, which was so unlike her his belly knotted even more.

The woman who had been both fiery and exposed was gone. Now he walked with a polite stranger and fuck if he didn't hate it more than anything.

By silent agreement, when they reentered the house, they avoided the main corridors and rooms where the other guests gathered. Laughter and music filled the hallways. Someone was playing the pianoforte, and though they played well, each note jarred along Dom's spine like metal bars being struck with a pewter cup by a prisoner demanding their release.

"Servants' stairs?" Dom asked Willa lowly as they hovered in the shadows outside the crowded parlor.

Expression tight, she nodded. Thank God he had studied the layout of the house already so he could easily guide them to the narrow stairwell without encountering anyone. He hadn't the stomach for anyone's sly looks or winks, and if anyone caught sight of his knees, they'd know precisely what Dom and Willa had been up to.

He didn't care if someone sniggered at the idea of him kneeling as he pleasured her. Hell, the idea was a delight. But it was *her* reputation that needed to be protected. She was still unmarried. Thanks to him.

They slipped up the cramped stairs, the wood protesting beneath his weight. Up and up they went, until they reached their floor, where they cautiously emerged into a main hallway. He peered out first to make certain everything was clear, and when there was no sign of another guest, he motioned for Willa to follow him out.

Then they were outside their respective doors. Despite the risk of being seen, they lingered in the corridor, their gazes holding, as if each of them wasn't quite certain how to part.

The devil knew *Dom* didn't. Words filled his mouth, so many words where he pled for her forgiveness again and again, where he vowed his eternal service to her, where he swore to give her anything and everything so long as he could be near her in any way.

You're my dream and my salvation and my torment. I want to claim you all for myself, and kill anyone who would touch you, but there's blood on my hands and shame in my heart, and my penance is living without you.

He said none of this. Instead, they continued to look at each other silently, until she straightened her shoulders and went into her room. The door closed behind her with a final click. She hadn't spoken a word to him since the pavilion.

Within his chest, his heart withered to a tiny husk, the kind of refuse you would kick away if you saw it in the street.

He went into his room, shut the door, and slowly stripped out of the foolish costume. Nude, he sat in front of the fire and watched the flames writhe, his soul thrashing in time with them.

Creaking came from the room beside him, her room. She was taking off her costume, getting ready for bed, and more flames shot through him at the mental picture of her stripping down to nothing.

Staying in this house with her was an impossibility. He wanted her too badly, burned too hot for her, and though they'd shared pleasure a mere quarter of an hour ago, the way she'd held herself apart from him afterward showed that nothing between them had been resolved. They were just as lost as they'd always been.

Yet he was trapped here. Trapped with his beastly desires and blood-soaked conscience and a woman who rightly despised him. Short of locking himself in his room, there was nowhere to go until one of the sodding boats came, and after the near-miss the other day, God only knew when that would be.

He sat up. There was *one* place he could go. Longbridge had pointed out on their trek around the island that there was a small cabin that was regularly maintained.

After dressing quickly, Dom left his room. Striding out of the house, night was all around him. The moon had set and there was nothing but shadow on every side.

A city bloke like him would be lost in this dark wilderness within a minute. There was a good chance he'd try scrambling up one of the hills and fall and break his neck, or else he'd wind up stranded at the bottom of a gorge.

Best to wait until morning, when he'd have a little light to guide him on his way.

He went back into his room and stood by the window, willing the sun to rise. As soon as the first gray streaks of dawn appeared on the eastern horizon, he'd exile himself.

Chapter 19

❧ ✳ ❧

$\mathcal{W}$illa stood with her hand pressed to the door of her room. It was morning, and she was supposed to go downstairs and join the other guests for breakfast. The guests who would include not only her brothers and their wives—who had engineered putting her onstage with Dom—but Dom himself.

She cursed and thumped her head against the wood.

Rash and reckless creature that she was, after last night's incendiary passion, she was terribly, terribly close to flinging herself at him and forgiving him his every trespass against her. Yet that would only leave her vulnerable to more hurt.

A shiver worked the length of her body as images from last night cascaded through her mind: Dom, his face flushed, his eyes glazed and mouth open as he stroked his cock beneath her excruciatingly aroused gaze. Dom, kissing her and thrusting his fingers into her. Dom, on his knees, looking at her quim with filthy reverence just before putting his mouth on her.

Her breath gusted against the wooden door as she fought a surge of desire. She hadn't been thinking clearly last night, nor had she tried to protect herself. She'd been too caught up in her need for him when she let him carry her off the stage. Afterward, tenderness had surrounded them. It was too easy to want more of this. To let herself be wrecked and ruined again—and now it would be completely leveling because they had grown even closer. He could hurt her badly, worse than before.

So, she'd retreated from him. It was either that, or else wrap her arms around him and refuse to let go.

The way he *touched* her. The way he *looked* at her. She never felt as beautiful, as important, as *necessary* as when Dom stared at her with his whole self in his eyes.

She shook her head. No. *No.* She wouldn't give in. She would stand firm and protect herself.

There was a sound next door, coming from Dom's room. He could be coming for her, when she wasn't ready to face him.

Moving without thought, she wrenched open her door and rushed out into the hallway. She passed servants going about their duties, and even Lakshmi, but she didn't slow when the young woman greeted her. Instead, Willa hurried down the stairs and dashed from the house.

She wasn't certain where she was going, only that her body had to be in motion. *Away* from Dom. When she hadn't been able to fight her battles, she'd run away, and today, she gave in to that old impulse.

Willa hadn't planned on going outside, so she had no shawl to protect her as blustery winds buffeted her as she headed into the craggy hills. Thick, iron-gray clouds hung low and ominous overhead. She also paid little heed to the shouts coming behind her, shouts that sounded suspiciously like Finn and Kieran.

Facing them right now was impossible. She could only keep going. Maybe somewhere on this island, she could stop and allow herself space and time to think, and to figure out what came next with her and Dom. God knew that at this moment, she was completely adrift.

She pushed herself hard, charging up one rugged mountain and down another, striding swiftly through the low stands of rowan trees, always moving forward, even as the wind began to blow fiercely, nearly shoving her to the ground with its force.

Something flashed overhead, and she started as it was followed by a deafening boom of thunder. And then . . . the heavens ripped apart.

Rain pounded down on her in heavy curtains that nearly made it impossible to breathe. Within seconds, she was drenched, her pink gown plastered to her and offering not a whit of protection or warmth.

"Fuck, fuck, fuck," she muttered.

What was she supposed to do? Already, she shivered with cold, her teeth knocking together. The rowan trees were far too small to take shelter beneath, but if she tried to make it back to the house, she'd surely perish of cold.

Looking around, she saw a familiar arrangement of rocks, and recognized the gorge in which she stood as the very same one near Mr. Longbridge's cabin. She remembered his instructions to reach the small house—it wasn't too far away—and she could take shelter until the storm abated.

As she followed Mr. Longbridge's directions, a loud roaring sounded ahead. She drew up short as what was promised to be a small creek had now swollen to a raging river. Thankfully, on the other side of the river stood the cabin, a cozy-looking structure with timbered walls and roof that appeared blessedly dry.

To reach the cabin, she'd have to cross the footbridge that spanned the river. It wasn't very sturdy-looking, though, and it appeared even more fragile as the water beneath it churned and foamed furiously, straining the wooden structure's integrity.

It groaned ominously beneath her weight when she stepped onto it. As she crossed the bridge, she glanced down to see the creek-turned-surging-river rising even higher so that it washed over the planks and soaked her boots. There was a terrible fracturing sound under her, and she flung herself toward the shore just as the little footbridge was washed away, its wooden boards immediately taken by the heaving water.

She scrabbled for a hold on the slippery bank as the rushing river pulled at her legs. Panic seized her and she screamed. She wasn't strong enough to fight the current.

A strong grip surrounded her, pulling her up to safety. She was lifted out of the water and hauled high—into Dom's arms.

She clung to him, tucking her head into the crook of his bare neck. He strode toward the cabin, carrying her up the steps, and through the open door.

Dripping, freezing, she shuddered as he kicked the door shut behind them. She pulled back and only then did she realize that not only had Dom rescued her from drowning, he was also completely nude.

DOM STRUGGLED TO hold on to a soaked Willa. "Stop squirming."

"P-put me d-down."

His heart still thundered from almost losing her to the river. "Not a chance."

"*Down,*" she insisted, kicking her legs. When he reluctantly let her go, she gaped at him. "Wh-why are y-you n-naked?"

"Had to take off my wet clothes. I was just starting to light a fire when I heard you scream."

Even though she shook with cold, her gaze shot to his groin.

It didn't matter that she'd seen his cock last night—this was broad daylight, in the middle of a squall, and, well, it was cold out, which didn't do a man's paraphernalia any favors.

He grabbed the closest thing at hand, which happened to be a stuffed owl mounted on a wooden base, and held it in front of his crotch.

"B-bit late for th-that," Willa remarked through chattering teeth.

His questions about what she was doing *here*, as a storm raged all around them, were forgotten as he saw the blue tinge of her lips, and the uncontrollable shivers that wracked her body.

Still covering his cock with the taxidermy, he strode to her and began pulling at the fastenings of her completely soaked dress. It had plastered to her body, but right now, he wasn't interested in seeing how it revealed her curves. The task of stripping her was made more difficult by the fact that he was doing it one-handed. Meanwhile, she tried to slap his hand away.

"What the h-hell are you d-doing?" She batted at him.

"Getting you out of these wet clothes before you die from cold," he said tightly. He wasn't making much progress.

Hell, there was no help for it. He put the bird on the floor and set to work undoing the buttons that ran down the side of her dress. *If* she would let him. She kept dancing aside and swatting him whenever he reached for her.

"Stand still, goddamn it," he growled.

"I'm n-not taking off my *cl-clothes* in front of y-you," she snapped.

"If you want to freeze to death, fine."

She looked torn, but a powerful shiver made her entire body shake. It must have convinced her, because she started unfastening her gown. Then she stopped.

"T-turn around," she commanded.

He rolled his eyes, but did as she directed, turning his back to her.

"Take everything off," he insisted. "Even your shift."

She hesitated for a moment, and then pulled at her clothing. As she stripped, he strode back to the fireplace and crouched in front of it. Thank God Longbridge's servants kept the little house respectably stocked with everything needed to start a fire. In short order, Dom had a decent blaze going, its flames small but getting larger.

While the fire grew in strength, he went to the cabin's sole bed and pulled the blanket off. Some bit of gentlemanly behavior won out because he turned away from her. As he waited for Willa to finish disrobing, he couldn't quite resist catching brief glimpses of bare flesh and silken limbs.

"Th-there," she said, followed by the sound of

her feet padding across the bare floorboards toward the fire. Wet fabric hit the floor. "I've l-laid out m-my clothes to dry."

"Everything?"

"Everything, C-commander."

He held out the blanket. "Put this on and get in front of the fire."

She did as he directed, taking the quilt from him and standing before the fireplace. He positioned himself beside her, trying not to think about the fact that she was naked beneath the blanket. Or that he, too, was completely nude.

She looked at his chest, and then quickly turned back to the fire. He resisted the impulse to scratch at the black hair that curled between his pectorals and ran in a line down his abdomen, leading right to the nest above his cock.

Her attention wandered lower, skimming down to his thickening flesh, and then quickly dancing back up to the breadth of his shoulders.

"Wh-what are y-you doing here?" she asked whilst studiously looking away.

"Trying to be alone." *Trying not to haul you into my bed and keep you there forever.*

She lifted her chin. "It wasn't m-my intention to d-disrupt your s-solitude. I w-went for a w-walk, and then Z-zeus decided to sh-show off with a s-storm that w-would drown D-deucalion. By th-the time the rain started, it was t-too late to go back to the h-house."

"You aren't getting any warmer." He clenched his jaw. There was no help for it.

When he faced her, Willa's eyes widened. And when he started to pull at her quilt, she demanded, "Wh-what are you d-doing?"

"We have to get you warm," he said through clenched teeth. "Best way to do that is if we huddle close—skin to skin. Don't argue, Willa," he added when it appeared that she intended to do just that. "I've seen men die within minutes when they fell into the Thames at winter and we hauled them onto the dock. I'm not letting that happen to you."

She pressed her blue lips together. For a moment, he feared he'd actually have to force her to drop the blanket and hold her struggling body against his.

Finally, she held the blanket open, and he went to her at once, pulling her tight to him. Her arms went around his shoulders, enclosing them both in the coverlet.

"Jesus, lioness, you're like ice."

"W-wasn't dressed for a d-deluge."

They were quiet together as he held her close, willing her shivering to subside. Fortunately, he always ran hot, and he hoped the heat of his body would quickly chase the terrifying chill from her. It was strictly for healing purposes that he cradled her to him, pressing his steaming flesh to her glacial body.

Gradually, her shuddering started to lessen. Color returned to her cheeks and lips. Her skin warmed. As his fear retreated, he became aware of the truth of the situation: they were both naked, and he could feel every inch of her lush form. Her pert little breasts, the nipples tight buds scraping against his chest, the roundness of her belly, her wide hips and thighs. And, Christ absolve him, the soft curls of hair on her mound.

"Are you . . . getting *aroused*?" she asked, looking up at him with wide, black eyes, before glancing down to where his cock was hardening. Under her gaze, it firmed even more.

"Can't help it," he growled. "Bodies do things, even without our express consent."

"You're not attracted to me?"

He stared at her. "Lioness, I want only you. Last night proved it. But I don't know if you want *me*."

"Don't want you?" She looked at him disbelievingly. "Despite my rational mind telling me I shouldn't, it's taking all of my willpower not to throw you to the ground and ride you like I'm breaking a stallion."

His heart pounded, and his cock went hard as steel.

"The way you retreated from me after the pavilion," he rasped. "I didn't know."

"And I don't know how to fight *this* any longer."

Dropping the blanket, she gripped his head with both her hands and brought his mouth down to hers. And then Dom ceased to think at all.

Chapter 20

❧ ✳ ❦

Dom growled into Willa's mouth, the thrillingly primal sound resonating deep in her body, as one of his hands curved around the back of her head and the other splayed across her lower back. Holding her tightly to him so that his hard, hot cock pressed into her belly and made her restless and achy with the need for more.

She couldn't remember a time when she *didn't* want Dom, and now that they were here in this moment, she would finally have what she desired.

"Delicious." His hand went lower, cupping her arse, and he rumbled, "All of you."

His old, rough accent was back, proof how lost he was to this moment.

"I love it when you touch me," she confessed.

"Only thing I've ever wanted is to touch you like this."

He made good on this, too, his hands now roaming

over her body, caressing her everywhere, from her throat to her breasts to her belly.

"Fuck," he muttered when his fingers brushed the damp hair curling on her mound. "You're already so wet."

She moaned when he slipped one thick, callused finger between her folds to circle her clitoris and entrance.

As he stroked her, his hips moved, surging against her, drawing streaks of moisture along her stomach that slicked from the head of his cock. She reached between them and wrapped her fingers around his length—forcing a long stream of praising curses from him. A deep, primal thrill shot through her at the feel of Dom in her hand—though there was a filament of astonishment at the sheer size of him.

The kiss went even deeper, becoming hungrier and more demanding. He caressed her, and while she panted and moaned, he slid one and then two fingers into her passage and worked them in and out, in time with thrusts of his tongue between her lips. Pleasure was a fiery net that engulfed her.

Her grip on his cock tightened, pumping him faster, and he made a desperate, animal sound of ecstasy. She loved that she could make him this wild, that *he* could make *her* so wild. The storm raged outside and within, and everything was unleashed. Her climax built with unseemly speed but she didn't care if she had become the veriest wanton.

She cried out into his mouth and he held her securely as she shook from the force of her release. He held her as if he'd never let her go.

Suddenly, she was in his arms, and he was carrying her to the bed. His lips never left hers as he laid her down, his hands all over her body. Huge and powerful, he leaned over her to gather up her breasts. He stopped kissing her long enough to lick and suck and pinch her nipples. She thrashed beneath him, clawing at the width of his shoulders and back as her arousal soared—as though he hadn't given her a shattering climax moments before.

"How do you do this to me?" she gasped.

"'Cos I'm made for you." His mouth trailed scorching kisses across her chest and belly. "And you're made for me."

"Dom." Her words were choked as her body ached with needs still unfulfilled. She couldn't have what her heart demanded, but there was one thing she *could* have. "Dom—please. I want more. I want everything."

He paused, lifting his head to stare into her eyes. Desire burned there, and emotions she didn't want to name. His voice was raw and rasping when he asked, "You sure?"

She kept her gaze even with his. "I want this. This choice is mine, and I'm making it. Only—we must be careful. I can't get with child."

"I'll make sure you're safe," he vowed. He kissed her, not hotly but tenderly, as if to seal his promise.

Then he stretched out above her, his body so much larger than hers, but he was careful to keep his weight from crushing her as he braced himself on his forearms.

She looked up at him, hardly able to believe that this was truly happening—the thing she'd wanted and dreamt of and pleasured herself to was finally going to come true. His own expression was just as dazed and reverential.

"Widen your legs for me, lioness," he instructed huskily. "Invite me home."

At once, she did what he asked, and he settled between her thighs. They both seemed to hold their breath as the crown of his cock teased her entrance. He moved his hips so that his shaft glossed between her folds, coating himself in her wetness. The sensation was so exquisite she could scarcely keep her eyes open. Yet she refused to close them, willing herself to witness every moment.

Slowly, he began to ease his cock into her. It was pleasant at first, but as the sheer magnitude of him entered her inch by inch, she couldn't stop her sharp inhale of discomfort.

"Don't stop," she urged when he went still.

"Hurtin' you," he gritted.

She couldn't deny that, yet, "I don't care. I want you all the way inside me, I want you to fill me up."

"Not if it means causin' you pain."

"Dom, *please*." She didn't care if she begged. "I'm desperate for you."

She made a noise of dismay when he pulled out. But then they were turning so that he was on his back, and she straddled him. His hands held tight to her waist as he stared up at her.

"Allow your body to tell you what it needs and when," he growled.

She spread her hands on his vast chest, digging her fingers into the dark hair that curled there, and gazed into his eyes as she adjusted her hips.

The head of his cock notched at her entrance, and she held her breath as she began to lower herself down onto him. Slowly, slowly, allowing her body to grow used to his proportions and being so utterly, completely filled. It was frightening—and wonderful.

"Breathe, love," he said, his own words gasping. His mouth was open, his eyes heavy-lidded. He looked like a man barely in control of himself, almost abandoned to pleasure if not for a thin veil of discipline holding him back. "Let yourself take all of me."

She did, exhaling long as she pushed her hips down even more. Until he was completely within her. A moan escaped him. Her eyelashes fluttered while she acclimated herself to having Dom's cock inside her. There was some pain, but mostly pleasure, pleasure that grew by increments until her entire being was permeated with it.

"Good?" he grunted.

"Impaled," she answered, breathless. "In the best possible way."

He gave a huff of low laughter that turned into a groan. "You feel so fuckin' good."

"Likewise. Only . . . I can't move."

"Kiss me."

They hungrily devoured each other, tongues swirling. As they kissed, one of his hands slid up to toy with her breasts, plucking at her nipples. More arousal flooded her, loosening her whole body with desire. Gradually, the pain receded and all she felt was rapture.

She *had* to move her hips, and she moaned at the sensation of him within her. Yet he held himself nearly motionless, letting her find the rhythm and speed that she liked best.

Tears gathered, and she blinked them back, yet how could she not be touched by his consideration and care for her? It frightened her, the way he could reach her needy, bruised heart in a way no one else could.

She thrust down harder so pleasure could banish her fear. And it did, until she lost control of herself and moved atop him with greater and greater speed.

"That's it, lioness," he rumbled. "Sit up. Ride me good and hard."

"Fuck me back, Dom," she panted as she sat upright. "Good and hard."

"Ah, Jesus." Cords stood out in his neck and

sweat slicked his skin as he held her hips and drove up with a force so strong, her whole body shuddered and trembled with gorgeous sensation.

The noises he made were delicious—lusty and base and completely abandoned to this primal act. He *was* loud, and she loved that he couldn't hold himself back. A steady stream of curses poured from his lips in his East London accent.

"Fuck, yes," he snarled. "Hell—that's—*fuck*."

She angled herself in exactly the right way so that her clitoris ground against him with each thrust. He kept one hand on her breast, taking her nipple between his fingers and gently squeezing. Bright strands of fire coursed through her, and then there was no stopping her.

"Dom, I—"

She came with a scream. There was no one around to make her strive for quiet, and even if there *was* someone nearby, she wouldn't have been able to stop herself from giving full throat to this engulfing pleasure that began with his cock deep inside her and had no end, expanding out to overwhelm everything.

Wrung out, she collapsed atop him. Yet he didn't relent, continuing to thrust up into her, pushing his hips into hers, until another orgasm harrowed her.

The world spun, and then she was on her back with Dom above her.

"Hook your ankles around my waist," he commanded, and when she did, he sank into her all the way to the hilt. "Good girl."

Why did that only sound right coming from him? "Or a very *bad* girl." She angled her hips up to push him deeper within her.

"Christ," he growled. Something flashed in his eyes, something far more profound than lust.

She didn't—couldn't—let herself see that emotion in his gaze, so she dug her fingers into the taut muscles of his arse, urging him on.

He was beautiful above her, glossed with sweat and dedicated to their pleasure. He reached down and caressed her clitoris with his thumb, summoning another climax from her.

A few more forceful thrusts, and then, with a groan that sounded like part torment, part ecstasy, he pulled from her. His release shot from him in a scalding arc, spattering across her belly and chest. He gave a long, loud moan as he came.

Moments later, he took a corner of the bedsheets and cleaned his seed from her skin, before rolling to his side, the bed groaning under his mass.

They panted together as the storm continued to slam against the cabin. But nothing matched the tempest within her, the clash of tenderness and desire and fear. And even anger.

"Damn it, Dom." Despite the fact that her entire being was wrung out from the number of orgasms she'd just had, she sat up and swung her legs around so that her feet touched the ground. Her fists clenched at her sides.

"Did I hurt you?" He was beside her, a look of abject worry on his face. "Did I do somethin' you didn't want? God, I'll fuckin' destroy myself if I did. I wanted to make it good for you."

She dashed her hand across her eyes, streaking tears across her cheeks. "It *was* good. It was *incredible*."

"But you're cryin'," he pled.

"We could have had this all along," she choked. "This could have been ours for the rest of our lives, but you . . . you *ran*. You didn't want me."

"Never believe that." His hand cupped her jaw, turning her so that their gazes met. "I've always wanted you, and I'll want you until I'm nothing but dust in a potter's field."

"I . . ." She struggled to speak, when part of her wanted to hoard the words and keep herself safe. But she didn't have to hold on to her strength forever. She could let herself take a risk, and be open. "I was in so much pain when you jilted me. And all I could think was that it was me, that I'd done something, or that I wasn't . . ."

She let the tears fall. "That I wasn't the kind of person anyone would want."

"Oh, lioness." He swallowed hard, and his own eyes shone with moisture. "You *were*. You *are*. But it's *me*. I ain't no good for you, Willa. Never have

been, and it was hubris to believe otherwise. If you
knew . . . you'd hate me."

"Knew *what*? Please, Dom." She seized his hand.
"Tell me."

She shivered. Dom rose from the bed, utterly
nude, and retrieved the blanket from the floor. He
wrapped it tenderly around her shoulders.

Then he sat beside her, bracing his thick forearms on his even thicker thighs. A long moment
passed, and when he spoke, his words were flat.

"I'm a murderer."

Chapter 21

❖ ✳ ❖

Dom's stomach knotted, and the sweat from their lovemaking that covered his body turned cold and clammy. He waited to see revulsion or shock in Willa's face. Surely any moment now, she would demand that he go, and never touch her again.

Instead, confusion clouded her dark eyes, but she was motionless and eerily calm.

Minutes before, they'd shared what was the most incredible sex of his life. Hell, it was the most incredible thing that had ever happened to him. The pleasure they'd created had both sent him into the ether, and also been powerfully carnal in a way that proved that there truly was no other woman for him—there was only Willa, now and always.

"Tell me what you mean," she said, remarkably collected.

His chest tightened. He stood and strode to a window, where rain lashed the glass like whips made of water. It was impossible to see more than a few feet, and at this rate, they'd be lucky if the nearby swollen creek didn't completely flood its banks and engulf the cabin.

"It was my seventeenth birthday." The words came out of him, cold and toneless, because he'd lived in this part of his past for so long, and sometimes he could convince himself that he'd been able to make peace with it. Even if he wasn't reconciled to what had happened, he had been able to fool himself that he could tuck it away, like a piece of meat rotting beneath the floorboards.

"Almost thirteen years ago," Willa noted, her voice coming from close behind him. He hadn't heard her approach.

"I'd been a man for a while," he said without looking at her. "Working at the docks since I was ten, and what coin I'd earned there went straight to paying rent and buying food for my family. Even so, turning seventeen seemed big. Like I'd truly crossed into adulthood, especially when I'd seen so many of my mates on the block not survive long enough to grow a beard."

He braced his forearm on the window and the icy glass chilled him even more than he already was. Willa had moved to stand beside him, yet he continued to stare out into the storm.

"I went out to celebrate with a few blokes," he continued, dreading what was coming next, but there was no avoiding it now. "The night was a blur of taprooms and gin houses. We got into more than a few brawls. Used to be one of my favorite sports, brawling. Never felt quite so alive as when you're dodging punches and landing your own, your fist connecting with a face or body. I go to a pugilism academy now, but it's not the same."

He was stalling now, and cursed himself for prolonging the inescapable.

"It was at the Blind Dog that it happened," he went on. "There was a bloke I knew, Tommy Frears. He wasn't my friend and he wasn't my enemy. Just somebody on the docks. Somehow, I got into a scrap with him and Tommy pulled a blade. We scuffled. I tried to dodge the chiff, but the next thing I knew"—he swallowed the bile that rose in his throat—"Tommy's knife was sticking out of his throat. There was blood everywhere, on Tommy, on the floor. On me."

"Self-defense," Willa said, breaking into his grisly memories.

He shook his head. "Some at the Blind Dog said so, but there was no way to know for certain. Could've been that I stuck the knife in, or maybe he fell on it. I wish to God I could remember, but the whole night's a drunken blur."

"Was the constable summoned?" she asked quietly.

A rueful laugh escaped him. "No one cares about anyone dying in Ratcliff. Tommy's people bore the body away, the tapster wiped the blood from the floorboards, and that was the end of it. Except," he added grimly, "it wasn't. Tommy was like me, he worked to support his family, and with him gone, I saw how they struggled to pay for food and cover their rent.

"I tried to give them money," he said, voice rusty like an old ax. "All of my wages, and my da had just started to turn a profit on leasing warehouses. Yet the Frears folk wouldn't take a ha'penny from me. There was no official inquiry, no trial, but they blamed me for Tommy's death, and they were right."

"Even though you don't know what truly happened," she murmured.

"There had to have been some way to keep Tommy from winding up dead," he growled, his jaw tightening. "I could've walked away instead of fighting with him."

"And risk his knife sticking out of *your* back." She rested her palm between his shoulder blades, but her touch was too comforting, and he shook it off.

"I tried to get on with my life as best I could," he went on. "Made sure Celeste never knew—she still doesn't." He'd had to cajole and threaten people in their neighborhood to keep silent, and that, too, had added to his guilt. Yet he couldn't let Celeste learn the truth about the brother she clearly—unreasonably—adored.

"And my brothers?" Willa asked.

He shook his head. "They were the only ones of the ton who would talk to me. I didn't want to risk pushing them away if they knew I was a killer."

"That must've been a terrible secret to keep."

"No more terrible than thinking myself a murderer." His jaw went taut. "Still, when Da made his fortune and we left Ratcliff for Hans Town, I didn't have the daily reminder that I'd killed someone on the floor of a filthy taproom. Got a huge new house that could sleep over a dozen families. Dressed up in togs that cost enough to feed us for a month. Went to university. Learned to speak proper and dance so I could become a gentleman like one of them nobs we used to mock," he said with deliberate use of his old accent. Then, his tone softening, he added, "I met you."

She made a soft noise, part chuckle, part sigh. "And we became engaged. But, Dom, when we pledged to marry each other, you hadn't forgotten what had happened in your past."

"I'd convinced myself that it was too far behind me to cause anyone any grief—especially not you. I thought, like a dolt, that I could be happy, that maybe I deserved to wed a princess like you."

"Something happened to change that."

His hand knotted into a fist. "Six weeks before the wedding, I was on the Strand, buying you a present, and I saw her. Tommy's mother. She was selling posies."

"Did she recognize you? You must've been greatly altered from the lad she knew."

"Oh, she knew me." His mouth twisted. "Savile Row clothes and boots by Hoby couldn't hide that I was still the same hulking brute who'd murdered her boy. She didn't say anything, but she looked into my eyes, and hate continued to burn there. I tried to give her all the blunt I had on me, but she walked away and the pound notes fell to the pavement. A crossing sweep grabbed them."

"Ah, no," Willa said on a long, mournful exhale.

"I thought about going to the law, confessing what I'd done," he said, stony. "But I worried what would happen to Celeste, to my da—especially to *you*—when the scandal broke. Magnate Ned Kilburn's son, a foul murderer. It would destroy everyone's lives, not just my own.

"That's when I knew," he persisted. "Marrying you was impossible. It wasn't only Tommy's killing on my conscience. I've done other things, bad things. I've thieved and cheated and lied, and I'm not worthy of happiness with you. And *you* didn't deserve to be shackled to such a vicious beast for the rest of your life."

There was another stretched-out silence that was like being drawn and quartered. Any minute now, she'd shout or weep or throw him out into the storm. But there was only sadness in her eyes, as if she bore the hurt that he'd carried for years.

He stared at her for a long time. "Ain't you disgusted by me? Horrified by what I've done?"

"I'm sorry that you went through that," she said

at last. "I'm sorry you've borne so much pain. But you don't disgust me, Dom. You don't horrify me."

"I'm a *murderer*," he insisted. "The foulest creature known to man."

"Perhaps you did have a hand in his death, or perhaps you didn't. It's impossible to find blame—and I think you've endured your share of suffering as a result."

He dragged his hand across his eyes as if he could wipe away the mix of compassion and distress he saw in her face. "I thought you would be revolted by what I've done. I kept it from you—didn't want to see you look at me with loathing."

"Dom." Her voice was a breath. "You truly thought that an accident from your youth would make me hate you? And that's why you pulled away before the wedding?"

At his jerky nod, her throat worked, and her eyes suddenly gleamed with moisture. The sight cut him as though he'd swallowed glass.

"When you left me like that," she finally said, her voice ragged, "I think there was a part of me that was expecting it."

"Hell, Willa," he rasped, hating the hurt she'd had to endure.

"I'd treated you like a wolf on a leash, and you treated me like a princess, and so we weren't being genuine with each other. Even so . . ." She moved to sit on the settee, and her gaze was distant. "I wondered if I was the kind of person anyone could love."

A strangled noise escaped him. His mind had long been filled with tormenting thoughts of what it must have been like for Willa, to have him jilt her, but he'd always believed that that pain was better than what she would have suffered in becoming his wife.

What she described, though, was far worse.

She turned her damp but angry black eyes to him. "I felt *broken*."

At once, he was on his knees before her.

"I'm sorry," he choked. "So incredibly, deeply sorry. I hurt you, betrayed your trust, and will spend the rest of my cursed life regretting what I did. It was never you," he continued urgently, his hands bracketing her. "I should've told you. I should've trusted you."

She pressed her hand to her chest, and there was regret in her eyes. "We didn't trust each other."

"The lioness figurine," he said lowly, "the one I carved for you. Did you keep it, or throw it into the fire?"

She looked faintly puzzled at this abrupt change of topic, but answered, "I kept it."

"You'd every reason to destroy it."

"You used to buy me so many expensive presents," she said after a minute. "They were beautiful and costly, and they all felt as though they were from someone else, *for* someone else."

He recalled a few of those gifts. Pearl earrings from Asia. Enameled boxes directly from Limoges.

Jeweled pins of Baltic amber and finely woven Indian shawls. Offerings to a goddess, not a woman. Not *her*.

"Should have given you sharp knives for throwing," he realized, "and humble pebbles from the paths we'd walked together and books about lady pirates sailing the globe."

"I don't know if, back then, I would've appreciated those things," she murmured, soft and sad. "I don't know if I was ready to receive presents from the *real* Dom to the *real* Willa. But now . . . the driftwood lioness . . . it was a gift of *your* heart to *my* heart. That gave it a value beyond measure. I couldn't throw it in the fire, any more than I could throw my heart into the flames."

His chest swelled. "Willa—"

She stroked her fingers along his jaw, and her eyes were as deep and profound as the vastness of the night sky. "We've spoken all there is to say, Dom. Take me to bed. There's been enough pain. All I want right now is pleasure."

Chapter 22

❧ ✳ ❧

*A*fter a moment, a slow, wicked smile spread across Dom's face. "Going to suggest something . . . with your permission."

Willa warmed from his willingness to cede control to her. But that warmth grew far hotter at the carnal promise in his eyes.

"Very well," she said as imperiously as she could manage, given the fact that Dom was quite, quite splendidly naked. His body truly was a marvel, so powerfully made, generously muscled as if he existed in the realm of myth. He'd made a perfect Hercules.

And just like the fabled strongman, there was tragedy in Dom's past. She'd understood, logically, that his life had been far different from her own, but she'd never suspected that violent death had scarred him. Whether or not he was responsible, no one would ever know definitively. But it had left a mark on him, one that blazed on his soul and made him believe that he was fundamentally unworthy of anything good.

It was a hard thing to hear, that he thought she'd reject him because of his crime. That he could think she wouldn't understand or accept him. God . . . she'd been so intent on protecting herself, the barriers she'd erected had shut everyone out. Especially him.

They knew each other now—not as the illusions they had each imagined and created, but as flawed and beautiful beings.

"I'll make everything ready for you, lioness." He rose to standing, putting her face level with his groin—and impressively scaled penis, astonishing even when it wasn't primed and ready.

She could hardly believe he'd fit inside of her, but then, sometimes impossible things became possible.

Dom moved around the cabin. From a small kitchen area, he grabbed a clay bowl, and then went outside to stick his arm out from beneath the shelter of the porch. She'd no idea what he was doing, until he returned with the bowl full of rainwater. He took the water and poured it into an iron pot, which he set up over the fire.

He had a surprisingly fluid grace, and she appreciated how competent he was in handling these small tasks. It showed that he was a man used to doing for himself, and was equally capable of taking care of her.

She valued her independence, yet there was something very primally satisfying in having someone attend to you.

"Are you making soup?" she asked. "Tell me what you're doing."

"Patience, lioness," he said, smiling over his shoulder.

Her heart seized at that brief but almost happy grin from him. It was a rare event to make Dominic Kilburn smile, and when he did, it was as though a gleam of light appeared in the middle of a shadowy thicket, guiding the way.

A few minutes passed, and then he removed the now gently steaming iron pot from the fire, setting it down on the flagstones on the hearth. He located some towels in a cupboard, and arranged them beside the warm water.

He strode to her in all his glorious nudity. Before she knew what was happening, he'd gathered her up in his arms and carried her to the fireplace.

"Is this when you burn the witch?" she asked, glancing toward the flames.

"It's when the witch burns *me*." His eyes shined as he laid her down, lying atop the blanket, which he carefully spread out onto the floor. He took the mound of pillows from the bed and tucked them beneath her head and around her.

"It's almost as if you've done this before," she said breathlessly.

He made no answer as he reached for one of the towels.

"Is this one of the steps in how you seduce someone?" She watched the firelight shine on his muscles and turn the hair curling on his body into tiny glints of gold. "Perhaps rogues have rules for seduction. Rule number one, always distract your lover with your impressive equipment before coercing them into doing something entirely wicked."

"You don't need coercing to be wicked." He dipped a corner of the towel into the pot full of warmed rainwater. "And all rules go on the rubbish heap when it comes to you."

"I'm learning that." Her breath caught as, kneeling beside her, he stroked the warm, damp towel over her body in long and languid caresses. She moaned as he slipped the towel between her thighs, cleaning her with soft but purposeful glides.

"Like that?" Despite his question, he smirked, already knowing the answer.

"This . . . is nice . . ." she murmured as he ran the towel over her breasts. "*You're* nice."

He snorted.

"Not the right word," she said with a low chuckle, which was a feat, considering how each of his caresses fueled her desire to rise higher and higher. "You're different. From anyone I've ever known."

"And you," he growled, following one swipe of the towel across her breast with a hot, trailing kiss, "are unlike anyone else in the whole world."

He sucked her nipple into his mouth, and she arched up as if she was a bowstring being drawn before being loosed. She gripped his head as he continued to lick her breasts, all the while he stroked the towel over her fevered body.

"Wait," she panted.

He stopped immediately.

"I want to do the same for you," she said, sitting up and reaching for one of the towels.

His jaw tightened and arousal flashed in his eyes. "Whatever the lioness desires, she gets."

She dipped her towel into the water. Cross-legged, they faced each other, and he held himself still as she softly rubbed the damp fabric across his shoulders, down his arms, along the broad planes of his pectorals, and then lower, over the corrugations of his taut abdomen. By the time she reached his cock, it was upright and thick.

He hissed, his eyes closing and his head tipping back, when she rewet the towel and wrapped it around his length before pumping him.

"Fuckin' hell," he growled. "Christ above."

"Always such profane language from you whenever your cock gets involved," she tutted, though she smiled at the fact that she could make him feel such pleasure.

"I ain't no saint when it comes to havin' you

touch my cock," he said, guttural. "I'll fuckin' level a city to feel you around me."

Heat spread through her at his words, her quim growing slick to hear how much he desired her, how much she affected him. It was a wonderful, beautiful power, to hold *this* man in her thrall, and it surged along her body with far more potency than the storm rampaging outside.

An urge seized her, so outrageous, so deliciously wicked, she lost her breath. And she knew with absolute certainty that Dom wouldn't deny her. Hell—he'd *encourage* her.

"If a mere towel on your cock can make you so blasphemous," she said, attempting to sound breezy and sophisticated but instead almost gasping with eagerness, "what would you say to my mouth?"

The curses he'd uttered before were as mild as a nursery ballad compared to the string of pure profanity that streamed from his lips.

"I take it that's a *yes*," she said wryly.

He stretched out his legs and widened them, giving her unfettered access to his now rampant erection. "That's a *yes*."

"I've . . ." She cleared her throat as she eyed his cock. "Never done anything like this before. I may be terrible at it."

"If it's *your* mouth on my cock," he growled, "it's going to be perfect."

She set aside the towel, and, after taking a

breath, bent down so that her lips hovered above the head of his cock. Even the feel of her exhalation on him made his shaft twitch, and that sense of power surged again. She could command him to do anything for her, *to* her, and he'd obey. Yet she wouldn't betray his trust.

Tentatively, she licked the smooth crown.

"Ah, fuck me," he snarled.

"Not yet." She gave him another lick, swirling around the head, tasting a hint of salt on her tongue that came from the bead of moisture seeping from the slit. "Let me enjoy this first."

More swearing poured from him as she grew bolder, taking the whole crown into her mouth. It was nearly as large as a plum, and she sucked on him eagerly. Yet when she tried to take him deeper, he was so vastly proportioned, she could only manage a few inches.

She made a noise of frustration, wanting to completely swallow him.

"Use your hand for the rest," he rasped. When she did, wrapping her fingers around his substantial girth, he grunted. "Good girl."

Any teasing she might have done about him calling her *good girl* again when she was clearly *not* being good was lost as she devoted herself to this crude and beautiful act. And the truth of it was, *she* was the one in control. He'd made himself utterly vulnerable to her, completely at her mercy. Having his shaft between her lips as he sweated and groaned, ensnared by the pleasure *she* gave him, roused her own desire. Between her legs, she was slick and aching, desperate for sensation.

Yet when her hand snaked down her belly so she might find some relief, he managed to catch her wrist.

"Let me see to that," he insisted darkly.

"But I don't want to stop sucking you," she protested.

He smiled mirthlessly. "I don't want that, either."

In a flurry of sweat-glossed limbs and soft instructions, he arranged their bodies so that he lay upon his back and she . . . she could scarce believe it . . . she straddled him, except her hips hovered above his lips . . . and she faced the other direction. She was aligned perfectly so that she could take his cock in her mouth, while he could—

"God above," she gasped when his tongue slid through the folds of her quim.

"Now who's being blasphemous?" It was a little hard to hear him, though, with his face buried between her thighs.

He held her hips securely as she lowered herself down to grasp his shaft. Pleasure permeated her as he·licked her while she slid his cock between her lips. Sensation was all around her, hot and wet where he ate her, in her breasts where the hard tips rubbed against his torso, and throughout her whole being as she sucked him. He filled her—she did her best to take as much of him in her, yet had to rely on her hand to fully enclose him.

The baseness of this act made her eyelids flutter with arousal. And when he slid two fingers into her passage, she cried out, the sound muffled by the thickness of him in her mouth.

Everything dissolved as she bobbed on his cock and he licked her while thrusting into her, expertly locating that engorged spot inside that throbbed with pleasure from his touch. All the while, he made the most glorious noises, as if he was devouring something profoundly delicious, mingled with sounds of his ecstasy.

Her release barreled into her with uncompromising force. She went taut as pleasure shot through her whole being, making her limbs shake and her breath sound like a sob.

She was learning that Dom was never satisfied until she'd come at least thrice, and he made good on this unspoken vow, consuming her greedily as he fucked her with his fingers. The fact that she had his cock in her mouth hurried each climax along, following one another like diamonds on a chain.

"Enough, lioness," he growled, taking his mouth from her and moving his hips so that he slipped from her lips.

"But you liked that," she complained, her words more a mumble from the sheer number of orgasms she'd just had.

"Too much. Was goin' to spill in your mouth."

"Maybe I'd enjoy it."

He swore again as he moved her limp body, positioning her so that she again lay upon the blanket. "You're goin' to fuckin' kill me."

"Then we'll meet our maker together."

He bent over her and kissed her, the taste of her own arousal upon his skin. And then it was as if those countless climaxes hadn't happened because she was aflame once more.

"Dom."

"Lioness?"

"Fuck me."

"Oh, I will." Kneeling, he placed himself between her open thighs, gripping her hips and lifting them up. Then, with one thrust, he was inside her.

It didn't matter that she'd taken him inside her less than an hour before. The size of him stretched her, filled her, so that she couldn't stop herself from gasping.

"Stop?" he growled, stilling.

"Don't you dare." This *was* how she was going to reach the end of her existence. She couldn't think of a better way than crammed full of Dom's cock.

She pushed her hips into his in encouragement.

"Ah, sweetheart," he said hoarsely. "This is where I belong. Inside you."

She swallowed against the rush of emotion that threatened to lead her away from her pleasure.

"How do you want me to fuck you, lioness?"

His voice was gruff. "Slow and easy? Hard and rough?"

The choice was *hers*. "Slow—at first. Then . . ." She moaned when he drew back and then drove forward in a thick, delicious thrust.

"Then good and rough," he finished.

"*Yes.*"

He did as he promised. His pace was, in the beginning, leisurely yet resolute. Each stroke into her was long and purposeful, his hips steady in their tempo and building sensation within her to gradual, dizzying heights. It was too much, and yet not enough.

"*Dom,*" she cried, nearly whining.

"Ready for a hard fuckin', lioness? *Tell me,*" he demanded, his breath serrated. "Tell me how you want me to fuck you."

"*Hard*, Dom. Fuck me hard."

"Whatever the lady wants." His already flexed body went even more taut as he drew back his hips and slammed into her. Once, and then again. His pace increased, until he hammered into her. She jolted with each thrust. It was rough and brutal and she *loved* it.

Every muscle on him stood out in bold relief as he dedicated himself to giving her exactly the kind of ferocity she craved. His mouth was open, his eyes glazed, as he panted and growled a litany of praise and curses.

She completely abandoned herself to pleasure. It

was her entire being, created by her and Dom together, and when he used his thumb to stroke her
clitoris, she screamed her climax, striking her with
even more force than ever. It crested and ebbed
and crested once more, until she was utterly depleted, her body going lax.

A moment later, he pulled from her. A wild noise
sounded from deep within him as seed shot from
his cock, landing on her steaming, slick flesh like
a brand.

She didn't quite know what happened after that.
Only that when she resurfaced from her haze of
pleasure, Dom had cleaned her, and she nestled in
his arms as they lay in front of the fire. His hands
stroked all over her body, soothing and grounding
her after all that had transpired between them.

"Did I please you, lioness?" he asked, his words
low and rumbling. He kissed the top of her head.
"All I want is to please you."

She buried her face against his chest, and felt the
curling hair against her cheek, the real, earthy es-
sence of Dom all around her.

What a complicated, troubled world this was, to
give her this man, and yet throw so many obstacles
in their path, so many perils that she did not know
how to circumvent or survive. The greatest threat
came from themselves, and their own untamed,
dangerous hearts.

At last, she said, "You pleased me."

Chapter 23

❖ ✳ ❖

"Where did you find all this food?" Willa asked. She dipped a piece of bread into the broth and ate it eagerly, making a little humming noise of satisfaction.

Dom could watch her eat all day. She had a way of immersing herself in the experience, giving herself to it completely as though nothing and no one mattered more.

Not unlike the way she lost herself in sex.

They'd been making love all morning and all afternoon, but his cock stirred with interest. He couldn't get enough of her, and, given the way that she kept demanding more, she couldn't seem to get enough of him—for the moment.

He wouldn't think about that. Now he'd just sit beside her at the small table, enjoying this very plain and humble meal of vegetable broth, bread, and cheese.

"Got excellent scrounging skills," he answered

without pride. He downed a spoonful of soup, and had to admit that it wasn't bad. "There never was enough to go around in Ratcliff, or to buy fresh food, so I learned how to nick an onion here, a bit of lamb bone there. Ma showed me how you could turn anything into a decent soup. Fortunately, it appears Longbridge's staff had been out here a day or two ago, and they left enough for a resourceful person to make good use of it."

Their clothes had dried enough so that he was able to don his breeches, and she wore her shift. The filmy undergarment did little to disguise the shapes of her breasts, or conceal the dark triangle between her legs. Given the way she kept eyeing him as he'd been moving around the small kitchen, she appreciated his nearly naked state just as much as he loved to see her in so scanty a covering.

The fire had done its job well, making the small cabin nice and cozy, so that they could lounge about in this state of undress, which suited him far better than any expensive suit from a shop on St. James's Street. And he definitely preferred an almost nude Willa to her swaddled in layers of silk.

In the glow of a lone candle burning between them, Willa smiled. "Who knew a strapping man wearing nothing but breeches as he cooks for you could be such an aphrodisiac?"

His large, burly body was merely his body—he'd used it as a means of hauling and unloading cargo, sometimes it was a weapon, and back when he'd been a rake, it had pleased his many lovers—but he couldn't help but preen to have *her* admire his physique. She'd enjoyed having her hands all over his bulk, too, so he couldn't be too upset that she liked him scaled as big as a warship.

"It's simple fare, though," he pointed out. "Not the fine stuff you'd get at a nob's table."

She made a scoffing noise. "As if I'd prefer to eat bisque de homard in a stuffy dining room with people I don't care about, rather than something you made yourself, at this homespun table, in this cabin, with you."

Heat filled his face—she truly *was* the only person who could make him blush. "You're only saying that because this is the first meal you've had since waking, and I fucked you half a dozen times today. Anybody'd be grateful for that."

"Well," she said, her own cheeks turning pink, "the soup *is* good. And so was the fucking."

Damn, how he liked hearing her say crude words. "Plenty more where that came from, my girl."

"Soup? Or fucking?"

"Both." He grinned at her, and her answering smile made something light and loose open in his chest. "You're going to wear my cock down to a sliver."

"That sounds suspiciously like a complaint," she murmured.

"Definitely not a complaint," he chuckled.

"Besides, you've got cock to spare. A little whittling down will hardly make much difference. And," she added wryly, "my quim isn't a lathe."

"Hell of a way to turn a table leg."

"And the production method is innovative, too."

Dusk had fallen, and the rain had barely lessened. He didn't give a damn. Hopefully, this would be another biblical flood, wiping out everyone else in the world except him and Willa. They'd stay in this cabin for the rest of their lives, eating soup and making love, and that would suit him very well.

Maybe he ought to pray for that to happen, just in case. He wasn't a churchgoing man, but he could change his ways if it meant being with Willa like this.

Later. Watching Willa enthusiastically eat the food he'd prepared for her and smiling at him with lust in her eyes inspired some very ungodly thoughts.

"This actually reminds me of a meal I had in Bruges," she mused after taking a bite of cheese. "It wasn't the most elegant meal, but I don't think I ate better than when I was there."

"Left an impression, did it?"

"Oh, it's a lovely town." Her eyes sparkled in the candlelight. "It's not as fashionable as Brussels—not yet. But I've a feeling it will become a place no traveler can resist. There are canals, and the most wonderful medieval buildings. It's as though you've stepped back in time, with only the clothing of the people to remind you that you're still in the modern nineteenth century, not the fifteenth."

"The decay of Ratcliff or even the new elegance of Hans Town is what I know best."

"I pictured you there, beside me as we walked Bruges's cobbled streets." Almost shyly, she added, "Wherever I went on the Continent, I thought about what you'd think of a place. How you'd enjoy it. What we'd talk about as we explored it together."

A warm, almost giddy feeling unfolded in him, as if he'd had too much whisky. "Thought you'd spent your whole time abroad cursing my name."

"I did," she said candidly. "Whenever I tasted a new food, like apfelstrudel, or saw a beautiful statue in a piazza, like the Fountain of the Four Rivers in Rome, I kept thinking, 'Dom's such a bastard—would he like this? I ought to tell that scoundrel about it.'"

He slid his hand across the table and wove his fingers with hers.

"Would you ever go back?" *With me?*

She stared down at their interlaced hands. As if she heard his silent words, she said sadly, "I don't know. I'll try to be satisfied with what I have and where I am at this very moment. No looking beyond tonight. Not even to tomorrow. Can we agree to that, at least?"

Tomorrow *would* come whether either of them

wanted it to or not, and if all joy in this world was fleeting, Dom would take his for as long as he could.

"You cooked," she protested as Dom took their empty bowls back to the small kitchen. "The least I can do is help tidy up. I'm really *not* a princess, you know."

"I'm well aware," he answered, "but tonight I'm taking care of everything."

"What should I do while you clean?"

"Look decorative," he teased, and was rewarded by her throwing him a rude hand gesture.

While he wiped out the pot and their bowls, she wandered around the cabin, poking her head into any available cabinet and closet.

"Curious as a cat," he said when she opened a trunk at the foot of the bed and crouched down to rifle through the contents.

"I don't think this is yarn." She straightened, and he nearly dropped a bowl when he saw lengths of satiny rope in her hands. "Unless it's for a very large cat."

He strode to the chest and peered down into it. There was more rope, as well as buckled harnesses, paddles, riding crops, and, yes, even a leather-covered phallus.

"Accommodating host, that Longbridge. He *does* keep this place well provisioned. Don't touch that," he warned when Willa reached for the artificial cock.

She pouted. "Why not?"

"I'm going to assume it's been cleaned, but even so, it's bad form to touch someone else's dildo without their express permission."

"I didn't know there were rules governing that sort of thing."

Dom scratched his chin. "More of an unspoken agreement."

"Can I touch this?" Willa held up a beautifully made harness that was adorned with elegant brass buckles. It jingled slightly as she handled it, and the sound shot right to his cock, along with the sight of her holding the contraption to her body.

A shudder of pure desire wracked him. It was too easy to picture her ripe form strapped into the harness, leather straps framing her breasts and clinging to her thighs, and imagine what he'd do to her if she wore such a thing. But he had to remember that, until a few hours ago, she was new to the world of sex, and rushing her into anything advanced could harm her both physically and emotionally.

"It's better if you don't." He plucked the harness from her grip and laid it back down into the velvet-lined chest.

"I've read about things like this," she informed him. "In the Lady of Dubious Quality's books." She studied the ropes in her hands, the black silky cords shining in the low firelight, and shooting more heat through Dom's body. "My curiosity was . . . sparked."

He raised a brow, much calmer on the outside than the riot going on inside of him. "Is it something you'd like to try?"

"I . . ." She glanced up through her lashes. "Would you think less of me if I did?"

"For one thing, lioness," he said fiercely, "*nothing*'s going to make me think less of you. And the other thing is that there's no shame in liking this kind of play. As long as everyone involved wants to be there and agrees to what they're going to do, and stops when they're told to stop, then do as you please."

"*You* seem to know an awful lot about it."

He shrugged. "No sense in pretending I didn't run wild in the years before we met."

"So . . ." Her cheeks went pink, and her smile was unusually bashful. She trailed the rope up his bare arm, sending shivers of heat through him. "You know what to do. How to do it properly."

"I do," he rumbled. "Would you like to try it?"

She opened her mouth, closed it, then started to speak again before falling into an uncharacteristic silence.

"I've an idea," he said, his breath already coming fast. "*You* take the lead."

He took a rope from her and wrapped one around his wrist several times. The cord was soft, rubbing slick and cool against his skin, and his cock immediately thickened. He slipped the free end of the rope into her hand, giving her control.

Her eyes went wide while her cheeks went even rosier. "I can . . . tie you up?"

"If that's what you want."

"I want," she said at once.

He grinned at her enthusiasm.

"I read a scene in one of the Lady of Dubious Quality's books," she went on eagerly. "The rake tied his lover's hands to the headboard of a bed, and she couldn't do anything as he toyed with her. Can we do that?"

"Lioness, I'll *beg* you to do the same to me." He typically took the more controlling role whenever he'd done such things, but putting himself at Willa's mercy made his cock hard and hot as a brand. And . . . he could show he trusted her.

"If I do anything you don't like," she said, gazing up at him, her eyes grave, "you *must* say so. I'll stop at once."

"You've an instinct for this kind of play." He cupped the back of her head and kissed her deeply, and she lifted up on her toes to press herself tight against him. She shook, but from excitement, not fear, and the feel of her anticipation stoked his need higher. "Tell me when you want to begin."

"Now," she said immediately. "Get on the bed. Please," she added with a saucy smile.

"Breeches on or off?"

"Off. Your thighs are too magnificent to be covered."

He looked down at the body parts in question and shook his head at how anyone could find his bulky muscles arousing. Even when he'd been a boy, he'd been called a brute and a beast, but it didn't matter anymore when Willa's eyes gleamed hungrily when he tugged off his breeches. She also avidly eyed his cock, upright as a mast.

"We haven't even started yet," she murmured.

"We started a long time ago."

She swallowed, her color rising higher still, and then flicked her fingers toward the bed. He climbed onto it at once, positioning himself so that he leaned against the headboard. As she approached, a silk rope in each hand, his heart threatened to pound right out of his chest. He could feel his pulse thundering in his cock, too.

When she took one of his wrists and pulled it up so that he was close to the wooden finial atop the headboard, he couldn't hold back his groan. Or the droplet of fluid that leaked from his slit.

"You're better at knots than I am," she murmured, eyeing the cord she held.

"Something simple will work fine." His voice came out in a rasp. "Keep it loose enough that it doesn't rub too hard. A taste of pain is good, but not too much of the wrong kind."

She nodded, and his gaze ricocheted between the sight of her tying a rope around his wrist and anchoring it to the headboard, and the focused, studious look on her face as she bent to her work, which inflamed him even more. Fuck, he could come from only this.

Once she had one wrist secured, she edged around the bed to give the same attention to the other. She was scholarly in the filthiest way as she gave the rope a tug to ensure that she'd bound him properly.

"I'm good and tied, lioness," he growled. "Now you can do with me whatever you want."

Her eyes darkened as she leaned close, digging her fingers into his nape to bring him in for a lush, deep kiss.

She pulled back abruptly and straightened. Her gaze roamed all over his body as if she owned every inch of muscle, and he writhed, aroused, beneath her possessive look.

"You can touch me," he panted. "*Please* touch me."

"Maybe I shouldn't," she said, equally breathless. "You said a taste of pain is good. I could keep you in pain like this."

"That'd be torture, not havin' your hands on me."

"I don't want you to suffer unnecessarily." She still wore her shift, and her nipples formed tight points beneath the thin fabric as her breasts rose and fell. Leaning over him, she hovered her hands inches from his already straining, taut body, and he held his breath. Waiting. Waiting.

He groaned when she finally stroked her palms

over his torso. Every nerve came to life beneath her hands, and he leaned into her caresses. She let her fingers play over his sides, before gliding over his pectorals. He hissed when she lightly scratched his nipples, but when she looked up at him with a question in her eyes, he gave a quick nod to let her know that he wanted her to keep going. Cautiously, she bent close to flick her tongue over his nipple, and when he growled, she grew bolder, drawing it into her mouth to suck. Hot sensation shot all the way from his chest to his cock.

He gave another groan when she smoothed along the muscles leading down to his stomach. She softly dragged her fingernails through the trail of hair leading to his cock, and into the thicker nest at the base.

Dom was sweating now, pushing his hips up.

"Fuck—I need to feel you on my cock," he said, voice rough.

She looked at him with a mischievous smile. "Like this?"

A long string of curses tore from him when she raked her nails up his shaft.

But she didn't stay there. Instead, she scratched over his thighs before going back up to his cock and lightly, lightly scraping up and down it, driving him to a frenzy.

"Where are you off to?" he demanded when she walked from the bed, toward the open chest.

Then he made a sound that was part torment, part ecstasy when she pulled the riding crop from the trunk.

She approached the bed with a cheeky grin, yet her smile faded when she got closer. "Is this all right? I don't have to use it if it's not—"

"Goin' to kill me, and I *love it*."

Her impudent look returned, and she lightly trailed the thin piece of leather at the end of the crop across his thighs. The strokes were soft, the leather cool, and he relaxed slightly before she swatted him. A quick, sharp strike that shot fire through him and almost immediately made a red line on his skin.

"All right?" she asked.

"Better than all right," he snarled. "Incredible."

She did it again, and again, raining a series of fast blows on his thighs. With each hit, he growled and cursed, his hips lifting off the mattress. Each strike was like a bolt of lightning that went straight to his cock. More fluid streamed from the tip, oozing down the head and shaft, glistening in the light.

He'd always been the one to wield the crop, but to be on the receiving end was unexpectedly ecstasy.

"You're so—*fuck*—damn—*Christ*—good at this."

"And you're so good at taking what I give you," she said, gasping. Color was high in her cheeks, her eyes were blown out, and her lips were parted as she watched the fruits of her labors with a glassy gaze.

He was on the thinnest of tethers, barely able to control himself.

"Stop, stop," he panted.

She did at once, lowering the crop. Worry creased between her brows. "Was I hurting you too much?"

"Not too much. But before I come, I want something from you. Untie me."

Her fingers were slightly clumsy as she undid the ropes. When he was free, he took her shaking hands in his.

Gruffly, he said, "Now *I* want to play with *you*."

Chapter 24

❖✣❖

𝒯rembling, voice faint from arousal, Willa asked, "Play? As in . . ."

"Bind you." Dom looked feral, sweat-glossed and wild. "Take control of you. Drown you in pleasure. That somethin' you'd want? Will you trust me?"

She hesitated. What he asked for was monumental. *Could* she trust him? Give over her body, having faith that he would only give her what she desired? A week ago, she never would have. Yet now . . . when he'd laid himself out for her in every way, trusting *her* . . .

"I'm a little afraid," she admitted. "But . . . I want to do it. I want to do this with you, Dom."

"Is that *yes*?"

"It's *yes*."

His nostrils flared, and he inhaled sharply before he gripped the back of her neck and pulled her lips to his. She braced her hands on his wide, slick shoulders as she gave herself over to his ravenous kiss, sinking beneath the waves while their tongues tangled.

When he leaned back, breaking the kiss, her head spun. Drunkenly, she asked, "What do I do?"

"Same rules apply, lioness. Anythin' you don't like, you tell me. Pick a word to say, any word, and the second you say it, I'll stop."

"*Embroidery*," she said.

"You need to know," he answered, grave, "that when I do this kind of thing, I take control. I get . . . controlling. Dominant."

"Dom *is* your name, after all," she said impertinently. "And I don't mind. I'd like to experience it, in truth."

A corner of his lips curved up. "There's my lioness." Then his expression turned serious again, his eyes hard and gleaming. "Take off your shift and kneel in the middle of the cabin."

Excitement moved in a tremor through her body, and her hands shook as she pulled off her shift. She moved to kneel, but before she did, Dom rose from the bed and slipped a pillow underneath her knees.

"Thoughtful," she said breathlessly.

"I want you obedient, not uncomfortable."

"There's a difference?" she asked.

"If it's done proper."

She thought he'd go right to her and do . . . something. Instead, he tugged on his breeches, but left the fall open so that his upright cock stuck out.

At her curious look, he explained gruffly, "You bein' naked and me bein' clothed . . . it puts a fire in me. I like seein' the difference between us. That I'm in control, and you're mine. Mine to do what I like with. Mine to pleasure."

She sucked in a breath as her quim ached with need. "I like the sound of that."

His eyes flashed, and his chest rose and fell. He went to the trunk and took a length of silk from it, the fabric pulling taut between his fists when he approached. He stopped, standing in front of her.

They gazed at each other, a fraught and electric current passing between them as he loomed over her, and she knelt before him. He towered above her, and yet power surged through her body to see his jagged breath, the flush of color in his cheeks, how his cock swelled even bigger, leaking clear droplets. *She* affected him. She might be kneeling, but she had as much power as he did. Perhaps, in yielding this way, she possessed even more than Dom.

"Look at you, bein' so good for me," he said on a rasp. "You could ask me to do anythin', and I'd do it."

"Put your cock in my mouth." The words were outrageous, shocking, and yet they felt perfect.

He growled. "Lioness, that's exactly what I'm goin' to do." He held up the silk. "But first, I'm goin' to cover your eyes. Block out anythin' that isn't me and my cock in your throat."

She nodded shakily. Arousal made it almost impossible to hold still as he tied the length of fabric over her eyes, the silk soft against her skin, the world becoming a place of darkness and sensation. The air in the cabin was humid and thick, and Dom's breath was ragged, louder than the rain that continued to pound against the windows.

This, she realized, was trust. The kind of trust she'd never given another person. Yet with Dom, at this moment, she was secure and safe. He wouldn't hurt her.

"How do I look?" she asked on a gasp.

He made another animal noise. "Fuckin' perfect. Now hold still."

"What if I don't?" she couldn't stop herself from asking.

"Then I'll punish you."

His stern voice made her shiver with anticipation. She jolted when his hand cupped her jaw, his thumb stroking over her lip.

"Open," he commanded.

She briefly debated refusing to follow his order, but she was too inflamed to refuse, and so she parted her lips.

"Wider," he demanded.

When she did, he slid his thumb and another finger into her mouth. The texture of his skin against her tongue was rough, yet she licked him, and was rewarded with his rumble of approval.

"That's right, my girl," he rasped, then pulled out.

She gasped when he slicked around her nipple with wet fingers, and then she moaned when he pinched the tip of her breast. Sparks traveled from the point of her nipple straight to her cunt.

"Keep your mouth open," he directed as he cupped the back of her head with his other hand. "Nice and wide so you can take all of me."

Her breath came hard and fast as the crown of his cock met her lips.

"Lick it," he ordered.

With an impish smile, she shook her head.

"You don't want to?" His voice had gone even deeper.

"Consider this me being disobedient. And I want my punishment."

He growled. "Later. Now suck me."

She shuddered with desire, then swirled her tongue over the broad, silken head, tasting the salt of his arousal. Without her sight, she was reduced to all sensation, and she was never more aware of him and her own climbing excitement than when he pushed the crown past her lips to sink his length into her mouth. Deeper he went, and deeper still, and she relaxed her jaw and throat so that she was completely full of his cock.

Pleased with herself, she gave a hum of satisfaction, and he groaned.

"Ah, hell, lioness," he rasped. "You're perfect."

His praise shot into all the hidden parts of her,

filling her with pleasure and satisfaction. Reaching up, she braced her hands on his thighs, which were hard as stone beneath her palms. She loved the texture of his breeches, reminding her that he was dressed, and she was completely nude.

"I'm goin' to fuck your mouth, lioness," he growled. "Hard. That's your punishment. And you're goin' to like it."

Nodding was impossible, so she made a sound of assent. He continued to hold the back of her head as his cock pulled almost completely from her, before sliding in once more. He did this again, and again. As he did, he made the most exquisite noises of feral ecstasy, and she abandoned herself to this moment—being used for Dom's pleasure, and yet completely in control of him.

"Fuck," he rumbled. "Yes. Fuck. Beautiful girl. I'm yours. Only yours."

She squeezed her eyes tight against the rush of tears that threatened to emerge. Whatever they said or promised now . . . she couldn't think about it. All she could permit herself was this moment, and the pleasure they gave each other.

His movements grew faster and rough and she sucked, drawing on him as she lost herself.

But then he was gone, pulling from her mouth. "Can't come. Not when I got other plans for you."

"What plans?" She had no fear, only eagerness.

"I want to bind you. Tie you up. If you'll let me."

"I'll do more than *let you*," she gasped. "I *insist*."

His lips were on hers, as he kissed her thoroughly, and then he carefully helped her to her feet, threading his fingers with hers, and led her several steps. She heard the sound of furniture scraping over the floor.

"Stay here," he said. "I'm gettin' the ropes."

She waited, and as she did, reached out in front of her to find that he'd positioned her to face one of the armchairs. Her knees bumped against its seat cushion. A thousand possibilities ran through her mind, but even having read the Lady of Dubious Quality's books, she couldn't fathom what Dom intended.

His footfalls were heavy as he approached. With gentle hands, he maneuvered her body, bending her forward, and resting her forearms on the chair's armrests. She exhaled when he wrapped a length of silken rope around her forearm, tying her to the chair. He did the same thing with her other arm. She was bound fast, and acutely aware of the fact that, bent over as she was, she was exposing herself lewdly. Surely, he saw absolutely everything. And she couldn't move, couldn't hide.

A tremor of arousal thundered through her. Her quim was wet and throbbing as she heard him take a step back to admire her.

"Jesus God," he growled. "Ain't ever seen anythin' so pretty."

"*Dom,*" she moaned. "Don't make me wait. Whatever you're planning, I want it."

"Made you wait long enough. Never again. But first, I don't think you've been punished enough."

His hand came down on the cheek of her arse. She gasped. He was . . . spanking her.

"No?" he asked gruffly.

"Keep going," she urged.

"There's my saucy wench." He slapped her arse again and once more, each strike bright and hot, and shooting directly to her quim.

She sucked in a breath when he gripped her arse cheeks, the warmth of his breath gusting over her quim, and then she cried out when he licked her with a long, hot slick of his tongue between her lips. He sucked at her cunt, devouring her, tracing her folds, nibbling on her clitoris. A scream tore from her when he thrust two fingers into her passage. As he feasted on her, he fucked her with his hand and used his thumb to stroke her nub. Her climax began to gather in hot, tight coils.

Then . . . his tongue found the tight ring of her arse.

She stiffened.

"Stop?" he asked, pulling back.

"Hell, no," she answered.

She felt his small huff of laughter—and then he bent back to his work. She moaned and gasped as he licked her hole, all the while continuing to fuck her quim with his fingers.

Release came in a storm, tearing through her body. Her legs shook with the force of her climax, yet the bindings on her arms and his relentless force kept her standing through the tremors of her orgasm, and the one that followed that, and the one that followed that.

He gave her cunt one more lick before withdrawing his fingers and replacing them with his cock. He circled her entrance with the head, then gripped her hips and slammed into her. She met his forceful strokes as best she could, pushing back into each thrust. His grunts and growls strummed along her back, and he cursed and praised in equal measure. When his fingers found her clitoris, circling and pinching it, she came again with a wail.

A heartbeat later, he tore from her with a roar, and his seed shot thickly across her back.

The storm continued outside, but all she heard was the gusting of her and Dom's breath, and the pounding of her heart.

He cleaned her, untied her, and took the silk off from around her eyes before gathering her up in his arms. After he put a cup of water to her lips, she blinked in the light to see him looking down at her with an expression that could only be called worshipful.

She'd trusted him, and he had trusted her, and in exchange, they had both been given something wondrous. Something that leveled everything else and left them alone together, in the ashes of a world that she didn't know how to rebuild.

"My lioness," he whispered, his lips pressing to her forehead.

She turned her face into his chest, overwhelmed, heart full to brimming, joyous. And afraid.

Chapter 25

❧ ✳ ❧

*T*he silence woke him. They were in bed, his body curved around Willa as she slept, one of his arms draped over her protectively. He must have shifted slightly, because she murmured something indecipherable before nestling deeper into the shelter he provided.

Soft gray light seeped into the cabin—it was shortly after sunrise. But the lack of sound made him lift up onto an elbow and cock his head, trying to discern what, exactly, was happening.

The rain had stopped. The storm was over. And instead of the roaring of the swollen river, he could just make out the quieter trickling noise of a much smaller creek.

Disappointment hit him, hard and sharp. There was no denying the truth of it: their time in the cabin would have to end soon.

Not yet, not yet, his heart demanded. He lay back down, staring at the timbered ceiling.

It didn't have to happen right away. They could enjoy these last few hours, wringing joy out of what they did have left.

He'd never let anyone strike him with a crop or tie him up before—it was exactly right that she was the one person he'd permitted to do it. And she'd been perfect.

Then, to give him such complete trust to bind her, to let him use her and pleasure her in new and forbidden ways . . . *God*, had anyone ever been given such a gift? One he'd cherish forever, as if she'd handed him his own missing heart.

He cradled her closer.

". . . have to be here . . ." a man's voice said.

". . . no other logical place . . ." a woman added.

Dom bolted upright. *Fuck*.

He knew those voices. Finn and Tabitha. Growing closer.

". . . never built a bridge before . . ." That was Kieran.

". . . did a lovely job, notwithstanding . . ." *Celeste*.

Dom leapt from the bed and tugged on his breeches. "Shit, shit, shit."

He ran to the window to see his two friends and their wives setting a roughly constructed short wooden bridge over the now diminished creek. Once the structure was in place, Kieran stepped onto it first, testing it beneath his weight. Unfortunately, the damned bridge held, and in a moment, he was on the near side of the bank, waving for the others to join him.

Dom spun away from the window and sprinted to where Willa's shift and gown were draped over a chair. He snatched up the garments on his way to the bed, where she still slept.

"Willa," he said, then, more insistently, "*Willa*. Get up. Get dressed. *Now*."

She barely stirred, and the blame was his, really, for wearing her out with bout after bout of love-making.

Though he hated to do it, he shook her. "Willa, you have to wake up."

One of her eyes cracked open. "Whass goin' on?"

"Kieran and Finn and their wives are here."

She closed her eye and nestled deeper beneath the blanket. "Thass nice."

"*Willa*."

Before he could do something drastic, like drag her from the bed and shove her clothes on, the Ransome brothers' voices grew nearer. In a minute, they'd be on the front porch. There wasn't bloody time.

He strode to the door just as a knock sounded.

Pulling it open, he did his best to try to block the view of inside the cabin, using his body as a shield. Finn, Kieran, Tabitha, and Celeste all stood on the porch, looking at him with bewildered expressions. Only when Tabitha reddened and turned away did Dom realize that he'd neglected to put on a shirt. All he had on was a pair of breeches, and since they'd been hastily fastened, they hung low on his hips. Celeste became very interested in the construction of the porch's roof.

Finn collected himself first. "Ah. Dom. Glad to find you here and not washed out to sea or shivering with a fatal case of ague."

"Hale as a cargo ship," he said with forced cheer. "Everything's fine. Nothing to concern yourself with. You can return to the house and I'll be along momentarily."

As he spoke, Kieran tried to peer around Dom, and Dom kept shifting, placing himself between his friend and the cabin's interior.

"Where's Willa?" Kieran demanded without preamble.

"She's fine."

"Dom?" Willa's voice floated out. And then, to his utter horror, she appeared beside him, the blanket wrapped around her. It was plain that she wasn't wearing anything beneath. She looked bleary, her hair mussed, as if she'd spent all of yesterday and into the early hours of the morning having athletic, enthusiastic sex. Which she had.

With him.

Finn coughed, and Kieran made a choked noise, and those sounds seemed to stir Willa from her grogginess. Her eyes opened wider and when she caught sight of her two brothers goggling at her, her face and whatever part of her body wasn't covered by the blanket turned pink.

"Oh, my God," she gasped.

Dom held up his hands. "It isn't—"

"I'll just . . . excuse myself." She turned away and moved deeper into the cabin.

"Give us a minute," Dom said to the brothers. "We'll join you when we're ready."

"But—"

Dom shut the door in the Ransome brothers' faces. He turned to Willa as she pulled on her clothes. "Let me help with that."

"I can manage."

Tautness gripped his spine and spread through his body. Of course she'd be distant when her family had just burst in on her, finding her wearing only a blanket. He and Willa dressed in silence, then left the cabin to find her brothers standing on the grass sloping away from the small structure.

Kieran and Finn looked damned pleased with themselves.

"For all your protestations," Kieran said with a smug smile, "our maneuverings couldn't have had a better outcome."

"A wedding *does* seem to be in your future," Finn added.

Dom searched Willa's face for a sign, anything

that might show whether or not she liked that idea. Yet she kept her expression unreadable.

"We ought to head back," Celeste offered cautiously.

"Let's go," Dom said. He didn't want to leave the haven of the cabin, but talking to Willa was imperative, and he couldn't do that here, with her brothers and their wives as an audience.

He walked quickly as they all made their way back to Longbridge's house. The sooner he and Willa could get some privacy, the sooner they'd shake off this choking net of tension that trapped them both. All the while, though, her brothers, Celeste, and Tabitha kept up a flow of chitchat, purposefully filling the tense air with words.

Finally, they reached the manor.

"Everyone's eager for your return," Kieran explained, heading toward the stone terrace at the back of the house. "Longbridge has planned a party to welcome you back."

Willa pressed her lips together in a thin, pale line.

"Tell him we're both exhausted," Dom said, "and the party's going to have to go on without us."

Without waiting for Kieran's response, Dom wrapped an arm around Willa's shoulders and guided her to one of the side entrances. They took the servants' stairs, but instead of leading Willa to her room, he went up, higher, until they reached the very top floor of the house.

"Where are we?" she asked as he pulled her out into a dark, narrow hallway.

"Don't worry—I know where we're going." Well, he did know in one way, but in another . . . he was lost.

He opened a small door, and sunlight poured in, briefly blinding him. Once his eyes got used to the brightness, he stepped out onto the roof and led her out to join him.

Together, they walked to the low wall, where they stared at the broad, steel-gray sea stretching toward the horizon. She had tied her hair into a loose knot, and dark strands had come free, blowing across her cheeks. Distractedly, she brushed them back, yet they kept trailing over her face. He wanted to wrap those curls around his fingers, feeling their heavy silk, but he kept his hands at his sides.

"Still not easy with the sea," he said at last. "The Thames, now, *that* I know. It's where I worked and made my blunt. When we'd be unloading ships, the river often stank, but it was a familiar smell, and it was comforting to hear the water lapping against the pilings or sludging up on the banks."

"You said men died in the river when it was cold," she said softly. "How frightening, to see that."

"Lots to be frightened about in Ratcliff. After Da made his fortune, the nobs and aristos were pestering me, but it didn't matter. Their words meant nothing, not when I knew how thin the line was between life and death. How easily something important can slip through your fingers. I know that now, better than I've ever known it before."

From their spot high up, they could hear the waves beating against the shore. At some other time, the sound might be lulling, yet he was anything but calm.

"It's a possibility." He braced his hands on the railing. "Marriage."

"To secure your inheritance?" She didn't look at him, but kept her focus on the horizon. "To make right the wrong from a year ago?"

He stepped between her and the wall, and her hands splayed on his chest. His heart pounded under her palms. "The hell with the blunt. And it's not about fixing the past."

"Then what *is* it about?" Her gaze was searching as it moved over his face.

"Moving forward." He cupped her face with his palms and stroked his thumbs along the curves of her cheeks. Her skin had cooled, yet there was heat beneath. "You're not a princess and I'm not a brute kept around only to shock the ton. We're more than that, and now we know. It can be a whole new beginning for us."

Her lips trembled. She leaned into his touch, rubbing her face against his hand. He soaked in the feel of her, soft to his work-toughened skin. But then she stepped back. His heart plummeted.

Her voice shaky, she said, "I *want* to give you an answer."

"But you can't," he said heavily as he dropped his hands.

She shook her head, and more strands of her hair fluttered in the wind, black wisps against the cloud-streaked sky. "My mind, my heart . . . I can't figure out what either of them need. What *I* need. The only thing I know is that I have to have time."

There was a hard, rending feeling in his chest, yet he nodded. "It's yours."

"That's not what you wanted to hear," she said with a sad smile. "But it's what I can say."

"I want you to be mine, Willa. Always." His chest rose and fell as if he was hauling heavy cargo. "That means nothing if you don't come to me with your arms open, with your heart open. And if it's time you need to do that, then I'll give you time."

In a life of brutal physical work, and gutting emotional loss, saying those words was the hardest thing he'd ever done. But he wasn't the same man who'd set foot on this island, and as he looked at Willa, her face turned again to the sea, it was clear that the only way to keep her was to give her the space to spread her wings.

HE FOUND THE Ransome brothers, predictably, in the billiards room. Except instead of playing the game according to its rules and using cues, they stood at the periphery of the room, lobbing the balls into the table's pockets.

Both brothers looked at him eagerly when he came into the chamber.

"Our parents will want a Town wedding, of course, at St. George's," Kieran said cheerfully, crossing his arms over his chest and propping his hip against the table. "Sometimes it's easier to just give them what they want than try to fight the earl, but you and Willa's wishes come first. However, St. George's doesn't hold good memories for anyone, so we could—"

Dom held up a hand, and Kieran fell silent.

"It's not going to happen, is it?" Finn asked gently.

"The choice is hers," Dom answered, firm. "It has to be hers."

When the brothers remained silent, he went on, "The ultimatum our families made, about getting married within a year or we lose our fortunes . . . I may cost us everything. Because if Willa doesn't agree to become my wife, I don't want anyone else. I never will."

Stoically, he waited for Kieran and Finn to object, or insist that he try to persuade Willa to wed him. Much as he hated disappointing his friends, he wouldn't be moved on this point.

"We know." Kieran's voice was gentle.

"And we understand," Finn added.

Dom stepped closer. "You don't care?" he demanded hotly. "That I'm costing you all that blunt? Not just you, either, now, but your wives, too."

"Two things," Kieran said. "The first is that both Finn and I have alternate means of providing for ourselves, and Celeste and Tabitha. Finn at the gaming tables, and me, with my publishing venture. But even if we didn't have a single groat between us, that wouldn't matter. Which brings me to my second point: we'd far rather that you were happy than for either of us to be heaped with cash."

Dom swallowed around the thick lump in his throat. "Without her, I don't know if I can ever be *happy*. If she doesn't want me—the best thing for you both is to stay away from me. I'll only drag you down."

"We're not going anywhere," Finn said firmly.

Kieran placed his hand on Dom's shoulder. "You miserable son of a bitch, we love you."

"Just like you to say something so daft." Yet Dom put a hand on each of the brothers' shoulders, overwhelmed by their care when he so clearly didn't deserve it.

There were so many things in this world he didn't deserve, and yet the Universe kept giving them to him. The trick came in not squandering those gifts.

As he looked back and forth between Kieran and Finn, he understood that the greatest gift he'd ever received was Willa, and he would do anything to keep her.

Chapter 26

❖ ✳ ❖

*B*y rights, Willa should be asleep. She had barely slept in the last twenty-four hours, and her body had done its utmost to keep up with the insatiable desire that blazed between her and Dom when they'd been at the cabin.

Yet after a bath that was supposed to be soothing, she'd climbed into bed and simply stared at the ceiling beams. Sounds from the house party crept faintly underneath her door. Music and laughter echoed as the other guests continued to amuse themselves with Mr. Longbridge's endlessly provided entertainments. Normally, noise never bothered her whenever she tried to sleep. But now it did. Same with the afternoon light that sifted in through the closed curtains.

She'd prided herself on being able to sleep whenever, wherever. And she truly *ought* to get some rest. Her body needed it, and her feverish, whirling thoughts could use the relief of unconsciousness.

Dom's offer of marriage ran like a rushing river through her mind, and even though she lay quietly in bed, her heart thudded in her chest.

Marriage. To Dom. She'd been engaged to him once before, awhirl in an immature infatuation and giddy with the belief that she was defying Society—and her parents. Hardly the foundation for a lifetime of joy. She and Dom had both acknowledged what a disaster it would have been, had they actually exchanged vows that day last spring.

Since then, she had evolved into someone else. Someone, she hoped, with a great deal more maturity and wisdom. And yet being wise where Dom was concerned . . . that was beyond her power.

They *could* be happy together . . . or they might be miserable, like her parents. Hell, she could find herself standing in front of the altar again, only to have Dom realize *again* that he was about to make a terrible mistake, and abandon her once more. And this time, the pain would be even greater, because . . . she loved him.

Willa sat up, pushing back the covers.

She *loved* him. And it terrified her. If she took what he offered, and if everything was to detonate once more, a trip to the Continent wouldn't help. Years in the country or abroad would do nothing. It wouldn't matter where she was or what she did with herself. She would be shattered, never to be whole again.

How could she sleep when the most monumental decision of her life stood before her?

The thought of joining the other guests made her stomach clench—but she had to do *something*. Slipping from bed, she strode to a small table where she'd set a stack of books. Perhaps one of them might distract her, or even provide an answer. Tabitha had recommended several texts to her, which could give some guidance. Yet when Willa went through the pile of borrowed books, they all had long, complicated titles with words such as *epistemology* and *ontology*, which made her head ache, although the Wollstonecraft seemed promising.

A knock sounded at her door, far firmer than Isla's gentle tap. It could be one of her brothers, come to check on her as was the habit of elder siblings.

"Come in," she called.

Dom stepped into her bedchamber, and she pressed a hand to her leaping stomach. It didn't seem to matter that she'd seen him only a few hours ago. Every time she was around him, her whole being came alive, as if a nearby fire had suddenly burst into existence and filled her with heat and energy.

Her gaze raked over him, taking in every small detail. The dark stubble on his jaw—he hadn't shaved since their return. The messy folds of his neckcloth—he had tied it hastily at the cabin and that, also, he hadn't attended to since they'd gotten back. His steel-blue eyes in the half-light of her bedroom as he looked her up and down, gleaming with desire. He stared at her from the top of her head to her bare toes peeking out beneath the hem of her nightgown.

God, how she wanted him. And he made her laugh, and she'd trusted him with her most unprotected self. But was that *enough*?

"Whatever you want," he said, rough but resolute. "That's what we'll do. We don't have to marry. We can live as lovers."

She started, unable to believe what she'd just heard. "What?"

"I've learned so much about you," he said solemnly. "About myself. I see your strength, and mine, and I see that we're also vulnerable. But it's not a bad thing, that vulnerability. It's good. Very good. Because it lets us feel, it lets us connect. And I'd rather link my soul to yours with or without the bonds of matrimony and feel the joy and pain of our connection, of all of it, than be without you. Because I love you."

Her fingertips flew to her lips. He'd never said these words to her before, and she'd never said them to him, and to hear them *now*, after everything . . . she could barely stand as happiness and fear buffeted her in equal measure.

"Not the princess," he went on, unwavering. "But the lioness. Who is strong *and* sensitive and so much more than anyone has ever given her credit for. I love you, and I *need* to be with you, Willa. In any way you desire me."

It took her several tries to speak. "Your inheritance . . . you won't get any of it if we don't marry."

"Fuck my inheritance," he said forcefully. "And fuck anyone who says there's only one way to love someone, only one way to be with them. This is about *us*." He stepped closer, and took both her hands in his. "It's not about what we represent, or anybody's expectations. It's just you and me."

The beat of her heart was a roar in her ears, and only the feel of his hot skin against hers kept her from flying into the air.

"My brothers would be disappointed," she managed to say. "They'd lose their money, too."

"They don't care, either. Finn and Key want us to be happy. But even if this made them shout and threaten and wail, it wouldn't matter. The only thing that matters is what you want."

No one had ever bestowed something so precious on her, the power of her own choice. And it made her legs shake beneath her.

"But *will* it make us happy?" she demanded. "Us, together?"

His expression was fierce. "All I know is that without you, I'm only meat wrapped around bones. I might live, but there's no meaning or purpose or point to it."

"I . . ." She wet her dry lips, struggling to speak,

to tell him the terrible truth and fully reveal herself to him. "I used to think I wasn't afraid of anything. But . . . I'm afraid now."

It was hard, so hard to admit it. She, the daring, the brash Willa Ransome, *fearful*. And yet, for all her fear, there was some part of her that knew she could trust him with her confession.

"I'm afraid," she said, choked, "and I can't rush this. I just can't, Dom."

His jaw tightened, but he didn't laugh and he didn't sneer. Instead, brow lowered, he opened his mouth to speak.

A quick, urgent knock sounded on her door. Before she could answer, it flew open. Celeste hurried in with Tabitha at her heels.

Celeste only blinked when she saw Dom in Willa's room, but she turned her attention to Willa.

"The boat," Celeste said breathlessly. "The reprovisioning boat, it's been spotted."

"It's estimated that it will be here in an hour," Tabitha explained, more level.

"Are you sure it's actually the right boat?" Dom demanded.

Tabitha said, "Mr. Longbridge recognized the markings and the sail."

Willa pulled her hands free from Dom's grip, and they stared at each other. The return of the boat meant that she could finally leave the island. Leave Dom. This whole episode could be put behind her, and she'd never again have to risk her heart with

Dom. She could resume her old life in London, or set off on another trip, far away from England and the chance of being near him.

But if she wanted to go, she'd have to make her decision. Soon.

"Think about what I said, lioness," he said, low and urgent. "Whatever way you want me, you can have me."

With that, he strode from the room.

Heart thudding in her throat, Willa stared blankly at the wall. She nearly ran from the room to watch the boat's approach—as though she couldn't believe it was truly coming without seeing its sails for herself—but her feet remained firmly planted on the thick carpeting.

"Willa?" Celeste's careful voice broke her daze. "What are you going to do?"

"I . . . I don't know." Willa pressed her hands to her temples as if she could find the answer on her skin. "He says we can marry, or not marry. But he wants us to be together, no matter what."

"There was a time I considered myself too analytical to appreciate a romantic gesture," Tabitha said with a self-deprecating smile. "I wanted facts and logic, not sentiment. As it turns out, it took a romantic gesture from the *right* person to make me feel something here." She pressed her hand to her chest. "Perhaps you ought to consult your own heart. It's surprising what we can learn from listening to our innermost selves."

"My innermost self is like Bartholomew Fair." Willa moved to her dresser, where the lioness figurine sat atop a silk scarf. She ran her fingers over the tiny figure's contours, rough in places from Dom's knife, but showing his care in making something so personal only for her. "Utter chaos. The thought of joining my life with Dom's . . ."

She dragged in a breath, then looked back and forth between Celeste and Tabitha. Being candid with her emotions and secret fears and feelings still didn't come easily. Would the other women be bored? Think her silly or flighty or foolish? She was Willa Ransome, the indomitable, and had played that role for a long time.

"You aren't my sister by birth," Celeste said, laying a gentle hand on her arm, "but I do think of you that way."

Willa dipped her head, humbled and grateful. "Always wanted a sister. Being surrounded by three brothers was an exercise in isolation."

"I've no sisters, either," Tabitha added shyly. "But the theory of them sounded so nice."

"*We* can be sisters and friends." Celeste smiled at Tabitha, and then at Willa. "And sisters tell each other everything. Believe me when I say that I know what it means to keep yourself carefully hidden because you're afraid what people might think of you if they knew who you truly were."

Willa felt her gaze fly to Celeste's, astonished by the other woman's understanding. Yet, it made sense that her poet brother would love a woman of deep insight.

"You do?" Willa asked.

"Dom had the privilege of being a man, and not being judged for his actions," Celeste said with a wry look. "I wasn't so fortunate. But Kieran showed me that there's so much more to gain when you take that leap. Granted, we must be selective when picking *who* we're revealing ourselves to. Still, Tabitha and I, we're not precisely the models of what the world considers ideal womanhood. If there's anyone you can trust, it's us."

"'*Learning to trust is one of life's most difficult tasks,*' Isaac Watts," Tabitha quoted. "It may be challenging, but the rewards . . . they're boundless."

Willa took a deep breath. She had transformed over the course of her time here, and if her brothers loved these women, she needed no other proof that she could love them, too.

"The idea of being with Dom fills me with joy," she finally admitted. "But how can I take that risk again? How can I leave myself open to the hurt he could cause me?"

Celeste stroked a hand down Willa's hair, a comforting, sisterly gesture. "I can't pretend that there *aren't* risks when loving someone. And Dom *did* hurt you."

"He might again," Willa said, forlorn.

"The greatest injuries are the ones inflicted by

those closest to us," Tabitha noted. "Yet the alternative is to keep everything and everyone at a distance, and while we might be protected, we'll never know the warmth of another's touch. We'll never experience how our souls vibrate with pleasure when someone sees beyond what the world believes of us. It's as if . . ." The scholarly, erudite woman searched for the right words. "It's as if we've finally come home."

"Home." Willa whispered the word. For all her life, it had been a fraught one, because the home provided by her parents had been one of peril and unhappiness. Yet *home* resonated, a place where she could be safe and loved.

She hadn't felt that sense of home with Dom when they'd been engaged. Neither of them had been where they needed to be in order to have that feeling of rightness for each other. But over the course of the past week, especially when they'd been at the cabin, she'd felt complete and whole, perhaps for the first time in her life. Dom had revealed himself to her, and she to him, and in that expansive, trusting openness, she'd found true happiness.

She went to the window and opened the curtains. Afternoon light streamed in, having broken through the clouds, and from her room she had a view of one of the gardens. Mr. Longbridge walked hand in hand with Baron Hunsdon, and the host laughed at something the baron said.

"It isn't perfect," Tabitha added, "when you give yourself fully to someone. There's still hurt and misunderstanding, and the words don't always come out exactly the way you want them to. But even when there are obstacles to overcome, everything is better because they're with you, and, in the end, they're there when you need them."

"He *wasn't* there," Willa had to object. She turned away from Mr. Longbridge and the baron's happiness to face the other women. "He *abandoned* me."

"You may think I'm obligated to defend my brother," Celeste said. "Yet I can say, objectively, that the man who I just saw leave your bedchamber would sooner tear his heart from his chest than be apart from you. You might not see the way he looks at you when you don't notice, but I do, and I've never in my life seen anyone have so much devotion to another being. Except," she added with a warm curve of her lips, "the way Kieran looks at me."

"Or how Finn gazes at me," Tabitha noted, her eyes soft.

"Three more fortunate beings, you aren't going to find," Celeste said. She placed her hands on Willa's shoulders. "Do you love him?"

Willa pressed her lips together. She'd admitted as much to herself, but the understanding was so new, so frightening. Summoning her courage, she confessed, "I do."

Happiness filled Celeste's eyes. "And he loves you."

"Is it *enough*?" Willa demanded.

Tabitha approached. "I've studied texts and treatises and essays and nearly every other form of written expression. Thousands of years of humans trying to decipher the mystery of love. If it's real. If it lasts. If it's the singular most important thing anyone can ever experience, or if it's to be avoided at all costs."

"Tell me the answer," Willa pled.

"There's a reason why people keep writing about love: because no one knows the answer. I had to learn that in the most difficult way possible."

"I see." A thick knot of disappointment lodged in Willa's throat. She was no closer to figuring out what to do about her and Dom—every direction only offered more questions.

"However," Tabitha went on, her expression sincere, "personal experience has given me my own answer. And that is that when you find someone who fills your days with joy and your nights with pleasure, when you are more yourself with them than you are with anyone else, when you would do *anything* to ensure their happiness . . . that's a rarity, and it's worth holding on to, as tightly as you can."

Celeste gave Willa's shoulders a squeeze. "You're battling your fear, and that's not an easy thing to do, but, Willa, you're also one of the boldest, most audacious people I've ever known. If there's something you want, *you go after it*. I always admired that about you."

Willa tipped up her chin. "I suppose I've been fearless in my pursuits, and now, when I need my courage the most, I should remember that."

"It took me so long to learn that I should hunt down my own joy," Celeste said. "I wish for you to do the same."

Willa stood on the cusp of something monumental. The most important decision she'd ever make in her entire existence. She could be safe on her own, cut off from the world and her heart, or she could join her life with Dom's. He was tempestuous and elemental, edged and dark, and capable of the most breathtaking tenderness. When he looked at her, he *saw* her. The vulnerable girl and the audacious lioness—and he wanted them both.

She knew what she had to do.

"You said the boat is an hour away?" she asked Tabitha.

"Likely less, by now," the other woman answered. "I imagine it will dock within thirty minutes."

Willa paced to the wardrobe and pulled out a gown, as her sisters-in-law exchanged uncertain glances. "Good. There's enough time for me to dress."

Chapter 27

❧ ✳ ❧

*F*rom the cliff above the dock, Dom watched the boat's approach as if the small vessel carried the fate of his soul. He'd loaded and unloaded cargo from every corner of the globe, yet no ship or craft ever held the same significance as this little single-master did. All his happiness depended on the reprovisioning boat, and the hell of it was, there wasn't a damned thing he could do about his fate. It was all in Willa's hands—as it should be.

The sunlight struck the waves like shattered glass, and he squinted against its glare. It was either watch the boat come closer or else pace outside of Willa's bedchamber, desperate for her answer.

He'd done everything he could to give Willa the choice she deserved. His whole body was taut, like he was prepared for a punch straight to his gut. How could he live without her? If she chose to leave him behind, he'd have to find a way to eke out a miserable existence. One stripped of color and light.

Tense, eager awareness danced through his limbs when her distinctive steps sounded on the gravel path behind him. Hungry for any glimpse of her, he turned as she neared, greedily taking in the sight in case these moments with her were to be his last.

She'd dressed in a blue gown, more vivid than the sky, her hair loose, and he purposefully burned the picture she made into his heart. He searched her face for some sign, a clue that let him know what her decision was, but she held her hand up to shield her eyes from the sun, and the shadow it cast made it hard to read her.

"The boat should be here in quarter of an hour." His voice came out ragged and harsh, as if he'd been shouting.

She stood beside him and gazed out toward the vessel, which had grown steadily larger as it came closer to the island. "It will take some time to off-load its cargo. There's still several days left for the party and they'll want plenty to eat."

"I don't give a damn if they starve," he burst out. "Nothin' matters except one thing—your answer."

"Dom." She said his name on a sigh, and his heart filled with lead.

"You don't want me," he said heavily. "I did my best, but I should've known that I fucked everythin' up too much to win you back." His throat was raw and the greatest challenge of his life was swallowing the tears that wanted to pour forth. He dug his knuckles into his eyes.

"Dom," she said again.

Her hands cupped his, gently pulling them down, and she gazed up at him. Was that tenderness in her eyes? The look someone gave another before saying goodbye? He shook as if he stood in the middle of a storm.

"I *do* want you," she said softly, and his heart shuddered in his chest.

"What?" he rasped.

"I want you, Dom," she repeated with greater strength. She smiled and the sight was the most beautiful thing he'd ever seen. "Because I love you."

"You do?"

Her fingers tightened around his fists. "I love every part of you."

He wanted to believe it, but was it real? Could he trust his ears? "Even though I'm rough and mean and come from nothin'—"

"*Especially* because you're rough and mean and I don't care about where you came from, I care about where *we* are going." Her lips trembled and her eyes glittered with tears. "And we're going to go so many places together. Even if we lived in a tiny shack together—"

"I'm givin' you a bloody *palace*," he insisted.

"Well, I won't object to a palace," she said with a

small laugh, "but truly, we could be anywhere, even living under a twig in the middle of a heath, and all that would matter is that we were together."

His breath gusted in and out and he couldn't understand what was happening to him, what this strange feeling was that filled him with brightness and strength and the need to roar to the heavens.

Happiness. It was happiness.

He'd gone so long without it, he didn't truly know what it meant. Back when he and Willa had first been courting, he'd believed that he was happy, and yet that was a pale echo of this all-consuming joy that filled him.

"I love you, Willa," he growled. "Lioness. My perfect mate."

"Depends on how you define *perfect*," she said wryly.

"Perfect for *me*." He crushed her to him, uncaring about the tears in his eyes. "I'll love you until after the stars have turned to coal."

"Let's try again," she murmured against his mouth. "Differently this time."

"I bollocksed everything up. I'd do it all differently."

Lips pressed to his, she smiled. "I wouldn't. I'll never want to go back, because we've grown and changed. This," she went on, deepening her kiss, "is so much better now."

Words were lost to them as their kiss grew hotter and more desperate. Hunger for her built and built, until it was wild, but it didn't matter if he'd no control over his desire for Willa. Not when she desired him just as much, and they had their whole lives to explore this miraculous thing between them.

Her hands roamed all over his body, but when she found and squeezed the curves of his arse, he chuckled.

"Let's get us inside," he said in a low rumble, "so I can show you good and proper how much I love you."

Threading their fingers together, they headed into the house. They were met in the hallway by Kieran, Celeste, Finn, and Tabitha.

The brothers took one look at Willa and Dom, and their still-clasped hands, and a grumbling Kieran handed Finn a wad of pound notes.

"You *bet* on us?" Dom demanded.

Glaring at Kieran, Willa said, "And you wagered *against* us?"

"Not so," Kieran said with a grin. "The bet was predicated on *when*, not *if*."

"So long as this is the *last* time you meddle in my life," Willa warned them.

"I thought it was family's purpose to meddle," Kieran protested.

"If Willa wants you to stop interfering," Dom growled, "then, *by God*, you won't do it again."

"But it worked out in your favor," Finn noted.

"You're lucky it did," Dom answered.

"I don't believe in luck," Finn said smugly.

"Then believe this," Dom said meaningfully. "If you two do *anything* against her wishes again, you'll have *me* to answer to. And I'm not a nice bloke. Not by a mile."

Willa's brothers exchanged a glance.

"We won't," they replied in unison.

"Swear it," Willa insisted.

"We swear."

"Good," she said with a nod.

"Now that the threats have been issued," Kieran said brightly, "we can get on with the business of celebrating. We have sparkling wine at the ready in the parlor."

Dom shared a hungry look with Willa. "We've our own celebrating to do. Alone."

"I'm just going to pretend that means you're off to tat lace," Kieran said as Dom and Willa hurried up the stairs.

"Don't be a hypocrite, Key," Finn said with a chuckle.

Dom stopped listening to the brothers, his attention completely focused on the woman beside him. They quickly reached their floor and rushed into her bedchamber before shutting the door behind them.

He pressed her against the door and kissed her passionately. They were voracious for each other, mouths ravenous, hands everywhere. She pushed her hips into his and mewled when, through the layers of fabric, the hard ridge of his cock pressed into her.

Her glazed eyes looked at him with surprise when he pulled back. "I'm not rushin' this. We're goin' slow so I can show you that I'm spendin' the rest of my life makin' you happy."

"You already make me happy," she said with a loving smile.

"And I'm goin' to make you even happier."

He led her to the bed and stood next to it. Slowly, they undressed each other, their hands tangling as they helped with buttons and fastenings and all the intricacies of their clothing. Even as impatience to get her naked burned him, he refused to give in to the need to hurry.

When they were both naked, he scooped her up in his arms, and gently laid her down before lying next to her. He gathered her close, kissing her deeply, and her fingers wove into his hair as she pulled him snug.

He held one of her hips as his other hand stroked down her lush body and caressed every part of her. His hand glided over her collarbone, then went lower to cup one breast and tease the nipple into a taut point. When she gasped against his lips, his tongue plunged into her mouth. She sucked on him, drawing forth a groan, and he slipped his hand down her belly to find her sex wet and swollen.

"This is *mine*," he said on a rumble.

"And *this*," she panted, wrapping her hand around his cock, "is *mine*."

"Thank God for that." Then he lost the ability to speak as she pumped him.

She gasped as he circled her clitoris with his thumb, while teasing and rubbing her soaked flesh with his fingers. Together, they pleasured each other, and she tightened around him, crying into his mouth when she came.

"Dom," she moaned. "I need you inside me."

"And you'll have me." He stretched out on his back as he lifted her up to straddle him. She braced her hands on his heaving chest, angling her hips so that the head of his cock teased her opening.

Their gazes held as she looked down at him. He felt the connection between them all the way into the deepest parts of himself, this woman, this force, who was everything to him.

"I love you, lioness," he said hoarsely.

"I love you, Dom," she answered, her eyes bright.

They both gasped as she lowered her hips, and his cock plunged up into her. He let her set the pace, slow at first, but then her speed increased. Her cheeks flushed as she rode him hard. His own hips bucked as he thrust into her welcome heat, overwhelmed with the need to be as close to her, as deep within her, as possible.

He gripped her thighs as she arched back and came with a long moan. His own release built, yet when he moved to pull out, she gasped, "Stay. Stay inside me."

His breath left him. "You—"

"Yes, Dom," she breathed. "I want to marry you."

He lifted up to cup the back of her head and pull her down for a hard, deep kiss. As they kissed, his climax ripped through him.

She draped herself over him as their hearts pounded against each other. He held her close, cherishing the feel of her.

"How is it possible that anyone so incredible as you could want me?" he asked, his lips in her hair.

She stroked a hand down his stubbled jaw. "How is it that so large a man could contain so gentle a heart?"

"Only with you, lioness," he said with a laugh. "To the rest of the world, I'm a mean bastard."

"And I'm a hoydenish virago. Which makes us perfectly matched."

"I'm only perfect to you," he said wryly.

"Isn't that what anyone is looking for? Just one person to see them as perfect?"

He glided his fingers over her face, soaking in the feel of her, reveling in all that she was. "Then I have everything I want."

Epilogue

❧ ✳ ❧

Three months later

"Do we have everything?" Kieran asked with unusual tension. "If there's something we've forgotten, we'll have to wait until the boat returns tomorrow, and then go back to Oban and—"

Willa laid her hand over her brother's. "There's nothing to fret over. Mr. Longbridge has provided all that we might need to perform the ceremony."

They stood on the tall grass that sloped down from the cabin on Mr. Longbridge's island, leading toward the calm, trickling creek. Summer was at its height, and the island had decided to bedeck itself with lush greens and azure skies, as if in repentance for the last time Willa and Dom had been here, and the harrowing storm that had brought them together in this place.

Now they were here again, moments away from formalizing their bond in a simple handfasting ceremony.

Though Willa's family wanted to parade their daughter's wedding before the whole of fashionable London, she and Dom had agreed that they wanted no part of that ostentatious display for others' benefit. This marriage was for *them* alone. And if her parents were livid about her decision to flout convention, she didn't care. Dom was hers and she was his, and only they mattered.

"I've brought the flowers," Celeste said, approaching with a small bouquet of white heather, as per Scottish custom. It was tied with a bow of white satin, which made Willa smile. If white was a symbol of so-called purity, then there was every chance the ribbon would burst into flames the moment Willa touched the fabric. Even in the three agonizingly long months between agreeing to wed and returning to the island, she and Dom hadn't been able to keep their hands—and all other parts of their bodies—off of each other.

She took the bouquet of heather from Celeste, yet the white ribbon didn't spontaneously combust. So much for Divine judgment.

"Why are you laughing?" Finn asked with curiosity.

"Better laughter than tears on one's wedding day," Tabitha noted. "I'm certain it's good luck, and if it isn't, it should be."

"I can always count on you to provide wisdom," Willa said with a smile.

"Are you nervous?" Celeste whispered, leaning close.

"It wouldn't be truthful of me if I was to say that I felt perfectly calm," Willa answered candidly. She had been in a similar situation once before, awaiting a wedding to Dom, and that had been a disaster. Something like trepidation now shimmered beneath her skin, yet there was eagerness, too, and the certainty that she and Dom were truly meant to be together and would never fail each other.

"Dom won't disappoint," Celeste said with conviction as she fussed with Willa's celadon-green silk gown, and her coronet of fragrant orange blossoms. "He's been nothing but impatient to finally become yours. He was up before everyone this morning, and I think he set out for the cabin not a quarter hour after dawn. But where *is* he?"

Willa looked around. The hills surrounded them like the hands of a giant gently cradling something precious. Sunlight poured down on the cabin and filled the grassy slope with green and gold. On the porch of the cabin stood Baron Hunsdon, and Mr. Longbridge, who would be performing the simple ceremony. Yet there was no sign of Dom.

"There he is," Kieran said, before adding in a mutter, "saving me the necessity of hunting him down."

Willa's thundering heartbeat became a song

when Dom stepped out of the cabin to take his place on the porch. He was dressed in a fine coat the color of midnight, and a silver waistcoat was snug around his torso, emphasizing his broadness, with buff breeches that clung to his thighs, tucked into gleaming boots. For all his splendor, nothing matched the magnificence of seeing the radiant love in his eyes as his gaze unerringly sought her out.

She and Dom would go through the world together, always beside each other. Always seeing who they were in the depths of their hearts. There would be fire and fury and passion and love, from the moment they met until their last moments on this earth, and beyond that.

"I'm ready," she said, her attention entirely fixed on him.

She was vaguely aware of activity around her, Finn and Kieran and their wives collecting themselves before they moved as a procession toward the cabin. Neither of her brothers had her on their arms—she walked herself toward her groom—because no one gave her to anyone. She was in command of herself, and *she* chose Dom.

As she climbed the low steps that led to the porch, sniffling sounded behind her. She glanced back, expecting to see maybe Celeste or perhaps Tabitha overcome with emotion. But no—Kieran wiped at his damp cheeks, and even Finn blinked at the moisture gathering in his eyes.

Willa and Dom stood before Mr. Longbridge, who was resplendent and solemn as he addressed them.

"I've been told by the bride and groom that we're to keep this ceremony brief," Mr. Longbridge said warmly. "Yet its brevity is only in contrast to the steadfast love between these two people, which has seen its share of tribulations, and in those tribulations, they have come to learn that their love is stronger and more enduring than anything ever created by humanity."

A tiny sob escaped Kieran, and Willa pressed her lips together when the smallest of smiles curved Dom's mouth.

Mr. Longbridge continued, "Let this love be solemnized here, at the place where it was at last realized. And I must note," he added for their ears alone, "it will always be open to you whenever you've a sentimental urge to visit."

Both she and Dom murmured their thanks.

"Now," Mr. Longbridge went on, "it's time to place the ring on the bride's finger."

From his pocket, Dom pulled out a plain, thin golden band. She knew that it had once belonged to his mother, and his father had given it to him before they had departed for the journey north. The sight of the simple ring, bought with a laborer's saved wages and symbolizing the tie that endured even after Mrs. Kilburn's passing, made Willa tremble, and Dom shook, too, as he slipped the ring onto Willa's finger.

"I understand the bride has a ring for the groom."

It wasn't traditional, but Dom had requested it. Finn stepped forward to hand her a wide golden band, and she could barely keep her hand steady as she put the ring onto Dom's finger. He stared down with a serious expression, a man making a silent vow to himself, before looking back up at Willa with adulation in his gaze.

"Join hands, please," Mr. Longbridge instructed.

When they did, she felt how deeply Dom shook, but she knew without a doubt it wasn't fear that made him tremble. It was something far, far richer and more joyous.

Baron Hunsdon gave Mr. Longbridge a length of golden cord, and he encircled it around her and Dom's wrists. Then the cord was tied into a knot.

A knot tied itself around Willa's heart, binding her to Dom.

"Repeat after me," Mr. Longbridge said, turning to her. "'I do take thee to be my husband.'"

"I do take thee to be my husband." Her voice began tremulous, but gained strength as she spoke.

"I do take thee to be my wife," Dom said without the need of prompting. His words were low but firm, wholly confident.

"Before the Almighty," Mr. Longbridge continued, "and in the presence of all who witness it, I proclaim that you are now married. Those whom the Almighty has brought together let no man put asunder."

Dom and Willa stared at each other, as if neither could believe that what they had feared and hoped for in equal measure had finally come to pass.

"Is that it?" Kieran asked in a stage whisper.

"I think it's enough for them," Finn answered in an equally audible voice.

"Might I suggest a kiss," Mr. Longbridge added, eyes twinkling. "It seems only fitting."

Willa and Dom needed no further urging, coming together for a long, deep kiss, as their closest friends and family applauded. Finn whistled, too, and a moment later, Tabitha whistled, as well.

"I feel a poem coming on," Kieran said, his voice thick. *"Something something scoundrel's last chance . . ."*

"I look forward to the rest of it, darling," Celeste said warmly.

"Maybe I could write a monograph about the philosophical implications of second chances," Tabitha mused.

"I wager it will be a brilliant one, sweetheart," Finn said with a smile in his words.

The scoundrels had all found their perfect, "respectable" brides, but no one knew that the appearance of respectability was merely that—a veneer that barely concealed the strength and power and rebelliousness of women who would always follow their hearts, with men beside them doing all they could to support their wives' journeys to greatness.

It had seemed impossible that Willa and Dom could ever find their ways back to each other after what had torn them apart. There had been moments when she would have sworn that no force on earth could have ever brought them together again. Except she hadn't counted on the force of her own heart, or Dom's. Two fighters who now faced the world's battles side by side.

They had gone through so much, and felt such pain, but that made this joining all the sweeter. She understood now that they'd had to endure all of that to arrive at a place that was far better, far stronger, like tempered steel. Nothing would break them apart now.

"You're mine, lioness," Dom whispered into her mouth as they kissed, "and I'm yours."

She held tightly to him, determined to be the fierce creature they both knew her to be, and holding fast to the elemental force that he embodied. Nothing in her life had felt so right as this, as *him*.

"It was ever thus," she whispered. "You and I. Beside each other, evermore. Two shooting stars burning trails of fire across the sky."

"Are you ready to ignite the world, my bride?"

"With you setting the blaze beside me," she said, her lips widening in a smile, "I'd like nothing better."

Find out how Kieran and Finn met their perfect matches . . .

THE GOOD GIRL'S GUIDE TO RAKES

and

HOW THE WALLFLOWER WAS WON

are available now!